Books by F. D.

The Pathways Tree

The Fairy's Tale
The Academy (2)
The Princess And The Orrery (3)

Stand Alone Novels

In The Slip

Praise for The Pathways Tree Series

"The world is Neil Gaiman, jokes are Terry Pratchett, and the politics are George Orwell, all originally made and sewn together by a brilliant wordsmith and storyteller who would please any fans of such authors." Miranda Kane, comedian.

"This is a complex, often dark but still comedic world. It manages to avoid both post-modern tweeness and intellectual abstraction with its earthy characters and F.D. Lee's humour." Andrew Wallace, author.

"If you like Terry Pratchett, or the Artemis Fowl books, you'll like this." Rhonda Baxter, author.

"F D Lee has crafted a wonderful world with a very interesting and wholly loveable protagonist, whose strength of character and self effacing determination to do the right thing made this book, for me, unputdownable." Reader review.

"Lee's imagined world of fairy godmothers, trolls, gnomes, ogres, witches, elves and much more besides living out a troubled existence in an Orwellian dystopia is impressively expansive and detailed." Reader review.

"Lee's witty, satirical storytelling carries the reader with a light touch through unexpectedly dark and twisty territory." Reader review.

In The Slip Copyright Page

All characters are fictional. Any resemblance to persons living or dead is purely coincidental.

In The Slip and all original characters, events and settings ©2019 F. D. Lee (identified as the author of this work). All rights reserved. No part of this book may be reproduced in any form or by any electronic or mechanical means including information storage and retrieval systems without permission in writing from the author, except by a reviewer, who may quote brief passages in a review.

Conditions of Sale
This book is sold subject to the condition that it shall not, by way of trade or otherwise, be lent, resold, hired-out or otherwise re-circulated without the author's prior consent in any form of binding or cover other than that in which it is published and without similar condition including this condition being imposed on the subsequent purchaser.

Cover designed by Jane Dixon-Smith
http://www.jdsmith-design.com/

ISBN: 9781072379508

About the Author

Faith is an avid reader, fan and geek. She lives in London with her husband and cats, who are engaged in a long running battle for the rights to the window sills (the cats, not the husband!)

Faith glumly suspects it will all end in tears, and she will be the one buying the kitty treats to make it all better.

Author's Note

I hope you enjoy this book. If you want to know more about the research for the Fracture, please sign up to my newsletter where you will get access all the inspiration behind it, as well as unpublished short stories, a free, unabridged e-copy of my bestselling novel, *The Fairy's Tale*, as a welcome gift, and more. You can sign up at www.fdlee.co.uk. If you're already on my mailing list, you can access the information now – check my newsletter if you've lost the link!

You can also contact me via faith@fdlee.co.uk or on Twitter (@faithdlee) and Facebook (@fdleeauthor).

Best wishes and happy reading,

Faith

Dedication

For James,

I love you, alltimewise.

In The Slip

Dear Anne,

Fight the future, save the past, alltimewise!

love
Faith
xx

worldcon 2019.

Loop 15.6

Want is the greatest crime we ever commit against ourselves, I reckon.

Which don't mean I'm a tempo sceever, I ain't saying choice is a problem. But you spend enough time in the slip, you realise the past ain't so different from the present, that people ain't changed. The lot of them are no-good, money-grabbing, cheating, lying sceevers now, and they were no-good, money-grabbing, cheating, lying sceevers then.

You get them all the way through the slip, pasttimewise and futuretimewise, same as you did before the slip was invented and folks like me called in to keep everything orderly. Take this kid in front of me.

Dirty, scared, rag-wearing. Lips wobbling like he's about to burst into tears. Yeah, this kid has a want, sure as silver. But that's an easy call, on account of him being when he shouldn't be, trying to change the future to his own benefit. What most other operatives won't account for is the fact this kid had it all anyway, only he thought he ought to have more.

It's all there in his design if they'd bother to see it:

Factor one: symmetrical face. Factor two: shoulders straight, legs long, torso wide. He stands at least one-ninety-eight, unnaturally tall. Factor three: his skin, pale like processed sugar, has a few little lines across his forehead and around his eyes. Tasteful, expensive; giving him some character, showing he's been lived in without giving away quite how long for.

But his eyes are the biggest tell. They're yellow, and not yellow like he's had work done, neither. Eye-dyes are too clean. His eyes are yellow with little flecks of silver and red. The kind of colouring that only comes from genetics. This kid's had invit work done and that don't come cheap. Parents are probably stockholders or copyrighters, to afford something like that for their foetus.

Kinda hard to have any sympathy for him once you know that. Also makes him easy to spot, for all his tatty costumery.

"You better come quietly," I tell him, knowing he won't.

"What do you want with me, brother? I've done nothing wrong," he whines in a shitty version of the local dialect, fire eyes dancing as he tries to watch me and reach, surreptitious, for the Holo on his wrist – official, too. Hard to get hold of on the black market. More evidence the kid comes from money. He's still an idiot, even so. His hand's shaking so much he might as well have shouted his intentions.

"Sure. And yet here you are, somewhen you ain't got no call to be, and here I am, and oh, look," I wave my official Holo under his nose, "Here's something about someone trying to alter the dioxomorphinate patent. Dioxomorphinate, ain't that the chemical they use to treat the water?"

We both know it is.

"Big business, that. Lots of capital."

We both know that, too.

The kid's made a mistake, sure enough, and now he's dealing with a Company operative. Sweat's beading on his pretty, pale invit skin, and his chest, for all its genetic superiority, is rising and falling in bursts, his lungs struggling to fill. Pressure's getting to him, right enough.

He tries to jump.

It's over quick, him laying out on the sidewalk, bleeding some, clutching at his side, wheezing through his teeth. He don't try to stand, just blubbers that he ain't done nothing wrong, that he's on the side of right, that we're all sceevers and criminals and the world ain't fair.

"That's what they all say," I tell him as I cuff him, fixing the bar in place to stop him reaching his wrist. "You ready to consent?"

The kid makes some kind of noise, which is good enough for me. Leastways, when I get the TnCs up from my Holo, he gives a good go at reading them. Lasts about five minutes before he consents. He's got no choice, but I gotta say I'm impressed he has a go at understanding them, especially given the state of him. Can't send him back to the One True unless he's processed right, which means until he gives his agreement he's stuck in the past, the weight of time on him. 'Til the pressure pops him, anyways.

Admin done, I open the slip, ready to send him back futuretimewise for processing.

"It wouldn't have worked," I tell him, once the Company confirms they're ready for him. "Diox is one of the biggest patents they got. Why'd you bother, anyways? You got money, right?"

"Listen, brother," the kid gasps, looking at me all soulful, eyes bruising, as if I'm supposed to be moved or something. "I forgive you. You don't know any better. You're just a cog in the machine."

"Sure, kid." I haul him up, shove him back into the future. "Ain't we all?"

That's the thing about the slip. You learn pretty quick that nothing anyone does matters anyways.

The bar is God-awful.

Noisy, dark, sticky. Kind of place you don't wanna touch with your bare skin, on account of all the people previous who've touched it with theirs. But this particular cog wants to stop turning for a spell. Wants to see its friend.

Besides, this bar ain't the worst place I've been. That honour goes to a corporate meeting room in what was the centre of the world. Some nut thought she'd upset the salt routes, destabilise the region, negate the need for the Sino-Amek International Trade Duty Alliance, and with it the refuelling bill that underscored the Arctic mining. Which, as it turns out, meant her company lost millions betting on the wrong horse, or, in this case, the wrong mine.

Same, same, same, sure as silver, alltimewise. I scan the bar for Lois. I ain't sure she'll be here, but I like to take the chance when I can.

And then my whole slip, the whole damn spaghetti mess of it, turns on itself.

Lois ain't here, but someone is. Someone I... someone I know, I reckon. A man, sitting at the bar in the spot I was hoping to find Lois, nursing a beer.

He's got Latin heritage, hair black as midnight from a time when the night was allowed to be such, falling against skin golden and dark as wet sand. Sitting there, frowning at nothing, shoulders forward. A sense he ain't really where he wants to be, like a tourist come to the wrong part of town but trying to fit in anyway. But then, I ain't exactly one to talk on that count.

I ain't never seen this guy before, I'd swear to it, but I recognise him in a way that hits you physical before your brain can register the thought, like a memory built into your bones.

This ain't right. There ain't no way I know this guy. Has something gone wrong with the slip? It happens. Things get turned around, people showing up where they shouldn't, an aberration somewhen changing their course. But even so, *I* should know when I met him. Shit. Is there something wrong with me? Did that tempo kid do something?

No. The pressure's getting to me, sending me screwy. Must be. I grab the tub of chloros from my pocket, pop a pill, try to think over the pain in my temples. Least there's one problem I can always solve.

There... that's it. Warmth building in my joints, working its way to my aching skull.

OK.

Breathe in and out.

Gather the factors, look for the want.

Factor one: there's nothing about this guy that marks him as being in the wrong part of the slip. No invit work I can see, though that tends to be harder to spot from a distance. Factor two: he's turned out nice for such a shitty place, wearing a pair of light pants and a button-up with long sleeves, tie loose around his neck. The cut and material of the suit fit the time. Factor three: there's a scar on his lip, running down to his chin; uncommon, but being mussed up ain't a crime. Factor four: no obvious tech on him, but Holos can be hidden easy enough. Hell, they can be removed if you're good with a knife and don't mind pain over much. Factor five: he's nervous. His big, soft body curled over his beer, fingertips whitening on the glass.

Want: he's waiting on something – a date, maybe?

That would go aways to explaining why he's dolled up so fine, but it don't explain the vibe I'm getting from him. The knot in my stomach could be some kind of sympathetic reaction – that's a thing I've read about, sure enough – but it don't chime right.

My Holo ain't got much to offer. It seems confused, lights blinking all over the place like it's having trouble fixing on me, but that's probably nothing. The damn thing is connected to my chip, so there ain't that much can go wrong with it. Roll my sleeve down, stand, think.

Best thing is to get back to the One True. Get checked over by the white coats. Hah. Get some sleep, have a few days off the chloros, clear out my head. God knows how many slips I've got rattling around.

Factor six: ...could be I'm hoarding timelines? I'll have seen someone like him in the past, and now I'm getting it all sideways. It happens sometimes, even with the chloros. If it ain't the pressure that gets you, it's the loose memories; hence why the Company cleans us out every so often, wipes us down and gets us shiny again. Stupid not to have thought of that sooner. In which case, I can have a beer, unwind in the dark and the dirt before heading back.

...Besides, if I'm up next to him, I can check him out for invit work. Yeah. I'll stay a spell, one beer, and then head back. If my Holo pipes up that something's wrong, I'll haul ass. The Company won't even know I was here if I'm quick in the slip, and I'm always quick in the slip.

I walk up to the bar, sit down next to the man, confident, order a beer. Robot obliges, takes my currency, wobbles off. Can't see anything unusual. No signs of invit, but it's hard to tell, peering at him surreptitious. Turn on my stool to fix him dead in the eyes – brown, like mine, but his are flecked with spots of amber. Invit or real? Hard to say. The colour ain't wild like invit. Lucky boy if they're real.

"Hey, how's it going?" I say in Bay Korean, the catchall language for this part of the slip.

"Hello. I fine. Am fine. Me," he replies, his accent untidy but still sounding, somehow, familiar. The inflection maybe. His BayKay, however, is shocking bad.

I switch to something I reckon he might speak better, based on his accent. "How's this?"

He smiles, nods. "Yeah, thanks. I can never get the tones right."

"Sure. So... we've met before, I think? I can't recall your name..."

His expressions flickers, something odd I can't place, except it makes me feel I made the right choice to check him out. He drops his gaze, hands tighten on his beer, lower lip pulls against his teeth.

"It's José Otero, with a *'juh'*. Portuguese." He pauses, searching my face like he's expecting me to do or say something. When I don't, he adds, "But you can call me Joe."

José's a neat name, but I like Joe, too. Whatever he prefers is fine by me.

What the fuck? Who cares what he's called? Stick to the factors.

"Right, yeah. I'm no good at names," I say. "Saw you sitting here, thought I'd say hi."

Joe smiles, but he don't seem happy. Ruining his date or ruining his plans for the slip? Sip my beer, play it easy. Hah. Remember I'm a cog. Just keep turning.

"Hey, did you, uh... did you..."

I shake my brains up, searching for a piece of news from this part of the slip, but all I can think about is the sceever tempo kid. Can't talk about him. Shit. Joe's watching me, no doubt thinking who's this idiot man talking to me, which ain't unfair. If only I could check my Holo for a José 'Joe' Otero.

Ahhhh! I got it. A case I worked on, pasttimewise – presentimewise, for Joe.

"...did you hear about that research company, the one that just bought the university debt from Barnes Int? Heard they own almost all the science debt now, ain't that a thing?"

He makes a face like he's eating something rotten. "Everything's for sale, nowadays."

"'*Sure as silver, good as gold, debt and profit never get old*'. That's what they say, ain't it?"

"There's a saying for everything, I guess." He stands. "Anyway, I've got to go. Good to see you-"

"Kong! Uh. Kong. My name."

He seems disappointed, somehow. "Kong's not a local name, right?"

In The Slip

"No one's from anywhere, where I'm from. But I got some Chinese in my blood," I explain, though it ain't so clear why. "A few gen back on my Pop's side."

"Well, it was, is, nice to meet you, Kong, but I've got to-"

"In actual fact, my first name's King. Kong's my family name. My Pop's idea. Stupid."

Why am I saying all this?

"Really?" Joe pauses in his escape. There's something in his face that weren't there a moment before. "Do you like it? Your name, I mean?"

"I guess it's what I got. It's supposed to be funny. Y'know." I make my face into an expression that feels like it could be the very dictionary definition of encouragement. "I usually say it the Sino way: Kong, King. But yeah, that's me. It's a stupid name, don't you think?"

"No, no. It's... unique. I'm happy you told me that, Kong." Crinkles around the corners of his eyes, good teeth. Nice smile. "God – sorry, yes. It's just..."

He bursts out laughing. I don't think he's laughing at me, though I ain't got a clue what else it might be. And, to speak plain, I don't care if he is.

It's a stupid name I got landed with, I know that. But it's the one I got, and I ain't never looked into buying a new one. Like it does for Joe, it strikes me somehow as being funny, and I guess that's why I've kept it. That and the fact it's been mine since I was born, weren't sold to me nor did it come with the job. It seems right that this thing that is mine is the very same thing that puts a spark into Joe's amber-flecked eyes and has him sitting back down on his seat.

"Your Pop sounds like an ass," he says. "Do you... how can I ask this... do you get on with him?"

"He had a sharp sense of humour on him, that's a fact. But he was my Pop, and you gotta love family."

His laughter dies away, which I'm guessing is on account of the fact he's clocked that Pop's done the same – died, I mean, not stopped laughing. Joe don't say nothing on it, though. Instead, he asks, "What's your business, Kong?"

"Ah, well, see... I'm a... a..."

I get ready to tell Joe the same as I told Lois, but somehow the lie don't feel as easy on my tongue as it did with her. Dunno. Just, I got a sense he'll know it ain't the truth and he'll hate me for it, and that don't sit right.

Take a mouthful of my beer.

Am I gonna go all the way with him? I wanna check my Holo, see if anything's come on the wave, but that really would be a step too far, somewhere crowded like this, in front of a native.

"Kong?" Joe asks.

What harm can it do to tell him? Besides, there has to be something wrong with my timelines. Yeah. That's the only way to explain this sense that I've met him before, that we already know each other. In which case, the Company will clean up and this conversation won't ever have happened, anyway.

"I'm a cop," I say, sitting up, making myself look all real and solid. "Pretty important one, too."

"A cop, huh? Do you have a badge?"

Madness for a moment as I consider showing him my Holo, the very thing I ruled out doing on accident. What's wrong with me, presentimewise?

"Nah, ain't got a badge. I guess... well, 'cop' may be too, uh, too *simple* a term. There ain't no police where I'm from. Not as you'd recognise them, anyways. I'm from the future, see. It's my job to come back in time and catch temporal terrorists."

"I see," he replies, stretching out the 'ee', grinning like an idiot. "I have to say, I didn't expect to meet a time travelling cop in a shitty bar like this."

He thinks I'm joking. Probably that's luck, him not taking me so serious. Then something changes. His smile shifts, taking on a sharpness that ain't aggressive, not as such, but sure as hell ain't innocent, neither.

"And am I on your hit list, then? Is that why you came over? Am I in trouble, officer?"

"Maybe you are, maybe you ain't."

"Are you worried I'll do some temporal terrorism?"

"Who knows what you might do?"

"Who, indeed?" He winks at me – the Goddamn man *winks* at me. Then, cool as you like, he returns his attention to his beer.

"So then, what's the future like?"
"What's it like... Well... See... It's...."
I look around, taking in the factors, presenttimewise:
Factor one: two women playing pool, laughing with each other and not seeming to mind that they ain't looking their best. Factor two: cheap teasers on the wall, some not even really selling nothing, just letting folks know there's a neighbourhood band here in a couple of weeks' time. Factor three: robot working the bar is behind the current trend, but it's doing well enough, serving up beers, whirling and clunking away in a restful manner. Factor four: dirty walls, the paint scuffed up from God knows what. Musak playing out of hidden speakers, some of it with real voices. The bar, sticky with old beer, has writing scratched into it: *mff loves ffm...*

Factor five: it's a shit hole in need of upgrading, lived in and used up by too many people, all of them leaving a piece of themselves on the surroundings.

What's the future like, compared to this?

"It's... clean. Really, really clean. Nothing old. Most diseases got a cure. Most people got work. You can buy most anything you want."

"You don't sound too keen?"

"What's not to like about freedom?"

Joe's eyes dance over me, a crease forming between his eyebrows. Then he lifts his glass in a salute.

"To freedom."

"Yeah. To freedom."

We talk on a while, Joe drinking the beers I buy him and me drinking the ones he buys me, arguing in a friendly type manner, him showing me he won't be pushed around on the things that matter to him.

And all the while I'm throwing out as much charm as I've ever had, which I'll own ain't much, but I'm doing what I can. Here I am, sitting with this man called Joe, who I'd swear I know from somewhere, somewhen, but whenever I try to place him my head gets to hurting, so I stop trying. Just enjoy a beer with a man who is laughing with me, and twisting 'round on his stool so's he can talk to me better.

Shit.

New factor, new want: I'm realising I desperately wanna bed this man.

I didn't plan on that, standing in the doorway considering what to do, but there it is. Hope he's gay. Most people are, right? Leastways, a little bit? It's fine. Anyways, folks in this part of the slip've got more important things to contend with than what kind of junk people like to rub up against. Joe's unlikely to get offended if I carry on as I have been, making jokes and eyes at him... although that don't exactly mean he feels the same way I do, neither.

To be truthful, Joe not reciprocating may not be so bad. I ain't looking to do nothing wrong. There's some as might say otherwise, what with the rule about fraternising in the slip, but they'd be wrong. It's not like I knew Lois wouldn't be here and this Joe would be, a person who makes me feel like I ain't never not known him, who seems happy in my company, who hasn't noticed all the things wrong with me...

No one can say I broke the rule when I didn't know this was gonna happen, is what I'm saying.

This is how it is: shit goes south pasttimewise, but the One True Timeline gets restored, and it all comes back to normal, or close enough. But here's the itch: pasttime and presenttime aren't the same thing, not when you live them both, and presenttimewise, here he is. And along with him, there's this oddness in my stomach, a sharp softness.

I don't know what's gonna happen.

So, I ain't breaking no rules, I reckon. Just... exploring this slip. Yeah. Gathering intel, clocking up new factors, working out new wants. Just so happens some of them are mine.

Joe brushes against my forearm when he reaches for his drink, and later, when I'm drunk enough, I press my hand on his shoulder. Conversation's fast and sharp and funny. Eventually, he excuses himself, makes his way to the john. I watch him walk away, imagining – remembering, almost – the feel of him on top of me. I know him, I'm sure of it. I could think better if my head weren't hurting again, a fine, high-pitched whine joining the tension across my forehead. Time pressure, must be. How long have I been here?

Chloros, that's what I need. Two in one evening? Shit, three, on account of the one I took before I grabbed that tempo. But I ain't feeling easy, and when the slip gets to you, you take a pill. One more won't hurt, I reckon. I got a tolerance to them, that's why they're wearing off so fast.

The little plastic tub winds up in my hand, sticky hot from my pocket. I bite a pill in half, washing it down with the rest of Joe's beer, and get the robot to bring us two more.

Joe returns. I help him onto his seat, my hand resting on his a moment too long, luxuriating in the feel of him. His skin's warm from the bar and the beer, fine bristles of hair tickling my fingertips. I wanna flex my fingers, spread that feeling all the way down into the palm of my hand, my wrist, my arm, my body.

Should I? Seems to me he ain't exactly averse to the idea, and in the dim light of the bar, he probably can't see what's wrong with me. Perhaps he won't notice at all?

Perhaps he *will* notice, but he won't care?

No, that's stupid...

"So, what's going to happen now, cop?" Joe asks, his hand all of a sudden on my knee. "You arresting me? If you're not, I'm free to go."

"Sure, that's your right, presenttimewise."

"Ah, but I could always confess. If I did, would you look after me? Make sure I get fair treatment?" His voice drops, his eyes meeting mine. "I'd be in your custody, after all."

That's a cheap trick, but I'll tell you this: it lands. Lands straight in my groin and settles there, which makes it about the only thing currently settled in that region. Joe leans forward, the heat of him so strong I can almost see it, like haze on tarmac, pasttimewise. He smells like a garden. A memory of... earth and trees and herbs... burning sugar...

"There's a lot of crime in this world, Kong," Joe continues, voice low and soft. "Perhaps you could help me? There's this... problem... I'm trying to fix. Some bad people are doing some very bad things."

I try to shake the sense there's something beneath my conscious, a taste, a smell. Focus. "People always do bad things, you ain't gonna stop them."

"But I'm not a cop, am I? Don't you *want* to help me?"

He smiles the way Lois does when she knows she's won an argument, and just like that I'm muddled, not sure where I am or who I am or what any of this is.

Quicker'n quick, he's kissing me, his fingers digging into my thigh, little points of pain that keep me from falling forward. His fingers catch in my hair, scratching my scalp, while his stubble scrapes my plastic-person skin. Sure as silver, he's got me beat, and we're kissing for all that we can, his tongue in my mouth, hot and pliant, brushing against my own; slow, confident, caressing the inside of my lower lip. The sensation speeds the flow of blood downwards, and I have to shift on my seat or else cause myself the kind of pain that ain't as much fun as that which Joe is causing me.

He pulls back, face flushed.

"See? I think we could work together pretty well, don't you? You and me, Kong, we could go through time, set things right."

"What?"

He leans forward, but not close enough for kissing, not this time.

"Kong, there's something I need to tell you. We have met before, you were right. I shouldn't... but I can't, either, you know? Shit. I knew this was a bad idea."

"I don't – what are you talking about?"

Something's going wrong. I can see it, a glass falling from my hand but I can't act fast enough to catch it.

Even in the slip, I ain't fast enough to stop what's happening.

"Please, Kong. You must realise how wrong everything is."

He's a fucking tempo.

I'm drunk, my head's screaming at me, and I've been sat for hours with a God damn tempo, making gooey eyes and kissing. How the hell did I get here? Is this why I thought I knew him – God, have I seen him on a case and forgotten it?

I only know I'm on my feet because suddenly I'm standing over him, and I don't know how I don't smash his face into the bar, but somehow I get away without causing the kind of scene that would get me in serious shit.

In The Slip

Damn it, I'm already in some serious shit. Do I bring him in? What if they ask me why I came here in the first place? I can't confess my friendship with Lois. I need to... need to think. Need air. He shouts something at me, but the whining in my head covers it.

Outside, the cold air hits me like a punch to the gut, forcing the alcohol faster through my veins. Footsteps. Joe? No. There's a woman behind me. She's attractive in a non-threatening way, dull and dressed neat in a black suit, dark hair tied up in a ponytail, skin pale and pink: Europhile.

"Having fun with your new friend?" She smirks.

Did she follow me out? What's going on? I can't breathe. Chloros. The tub shakes in my hand. Get a grip. I ain't done nothing so wrong. Flirting ain't risking the One True. No babies. No deaths. No copyright infringements. Get rid of this woman, call it in.

"What's it to you?"

She shrugs. "Nothing at all. If he wants to make himself miserable, that's his lookout. Personally, I'm with Juliet – what's in a name?"

"What?"

"Just my little joke. Anyway, let's get this over with. Do you know who I am?"

"I ain't never seen you before in my life."

"What about the guy in the bar? You know him?"

"I – No. Course I don't."

She shakes her head like I failed some kind of test so obvious even a dog could've done it.

"You really are a total shit, Kong."

And then she shoots me.

F. D. Lee

Reset

My Pop sits me down on the sofa and ruffles my hair. He's off out to save the world, he explains. Mom stands in the doorway, watching him, a smile on her face, proud.

Pop reminds me of all the wonderful things we've done together – visiting the zoo and seeing the animals, trips to the mall, flying kites and climbing mountains. Playing catch in the backyard. Buying a new big screen and watching the teasers together. Horseback riding. Soccer games. The time he caught me with a boy by the bus shelter and brought him home and introduced him to Mom. Buying my first razor. Learning Mandarin and Spanish and French and English and German and Italian and Portuguese and Korean and Arabic and Punjabi and Hindi. Taking me to the Museum of Commerce. Him sitting on my bed, going through all the Patent holders before the big test. Helping Mom bake a cake. Playing with the family dog. Walking along the Skyrail, looking out over the city. Ignoring the bones that fly, dust and ash, outside.

Pop asks me how old I am, and I tell him. Asks me what I like the most, and I tell him. Asks me how he dies, and I say, *Pop, you ain't never gonna die so that don't matter.*

He smiles at that.

Loop 16.0

I wake up in the tank, head full of fireworks.

Turns out getting shot in the gut hurts – who'd have thought, huh? I try to bring my hand to my abdomen, instinct wanting me to check everything's still where it ought to be, but the gloop in the tank is thick and holds me in place.

The movement alerts the white coats. Light shines in, distorted by the viscosity and the darkness, looking like the moon did before the night went neon.

"Don't move. We're just finishing the cycle now," says a tinny voice through the tank's speakers.

I don't answer, naturally. No one wants a mouthful of this stuff; tastes like turpentine mixed with brine, and if you vomit all you got to look forward to is your own puke caught in the gloop, inches from your face. And that's if you're lucky. I heard stories about agents puking up in the tank and the gloop trying to reattach their vomit to their insides.

"You were shot six months ago, point blank range, causing damage to the inferior vena cava," the voice tells me. "Hypovolemia escalated to 40 when we picked you up."

I fix my expression in such a way to communicate that I'm aware I got shot on account of the fact it was me who took a bullet. I doubt they can see it, but sometimes you gotta express yourself.

"You're lucky we found you, all things considered."

And these idiots are supposed to be in charge.

They move me to a medi, a nice small room with coconut air and clean surfaces, the halogens washing a faint blue over everything. First thing I do, once I'm clean and my eyes adjust to the One True, is stand in front of the mirror above the sink. I don't know what I expect to see, but I'm disappointed by what I get.

My face is much the same as it ever was. A touch paler on account of being in the tank so long, and a little thinner for the same reason. I study my torso, poking at the muscles above my belly. No scar. Dull, plain skin over dull, plain bone.

I keep on gawping at my same-old-same-old self. And yeah, I'm disappointed, which don't make no sense. If an agent for the TTCP, that's the Company, had themselves a slashed-up shell, well, that just wouldn't work. Travelling the slip is all about blending in pasttimewise, boring and regular like all the rest of them. The Company employs us with that spec in mind. If you're too tall, too well-fed, if you've had surgery or parents that could afford invit, you'd stand out, pasttimewise. It's why the Company's so careful who they take on, why they get us young and alone.

Sudden pain around my knuckles, stinging and throbbing, making me press my hand under my armpit to silence it.

I punched the mirror.

The glass is shattered, a flower of thin lines, but the mirror itself held. My hand took most of the damage, sticky blood lumping between my knuckles, flashes of white that might be from the mirror or, if I'm lucky, is just bone. I don't much fancy an afternoon filling out insurance forms and evaluations to make sure I ain't gonna smash up something that might actually matter. Besides which, I don't recall the impulse to punch the mirror. I ain't sure how well that'd fly in a return-to-work interview, but I can guess.

I wash my hand, flexing it in the clear, clean water, expecting it to hurt more under the heat – and it does, but not nearly so much as my head. There's this tension around my hairline, like the skin's too tight or my head's too big for it.

Naturally, it's at this point the nurse walks in. Like I keep saying, some things never change. Her eyes shunt from me to the mirror, a look of disgust on her face that a better liar would have been able to hide.

"You'll be charged for that," she says, not quite looking at me. It's tempting to try to duck and weave into her line of sight, if nothing else but to see how committed she is to her avoidance. The citizens of the One True don't like reminders, see. That's why she ain't so keen on me – none of them are. Not that I can blame them, nor call them out on it. The mirror speaks to my own thoughts on my appearance, after all.

In The Slip

At least people like her got the chance to amend themselves. This nurse, for example, got herself some pretty tidy aesthetics done: her cheeks are augmented with under-skin implants to make them dollishly round, her chin filed to a point, her eyes enlarged. She looks like a doll, except for the teddy bear ears wiggling on top of her head. Expensive. Stylish. What a good girl she is, and she's stuck with me.

"Give me your hand," she instructs.

"It ain't that bad."

She grabs my hand and slaps a Kwiq-Dissolve on it. Healing done, she passes her hand over her wrist, accessing her chip, and a screen appears in the air in front of her. She ain't got a Holo covering her chip, which always looks strange to me, no matter I seen it a thousand times. Without the slim, black, beetle-shaped Holo covering it, you can't hide the fact the tech is inside you, all the wires and whatnot crawling around your muscles and nerves, all the way to your brain. Folks in the One True make a feature of their chips. The nurse has little unicorns cosying up to the strip of metal.

She starts tapping at the screen projected from her chip, asking me the usual detanking questions. It's a routine I can rattle through easy as pie, and if she knows I'm only mouthing along, she don't seem to care. I catch my eye in the broken mirror. My face is all splintered. I smile at myself and my reflection smiles back, my mouth split across the petals of the glass flower. Stick my tongue out to the same effect.

"All seems well. Is there anything I can get you?"

"Chloros," I say quick, snapping back to attention.

She hands over a bag with a couple of tubs in it, obviously expecting the request, then produces a TTCP branded storage box.

"I've got your clothes. But... I think they got damaged?"

I shake my head, start pulling on my jeans, buttoning up my shirt, et cetera. The nurse watches me, eyes following each item I pull on like a cat that's just had its ass handed to it by a mouse. When I take my old boots out of the box, the heavy material scuffed and fraying, she looks like she might faint or throw up.

"I could make an order for you," she offers. "You can reimburse the Company."

"It's fine," I reply, shrugging on my grey overcoat and – I'll own – making sure she notices the patch I sewed on the elbow.

"Only Murdache wants to debrief you and-"

"It's fine."

I almost add that I wish I'd smashed my head into the glass instead of my hand, but I reckon it'd send the nurse into palpitations. And what's the point? Alltimewise, folks been smashing their heads into shit, one way or another.

It don't seem worth the effort when you think on it like that.

The elevator takes me up a few dozen floors, the journey made all the more pleasant on account of the chloros also taking me up. Doctors and nurses ain't my most favourite people, but I can't deny they got their uses.

The elevator stops where it knows it should, having read my particulars from my Holo. I got clearance up to the eighteenth, but right now I'm being halted on the forty-first, where Nafre A. Murdache resides.

Murdache's office is a perfect piece of Regeneration styling; a line drawing actualised in silver and glass and marble. She's waiting for me, neat and tidy, her skin a lilac blush with a logo flecked in discreet gold point on her throat, ebony hair pulled back in a precise knot. She's standing in front of her glass wall, looking down over the world she helped create – with my help, though God damn if she'll ever recognise that piece of factual information.

Perhaps I shouldn't have taken the chloros if that's my first thought on seeing her. Being rowdy ain't gonna help me out. To speak plain, I ain't even sure why I'm feeling so disinclined to be courteous to the woman. Debriefing is common after every trip in the slip, and that's without spending time in the tank. I shouldn't be surprised Murdache wants to see me, it's just I got this feeling she's to blame for something.

"Kong," she says, looking me up and down, showing she ain't bothered by me. "Take a seat. We're very concerned about the incident that occurred on your last contract. Someone shot you?"

"Yes, ma'am, they did."

"But it wasn't the tempo you were sent for?"

In The Slip

The pain in my head worsens, but there ain't much point complaining. Murdache damn well knows what happened, she'll have read my feed – it's not like I got skulled or nothing. Just she wants the details from me. I struggle through the fog, looking for an answer.

"No... It was a woman. Yeah, a woman with dark hair. Europhile."

Murdache nods, stares a while, face all stony and hard. Then she accesses her chip, scans the screen that appears. No Holo for her, either; the bosses don't risk the slip.

"Well, you passed your assessment, so it doesn't seem to have done you any damage. We'll add your description of the woman and anything we can salvage from your feed to the database. Bloody tanks," she adds, shutting down her screen. Easy enough for her to say, she ain't never been in one, never had to deal with the scramble they make of your brain while everything settles back down. Well, mostly everything, anyways.

"I want to talk to you about an upcoming mission," Murdache continues. "We're very close to patenting a new design of chloroxamphamine. If we're successful, they should alleviate the time pressure even further." She taps her fingers against her thumb like she's following a beat of music, gaze locked on some internal thought process. "We could go back farther. Maybe even pre-Fracture."

I sit up straight. Ain't no one ever gone back before the Fracture, the pressure's too strong. New chloros. Well, well, well. Those tempos won't stand a chance, not if we can go so far back. No, sir. No, no, no.

...Wonder when they'll let me have them...

"Really, ma'am?"

"There's no need to 'ma'am' me, Kong. You've already been put forward to trial them." A pause as she eyeballs me. "I hope you're up to it. Six months in the tank and, well, all this... *you*..."

"I'm good in the slip, ma'am. The best."

That don't seem to satisfy her the way I hoped it might. It's a fact that Murdache ain't a cheerleader of mine, but I'm good in the slip and she knows it. Why's she making faces and pretending like this is some kind of debate?

"I'm sending you home," she says at last. "We're a while away from a pilot jump. In the meantime, I'll contact you when a case becomes available."

"Yes, ma'am."

I'm so close to the door I could spit on it and not miss when Murdache calls out:

"And fix that fucking accent, Kong."

Outside the Company, the city is bright and beautiful, teasers flashing pretty colours all around. Tall, clean buildings towering over me, white and glass, going on for miles in every direction.

Say what you like about the One True, but it sure is packaged right. Alltimewise, folks strive to be clean and healthy, sexy and appealing, and the city's job is to represent that desire, just in case you're ever in danger of forgetting it. The air smells fresh, a hint of something on it I think might be sea foam, though there sure as silver ain't no seawater nearby.

Before I went out on that last mission, the air smelled of cinnamon and sugar. Not my favourite, but each to their own. Besides, if you don't like the current fashion, you just gotta wait. The city's always upgrading, always improving. Basic air's still free – but folk can buy the scents for their home ventilation if they feel so inclined. Most do.

Choice and the freedom to choose. What's not to like about that?

I stand on the Company steps, stomping my boots into the giant Trans-Temporal Copyright Protection logo – a penguin of all the dumb-ass things – a little harder than maybe I should on account of Murdache pissing me off, and try to get my bearings.

Tanks screw you up. Like those times when you wake up in the dark, but you ain't sure if you're dreaming or not. When you drift in and out of strangeness, not knowing where you are or who you are, and then in the morning all you can remember is the uncertainty. Six months has got to be a record, I reckon. If I could face a conversation with one of the other operatives, I guess I could find out. To speak plain, I'd rather go back into the tank than-

In The Slip

I'm talking with a woman. Lovely lines across her forehead that make me think she's one of those types that likes to lift their eyebrows up, expressive and easy with their features. Lois. It's Lois! She found me in the darkness!

She's telling me things I can't hear right, but she keeps on telling me, her mouth moving faster and faster, and, yes, her whole face moving with it, eyebrows dancing a jig, leaping up her forehead and coming together in a frown.

Black snakes squirm and coil around her feet, trying to climb up her. She turns and runs, shaking them off.

My head spasms, pain rocking through it so fast and nasty I think I'm gonna throw up. I crouch on the Company steps, take a few breaths of salty air, wait for it to pass. Once I know I ain't gonna puke, I take a chloros for the pain, pull myself back to my feet. No one seems all that bothered by my display, or leastways, no one's looking my way.

Lois! I was dreaming about Lois in the tank. How could I have forgotten her? See, that's what six months will do to you.

My head still hurts something rotten, but I remember it all now. Remember meeting her at that corporate auction at Barnes International University, remember her coming up to me full of wit and anger at the world. Smart, and different from the rest of them. Lois's got eyes, and she uses them for thinking, not just for seeing. And she's got a brain that she uses for seeing, not just for thinking.

I remember us talking all night long about how fucked up everything is. How the world went wrong – *is* going wrong, from her presenttimewise. About how things should be, and all them sceevers who are too dumb to realise it'll never, ever be like that. Meeting her in the dirt bar, clandestine, to set the whole mess of it to rights over glasses of cheap beer, though God knows there ain't no setting anything right, not really.

Lois. My friend in the slip. My secret. Mine.

Thank God the memory didn't come back when I was with Murdache.

I step off Company property and onto the street, this one owned by a soft drink manufacturer. I last about a block before the teasers start annoying me. Every step brings up a little jingle for this raspberry sugar water or that prune soda pop. Don't get me wrong, I know the importance of choice, and teasers help provide that. But I'm in too good a mood right now to be tempted by them. Speaking plain, I ain't sure sometimes how people can claim to enjoy them, but hey, it's a free city.

I access my chip via the Holo, and the sidewalk TnCs appear. I walk the rest of the way home in blissful silence, reminiscing about my friend Lois, each step costing me point zero zero five of a pennycent.

Loop 16.1

There's some tall, suit-wearing sceever with tasteful purple-black skin standing in the narrow hallway of my floor. Clearly, I missed the purple trend. He looks anxious as sin, hanging around like he's about to sell me insurance or religion, one of which I got and the other I ain't in the market for.

"What you doing here, mister?"

"Nice block," he says, looking around in a polite way, as if he ain't already been staring at the walls. He's got nice eyes, dark brown like mine. Not that I'm interested in making connections, but it don't hurt to stay aware of the market. Commerce is constancy.

"You looking for someone?"

There ain't no point asking how he got in the building. The entrance downstairs is chiplocked, but that don't mean nothing if this guy's a high-level sales person. The Church, for example, got enough clout for access to most places. Would account for his expensive dye job and neat suit, too – ain't nothing sells like what you could be.

"I am, yes," he answers. "I've got... news."

"Right. And that would be the 'Good News', huh?"

He beams at me. "Yes, in a way."

Chances are he's waiting for me. He's right about the block being a good one. The Company leases apartments to its workers and this one's much more expensive than I could afford, even on my salary. Straight lines everywhere. No dust, no stains. There's minimal teasing inside and what there is, is nicely done: the art on the walls is a series of photographs with discreet messages along the bottoms, telling which tech they were shot on and a wave port to purchase it.

What really gives the building away as being desirable, though, is the space. There are only three apartments on this floor, including my own. One's owned outright – *owned*, not leased – by an old woman called Catherina Fedorov with white hair and blue eyes, her skin covered with tea-stain age spots which I try not to stare at, they're so pretty. The other apartment is leased to a young couple who work code. They work from home but I never see them. Toiletries, groceries, those kinds of things, get dropped off – I hear the door opening and closing in the night. Sometimes I like to look through my spyhole and catch one, all pale as they wave their wrists and grab their food. Ghosts.

And that's the floor I live on. So, given such a stellar line-up of potential customers, I don't reckon it's too much to be thinking the God man is here for me.

I guess folks pasttimewise might have expected things to be different here in the One True. Like we'd be beyond superstition. But the Fracture fucked a lot of people up, even now, and God's always been a big seller. When you think on it like that, makes sense we'd have Him here.

"I ain't buying," I say, pushing past him to my door.

"Are you... don't you live here?"

I fix him with my idiot glare and wave my wrist against the panel. The light, naturally, goes green, and the door unlocks. "Don't play dumb. I told you, I ain't buying."

The suit guy looks befuddled. "I'm not here to sell anything. I'm here to meet you, Mr King."

"Kong. What do you want with me if you ain't selling God?"

"Selling God?"

"What *are* you selling, then?"

"I'm not – are you Mr King or not?"

"Kong. It's on my fucking door. What is it, then?"

He brings his hand up to his face, rubbing his eyebrows, first the left and then the right. Weird. "It's my mistake. Have a nice day."

I watch him walk towards the elevator, his shoulders all slumped like he just found out his credit rating tanked. And then – I don't know why – I call to him.

"You sure you ain't selling?"

"No," he says, turning back. "I just want to talk to you. Uh. No charge."

I don't know if it's getting shot or six months in the tank or even the fact I'm still happy to have remembered Lois, but I find myself holding my door open. "Fine. Come on."

In The Slip

I don't usually have folk inside my place. I'm not here that frequent and, well... the couple of times I did have visitors, they tended not to want to stay.

I watch this guy's expression twitching as he tries to take it all in. I like to collect stuff, I guess. Pick things up. Ain't a problem for the slip – I pay for what I take, or I take what's already been thrown out and fix it up. No harm in it, I still spend my paychecks. But it tends to make other people nervous.

Suit guy steps around one of my tables, this one covered in old books I picked up in the slip, and then he's on to the next, stopping to stare at the sewing machine and the bits of material strewn across it.

He looks up at me. "You fix your clothes?"

"Just as a hobby."

"That's... How long have you been, uh, doing this?"

"What's it to you how I spend my free time?"

He rubs his fingers against his thumbs, shakes his head. Never seen a man with so many ticks – it's like he's trying to find new ways to fidget.

"I didn't mean to be rude," he says. "I'm just curious. Don't you think you should buy new?"

"You trying to insult my citizenry?"

"No, no, no, of course not. Sorry."

He picks up the jacket I was last working on, brings it up close to his pretty eyes, inspecting the seams on the shoulder.

"You've got good stitches. Strong." He glances at me. "But the thread isn't right, I think. You need something with elastic or you won't get much movement."

"You a fashion maker, then?"

He puts the jacket down, licks his lips, scratches his collar bone. "In a sense, I suppose. This is a fascinating home you have. I don't think I've met anyone with so much stuff. I mean, people have possessions, of course. I'm not saying you're... but some of this looks really old. What's that?" He's moved away from my sewing table to an old silver machine on one of the shelves along the far wall.

Something in my stomach shifts. "It plays musak, that's all."

Tall like most folk in the One True, he reaches and grabs a plastic case from the top shelf with ease. "These things? How?"

I try not to stare at the disc he's selected. "You, ah, you put the disc into that machine there, turn it on, and it'll play the songs. It's all old voksac, mostly. Ain't very interesting to a fella like you, I reckon. Why don't we go-"

"You like to listen to the voices?" he interrupts, turning the case over in his hands. "I've never seen one of these before. It seems very... bulky? How many songs does it hold?"

"Twelve."

"Only twelve?" He takes the disc from the case, his face distorted in the reflection.

"Some of them went to fifteen, eighteen. But mostly twelve."

"Could we listen?"

"Uh, yeah. Yeah, OK."

I grab the disc and put it in the player. Suit guy closes his eyes, listening. For the first time since I met him, he's stock-still, head cocked slightly, like he's trying to work the sounds out, somehow. I watch him, trying to work out how the voices, the instruments are making him feel. But he's just standing still, empty. Blank. Unreadable.

Me, I like to turn it on full blast, grab a bottle of whiskey, sit in the centre of the room, between the speakers. Let it drown me.

The song ends and suit guy's eyes open. He looks over my collection as the next track plays. "You like it raw like that? All those... feelings?" He says this like it's something he didn't expect; like he had an idea already what I should listen to.

"What's it to you?"

"Nothing," he says, smiling. "I just don't have the intelligence for it, I suppose. I find it a bit too untidy."

"You wanna tell me why you're here?"

"I know you work for the TTCP, in the slip."

"And? You only gotta look at me to know that."

He straightens up and fixes me in his sights, his foot tapping the floor. "This might seem a little odd, but... Have you recently been shot in the stomach by a dark-haired woman?"

What...? Who is this guy? How's it he knows about that? I've only been out of the tank a couple of hours, and there ain't no way the Company's been holding press conferences on one of their operatives getting shot.

I'm struggling to find something to say. I ain't had training on being asked by a stranger if I've recently been shot in the stomach by a dark-haired woman when I've recently been shot in the stomach by a dark-haired woman, and it shows.

We stare at each other while the voice of a woman long lost in the slip washes over us.

Luckily, amongst all my collectables I happen to have an alcohol cabinet. I make myself a strong drink, down it, then make another. They'll mix bad with the chloros and the tank, but I think I need it. Futuretime Kong can work out the kinks. Suit guy watches me, no longer so fascinated with my musak tastes. He's got enough of a head on him to work out the answer to his question is 'yes', I can tell from his expression.

He waits for me to finish my second drink and says, "Her name's Karen. Karen Krezzler."

"And how do you know all this? She shot you, too?"

"No. But she's been looking for you."

"That don't make sense. I ain't anyone."

He looks away. "It's not easy to explain."

"Well, you wanna try for complicated, then?"

"No, not really. Not yet."

"In that case then, mister, you might as well take your leave. I ain't got time for mysteries and I sure as silver ain't interested in them, neither."

This is something of a gamble on my part; I'm hoping a bit of reverse psychology might open him up a touch.

It don't.

"I'll go now, but we'll speak again soon." He pauses at the door, fingers tapping the frame. "Everything will work out, don't panic. And don't do anything... noticeable."

And then he's gone.

I think perhaps I might follow him, but the drugs and the liquor got me good. Besides, what difference does it make? So I got shot by some sceever. The Company knows about it. If it winds up mattering, they'll get involved. If not, well. Here I am. Tank fresh and ready to go again.

F. D. Lee

I make myself another drink and fall into my chair, down into my dreams, into the darkness.

Loop 16.2

"You don't know who this man was, then?" Catherina asks, lifting her head. "He was just waiting for you?"

I nod, taking the tray from her and set it on the coffee table in the middle of her apartment. I'm at my neighbour's dropping off some medicines and groceries. Don't know why, because it don't matter at all, not one bit, but I wound up telling her about the suit guy.

She wipes traces of powder from her reddening nose – no dye jobs for her. "But he knew about you being... unwell?"

Hah. 'Unwell'. For whatever reason, Catherina finds the ideas of the tanks upsetting. At first, I put it down to her age, but that idea got wiped once I got to spending more time with her. She's got an anxiety kink, see. Likes to get all worked up over things and then take her medicine to straighten herself out. Good thing she can afford to keep her privacy up 24/7.

Privacy is a hell of an expense – it keeps you safe not just from the teasers, see, but from the TTCP as well. A little hidden bubble of time no one can access. Something only the real-deal, big and proper patent holders can afford, those that, normally at least, choose to live up above the city, near the roof of the dome. Means Catherina can live free – hell, probably no one even knows she exists anymore, judging by the age of her. Makes her a bad citizen, true enough, but I ain't exactly in a position to judge – I come over here as often as I think I can get away with it. And I like her company, erratic as it is.

"Yeah, he knew all about the woman who shot me," I answer. "Even gave me a name."

"Oh?"

"Krezzler. Karen Krezzler."

"Sounds made up, like yours," she replies. "None of it's real. It's all a lie, they change you to make the lie work. I expect she's some kind of double agent. Probably she's been following you. Learning all about you. That chip of yours giving away all your secrets, recording your brain. You should put a gun to your head and break the connection. Can't read what isn't there."

"I ain't skulling myself, Catherina."

"You used to take my advice."

"Sure." I smile, trying to lead her away from the fit she's working towards. "But if I skulled myself, who'd keep an eye on you?"

"They watch you, you know? You think they let you live in that apartment because you're special, because you're so good?"

"Sure, why not?"

She snorts out a laugh. "This man tell you anything else?"

"Other than the name of the woman who shot me? No. All I remember is being in the alleyway and then her coming out of nowhere."

I don't mention the way this Krezzler looked, in part to avoid Catherina's panic and in part because I can't remember it all. My memory's still hazy from the tank, bits and pieces coming back in odd, indistinct flashes, like going to the edge of the city and looking through the viewfinders at the sandstorms, trying to make out shapes. But I do remember more than I did a week ago.

The woman, Krezzler, had the look of an operative. She was wearing the plain-jane clothes they make us wear, had the same nothing-type face they aim for in their employees. No wrinkles nor marks that I can recall, though that kind of detail is hard to place after the tank. But still... the best way to spot an operative is to look for what ain't there that should be. That's the truth of it: we all look wrong for looking too right. And Krezzler? I'm almost certain she fits that bill.

A rogue operative working the slip for the tempos is damn near the worst possible thing that could happen, for obvious reasons. I've informed Murdache, of course.

Catherina shakes her head. "My great-grandmother, Baba, used to tell this story-"

"-about life before the Fracture. Everyone had everything they ever needed, homes and health and education and all the rest? We got all that now. We got it better. When was the last time you heard of some disease washing through the population?"

"It's not the same," Catherina replies, pursing her lips. Wrinkles crack the skin around her mouth. Ugly, I suppose, but I like them. I like the ones on her forehead, too, and the way her hands crinkle when she moves her fingers, and the blue veins that run up her arms. She does this trick where she presses down on the big vein along her forearm, holds it and releases it, and you can actually see the blood flow back, her skin's so thin. I wonder if the reason I like her so much is on account of the fact it's so clear she's dying a little bit every day, time piling on her body like sand on the dunes outside. Tick tock.

"I don't know why, but I know it's not the same," Catherina continues, her eyes dancing as she thinks. "Baba used to say it shouldn't be like this. We should be outside."

"You taken a look outside the dome? They did that, your 'Baba' and mine, all of them. They caused the fucking Fracture, not us."

Damn it. I answered harder than I ought to, and now she's gonna go off about all the dead animals and people, the sea bubbling white toxic foam, the sandstorms and food droughts. But instead, she pushes herself up from her seat, refusing the hand I offer, and shuffles over to her bookshelf.

"Do you remember this?" she asks, pulling out a musak case, the plastic cracked.

I've been tanked a few times in my career, and Catherina knows some things come back and some things... some things stay lost in the black. I got in the habit of leaving her with stuff I don't want lost. Ain't foolproof as her meds steal from her almost as much as the tanks take from me, but it's better than nothing.

She passes me the case, her hands shaking and her pupils blown. Five minutes and she won't be in the room anymore, not in the way that counts.

I don't know what exactly I was expecting, but it ain't this. There's a man on the cover, prancing in the middle of a forest clearing, a crown of leaves around his head and his chest bare. He's playing a flute, while around him a load of woodland critters sit calmly watching – not a one showing any signs of surprise that some asshole decided to dance around like a jackass in the middle of their living room.

So ridiculous is the man it takes me a second to realise that the tree in the centre of the image has a woman growing out of it, her hair billowing into the branches, flowers strategically covering her breasts and a look of constipated enlightenment on her face as she watches the cavorting lunatic lolloping around in front of her.

I burst out laughing.

"*Love Across Time: A Collection of Traditional Love Songs?*"

"You don't remember it, then?" She grins at me, activating a whole new set of lines. I love her face. Every new expression gives away something about her life, her personality. That's why she keeps them, I reckon. How can you ever say your body's yours to own if it don't carry the marks of your choices on it?

"I listened to this?"

"I suppose so. You left it here a while ago... before you... before they got you. I meant to give it back, but I was scared. They stole some of my privacy... I know they did..."

I take that at face value, letting her ramble on a spell. There's no point pressing her when she starts talking about *Them* and *They*. I hang around for another thirty minutes or so to make sure she doesn't work herself up, but she settles down quick, switching through channels, chatting nonsense to her big screen. I read some of the lyrics on the inlay of *Love Across Time,* waiting for her to crash. It's all hippy, commierot trash – schmaltzy nonsense about true love and sacrifice, destiny and nature. Why'd I be listening to something like this? Waste of time, waste of thought, waste of hope. It's the kind of nonsense that can derail a person – if you let it, anyways.

Catherina finally blacks out. I pull a blanket over her and order some breakfast to be delivered in the morning.

I take the musak disc with me when I go.

Murdache sends me a case two weeks after I'm de-tanked. I ain't boasting when I say I'm good in the slip, and there's always something the Company needs done.

The case itself is easy; the slip's the problem. It's just far enough back to make it hard for the other operatives. This is my hunting ground, my part of the slip. The strange no-man's-land when folks still thought something could be done to bring the world back as it once was instead of accepting what it had to become. After the point of no return, but before the deaths *really* start to mount up,

In The Slip

leastways in the places that matter. Time pressure's heavy, but it's nothing I can't handle. I got my chloros, and, as I say, I'm good in the slip.

These are the factors:

Factor one: a corporate headhunter is trying to steal the brains behind the purification tech that'll be adapted to make Clear2o. Factor two: Clear2o is the best drinking water available in the One True. If they lose the copyright, we lose the water. Factor three: some idiot is gonna try to do a bit of under the table dealing. Simple case. Even the want is obvious, boring: money. Status. Yadda, yadda, yadda. What's interesting is that my mark's prepared to take the risk.

See, in this part of the slip, there're still enough independent companies for there to be actual competition, and talent's got some freedom to choose who they wanna work for. But some folk figure they can have both – keep their job *and* trade their idea elsewhere. It's a risk. See, presenttimewise, the law is such that anyone caught trading corporate secrets is looking at ten years inside and a blacklist when they get out. That's a hell of a gamble.

Course, in the One True, these laws appear kind of cute, on account of how tame they are.

So this is where I come in, to give the ones with guts – like my mark – a bit of friendly advice. And if that don't work, well... Sometimes things get less friendly. Ain't my idea of a fun time, speaking truth. There're some operatives get a kick out of kicking, the ones who've forgotten that the past ain't dead when you're in it. Me, I try to keep it on the friendly side, best I can.

Besides, most folks ain't keen on a fight, whatever they might say after they've sunk a few beers. Most times, all it takes is a few choice words, maybe a bit of swagger, and the case is done before my chloros run out. Normally that means I'll try the dirt bar after the case wraps, see if Lois might be there. But I guess it might be sensible to play it proper for a while; don't wanna mess up my chances of landing the chloros pilot.

I'm here early, waiting in a café for my mark to show. Don't want no mistakes. Other operatives don't bother with this kind of leg work, but it helps, I reckon, to get a sense of where you are, see what you can see. They take too much on trust, blasting in and out of the slip, never pausing to check the factors. Plus, the way I see it, one of the perks of the job is that you get to enjoy little things like a cup of tea without having the damn fool cup teasing you.

Presentimewise, the air's just about breathable thanks to huge fans caught in thick metal structures above the city. We're still years out from the domes and proper safety, but it ain't so bad. Not too many people, naturally. Food is expensive, disease is rife, everything's covered in sand. But that's the slip for you. What you gonna do?

Inside the café, the aircon hums away pleasantly, mitigating the 60°C outside, and the radio's playing more songs than teasers. You still get voksac in this part of the slip, and I take a moment to listen. It's barely even voksac, leastways to my ear. Tinny, electronic, the same words repeated over and over again. A sign of what's to come, but then the whole slip works to being a sign of what's to come, so there ain't much point getting all sombre about that.

The mark comes in: a woman in her mid-sixties, though she's had some work done. It's messy compared to the One True, but in this part of the slip it probably cost her a couple of months' wages. She settles herself at a table, pulls out her screen – physical, no chips here – and sets to doing whatever is it she does when she's on her own pennycent.

Time to have a few words.

And then who should appear but Karen fucking Krezzler.

She walks straight up to my mark and sits down. They talk a spell, the mark's face losing some of its pretty brown colour as Krezzler speaks. The mark shakes her head, looking for all the world like she'd shake it off her own shoulders if it weren't so well attached. Krezzler leans forward, the mark leans back, more words are exchanged, and then Krezzler pulls out her own plastic screen, points to something. My mark looks like she's gonna throw up. Her fingers get to dancing across her screen.

I wanna pull up my Holo, check the history feeds. But the café's crowded and there ain't no way I'm risking a tech-reveal in a place like this. I'm reduced to watching as my mark finishes typing and waves her hand over her screen, sending whatever she's done to Krezzler's. Krezzler checks her device, smiles, and then she's up

In The Slip

and out. The whole thing lasts about five minutes by my reckoning, but my mark looks like she just spent a week in the hospital, waiting for a loved one to die.

Follow Krezzler or check on my mark? If I go after the sceever, I could find out why she shot me as well as what the hell she's doing here and how it is a tempo is able to get hold of chloros good enough to bring her this far back.

The two-bit, shake-and-hustle tempos, the ones that save up everything they got for a bootleg Holo and cheap chloros approximates, flooties or the like, they can't go too far back, not with the time pressure. Even the tempos with money, like that kid I brought in, can't go manage much farther back in the slip. Sure, they might get themselves some black market chloros, sometimes even official Holos, but they ain't used to the pressure; the shakes give them away soon enough.

See, it's all about how far back you can get. The further back, the harder it is for the Company to unravel the changes. A race to the past in order to control the future. Gotta be the past, too. Be easier to lock onto the future, back-engineer it. Hell, the Company toyed with the idea, but they had to bin it. Can't get to the future. Not on account of the pressure – if going forward was a problem, we'd all be screwed. It's the uncertainty that's the risk. The world outside the domes is bad enough if you're out in it for more than a couple of minutes without a bio-suit and a shit load of meds – God alone knows what you might find a hundred years forward. One jump and you could be soup.

So the past is where it's at, and the Company always has the edge. The tanks, the drugs, the Stasis Bank to alert them when things seem to be changing. But most of all, the Company's got proper, trained operatives who can handle the slip.

And Krezzler, well, she looks to be handling herself just fine. To be this far back, she's gotta have the real-deal chloros, and she's got to have training. Adds weight to the conclusion she's a turncoat. Also suggests there's a mole in the Company.

Shit. I wanna follow Krezzler. But my mark looks like she's about to do something stupid, and the Company'll be less than thrilled if I lose the Clear2o copyright – hell, that's the kind of mistake that could get a man's credit rating tanked, and I ain't

F. D. Lee

looking to spend the rest of my days stuck to the pavements, begging for scraps with only the teasers for company.

I need to make a choice fast, and I need it to be the right one.

Now I'm here, I can't come back. Can't have two versions of the same person in the slip at the same time. I guess they could send another operative for the mark, but I don't want Murdache to get riled, don't want to lose the chance to road test the new chloros. Besides, Krezzler's in the system now, and she's clearly active in the slip. There'll be another chance.

I go up to the counter, order a cup of jasmine tea, take it over to my mark.

"You alright, ma'am?" I ask, my Hindi accented something horrible.

She looks up at me, and it's a testament to whatever's just passed that she don't seem at all alarmed to be approached by a stranger.

"I... that woman..."

I take a seat, nudge the cup closer to her. "Drink this, it'll make you feel better."

She takes a sip, and then another, her hands grasping the tea like it might be the only thing in the world that can save her.

"Ma'am, if you don't mind telling me, what happened just now?"

"That woman... she knew... she knew it all," the mark says between sips. She's full of panic, not thinking clearly about what she's saying or who she's saying it to. If I'm quick, I can get it out of her before she starts being a bit more sensible.

"Knew what, ma'am?"

"Everything. The merger, the factory in Tamil Nadu... all of it."

"Did she threaten you?"

"She wanted me to give her access to our financial records. Oh, God. Do you think she's going to go public?"

Truth is, I ain't sure. I can't recall a record in the One True of a scandal hitting her company in this part of the slip, and while the tank scrambles things, somehow the corporate stuff just sticks. But then, if the slip were impervious to change I wouldn't have a job.

"Did this woman want anything else?"

"No, no. She just wanted access to the finances."

I don't bother asking the mark if she gave it, some things not needing confirmation. "Listen, ma'am," I say gentle, reaching over and covering her hand with mine. "Truth is, I'm after that woman. I was here waiting on her."

Her eyes fill with relief. "Really? You're from the Beijing branch?"

"Sure. I'm over here special. But I need you to do something for me in return, OK?"

"Anything – if they find out I gave away access to the accounts... I wouldn't survive in prison... Oh, God..."

"If you do what I say, you won't have to worry about that. Now, listen. You're gonna get approached later today by someone from Intek looking to recruit you. They've heard about your work, the stuff you're doing with water purification." I give her hand a squeeze, just hard enough to feel her knuckles grind. "Turn them down, ok?"

Her relief evaporates, pain boiling it away. I almost feel sorry for her.

"How do you-?"

"It don't matter. Just turn them down and then you and I won't need to see each other again."

"You'll get the access back from that woman?"

"Sure, sure. You got my word. But you gotta say 'no', right?"

"Absolutely. Yes. I promise."

I leave her grasping her hand to her breasts, her eyes shiny.

First thing I do when I'm alone is check my Holo. It struggles, the link with the One True weaker this far back. Pop a pill while I wait. My head ain't so bad, only a gentle ache that could be mistaken for dehydration, but prevention is better than cure, ain't it?

Holo pipes up, and I see that all is as it should be. Whatever Krezzler was trying, either she didn't succeed, or it wasn't anything to do with the Clear2o copyright. Thank God the Company got a Stasis Bank to keep track of what is and what should be.

Some things, however, ain't so easy to track. Now, if I were a superstitious person, I might be wondering about Krezzler crossing my timeline twice, but... yeah. Superstition is like religion, ain't it?

F. D. Lee

People come up with these things because they need to explain the unexplainable. Slack-jaw, know-nothing types. Thinking like that, that's what got us the Fracture, to my mind. Too busy believing, wishing, *hoping*, to look around and do anything. And yet it ain't exactly normal to have the same person turn up twice in your own timeline. I mean, sure, there's Lois, but it's not the same. I seek her out, and she ain't got no idea who – what – I am. It ain't fate nor nothing like that.

Maybe Krezzler is seeking me out, too? But she didn't seem to know I was watching her…

Reckon I need to find out who this Europhile tempo sceever actually is.

Back in the One True, I get to my plan. The Company have the best records, but you need permission to go searching, and I don't fancy asking Murdache for it. I want to be part of the chloros pilot, and rocking the boat ain't gonna ingratiate myself.

Instead, I visit one of the cram schools.

I ain't been to one before. Never needed to. I started working for the Company after my Pop died and they gave me my education. Most corporations are the same, grabbing young and educating right, but the cram schools exist for those with the cash to better themselves.

I choose a Mall close to the Company, find the best cram school I can for my price range, pay, get assigned a desk, rest my Holo over the scanner and I'm linked. Fifteen minutes begins to countdown on the screen, and I'm invited to choose what is it I want to learn.

They're making me pay to read the menu? God damn sceevers…

Right. Focus. The options are business courses mostly, some finance, some engineering, some history. What do I choose? Can't just search for Krezzler – if she is rogue, likely the Company will have wiped her from the public feeds to save face.

After what feels like too long deciding, I open up the history sub-menu for '*City 1 Records*'. Get a few more pre-selected options, stuff about the Fracture, when the world tipped too far to be salvaged. The resulting wars, the mass migration as whole countries became unliveable, the sand storms and water riots, the

In The Slip

food droughts, the diseases brought back to life as the medicine failed and the ice-caps melted. The eventual dissolution of individual governments, the rise of the Industries to take their place, the five cities and the dome tech, the lotteries to decide who got in, and the birth of the One True. That's it. Stuff any kid knows.

Twelve minutes left, and I still haven't started the cram. Shit, shit, shit.

I go back to the main menu, try the *'Corporate Information'* option, and two sub-screens later I get the option to learn about the TTCP. From here, I'm able to access public information on tempo terrorists.

Ten minutes left. I gotta choose. Choice and the freedom to choose. Ain't that the kicker.

Fine. This is as good place to look as any I'm being offered, though I'll admit I ain't expecting to find a file with Krezzler's face and home address stamped across it. I select the 'download' link on the top of the screen, my brain sending impulses down the wires into my chip and through my Holo, letting the tech know I'm ready for the cram.

The world goes white, a high pitch screech and a feeling like ice hitting my brain accompanying it. I think I hear myself yelp, somewhere behind the pain.

I'm inside a room, faces all around me, data streams spooling, except for one wall which is just a giant image of a burger and fries. A clock pings up on the ceiling, counting down from nine minutes, 22 seconds. OK.

"Women."

A spinning circle appears, showing the machine's thinking. One minute later, the men disappear from the walls.

"Europhile."

Circle. Another minute. About seventy percent of the remaining women vanish.

"Brunette, white. Early to mid-thirties."

Circle. Another minute. Reveal – twenty women remain.

Check the ceiling clock – just over six minutes left. Jesus, no wonder so few people bother with the cram schools. The image of the burger starts to flash, the room filling with the smell of frying onions, fats, and carbs, tugging at the mammalian part of my brain that still craves such things above all else.

"No scars nor other marks."

Circle. Wait. Five minutes left.

Four women appear, all processed, three of which I arrested myself. My stomach rumbles and I'd swear the light in the room is getting brighter, hurting my eyes. The burger stench is stronger, that's for damn sure. I scour through the women, selecting and rejecting files, trying not to rush, trying not to miss anything. There's nothing here. Nothing to help me.

Three minutes. I'm wasting time.

Think, Kong, you dirty sceever. What are the factors that ain't being attended to? What might have been missed?

Ahhh. Maybe...

"Same criteria – unsolved cases."

The clock above ticks down as the tech thinks, searching the public feeds. It's a long shot, and I don't expect much to come of it. God I'm hungry.

One minute twenty seconds.

The three walls fill abruptly with information, a list of deaths. All of them operatives, all died in the slip. They ain't Company files, they're insurance claims. Records kept public to ensure rates are maintained correctly.

Fifty-seven seconds.

I pick one at random, skim the details. Sceever got skulled, head blown to pieces by an unknown assailant. Skim another, same thing. All happened in the slip. Work-related deaths, compensation paid to the TTCP to the tune of-

The walls white out completely, a deafening high-pitch wailing filling my whole universe until I can't see nor hear anything.

My sight comes back slowly, the screech fades, and I'm back in the cram school with a headache and the overwhelming desire to buy a burger from the food joint across the Mall. Fucking teasers. I make a deal with myself to go eat as soon as I'm done, and the sensation dies down – doesn't leave, no sir, but becomes less needful.

There's something going on, I'm sure of it. I sit back, unlink, and take a chloros to melt away the pain behind my eyes. My palms are

In The Slip

sticky. I dug my fingernails into my hands so hard I've left little crescents of blood in my flesh. I'll have to get that fixed now, as well as buying a burger.

My stomach rumbles on cue. I ignore it, go up to the front desk.

"Hey mister," I say to the receptionist.

"What?" His eyes are glued to a magazine show on his screen. The light flickers on his face, dancing shadows on top of the green ivy he's had pigmented onto his cheekbones. Makes him look like he's got some kind of expression.

"I paid for a cram but I didn't get enough time to see it all."

He breaks contact with the screen long enough to nod towards the scanner on the desk. "You can always buy another session. It's a free city."

And that seems to be all I'm going to get out of him, leastways without resorting to violence, which I'll own is tempting. But I don't want any attention on me, meaning I can't pull this sceever's head off.

I walk over to the burger joint, order, chew over my thoughts as I chew over my burger – vat-grown beef, nut-cheese, salad, ketchup, fries on the side. Just like the teaser, but damn it tastes good. Pasttimewise, they'd rather eat the cattle than fix the world, even when they knew what was coming. Slack-jaws, no wonder so many of them didn't make it. Chew chew chew, here comes the train to deadsville. Hah.

I can't figure out why the Company's kept quiet about the dead operatives. Seems to me they should have us out there hunting whoever did it – and I'm sold on the fact it's Krezzler who did the deed. She may not have skulled me, but she still shot me. Plus, she's shown already she can work the slip almost as well as I can, which is a damn sight better than the other operatives. Sure as silver, she's the one.

Being an operative, you get used to having a level of certainty about things. You get to see the same types of folks making the same types of mistakes, and it gives you a kind of, I don't know, comfort, maybe? Like, everything is a steaming pile of garbage, always was, always will be, but at least you know it. At least you ain't living locked up like Catherina, pretending pasttime was better than presenttime. Or pretending you can do anything about it, like those tempo sceevers, risking it all over something that can't be changed, anyways. Hell, or ignoring it altogether, like folks in the One True.

I swallow, the burger slimy on my tongue. It don't taste so good anymore.

The truth is, I want to see Lois. I've been stuck in the One True for almost a month, not counting the mission just done. I want to escape for a few hours, go somewhere that's ain't so bright and clean, that smells of something other than bubblegum, the current on-trend scent. Talk to someone who gets it, who understands how awful everything is. But the only place I know to find her is that dirt bar, and I reckon heading back there would raise questions like 'Why go back to the place you were shot?', 'Why were you there, anyway?' or, worse, 'How many times have you been there?'

Operatives are allowed time in the slip. It's a perk, I guess. We don't fit in wherever we are, leastways that's how I've always felt. Some of the others, they spend time together when they're in the One True. I see them. Laughing and shopping and being all pally. Pretending like they don't know better, that they ain't realised the truth. Or perhaps they genuinely haven't, which is even worse.

Anyways, we're allowed time, long as we don't make trouble back in the One True. This last factor comes to being something of a hidden prohibition. See, if you spend too much time in the slip, get friendly with someone, it becomes more likely you'll cause an aberration, screw up the One True. Say something you shouldn't, know something you ain't got no way of knowing. Show off a bit of tech that don't exist in the current presentime. That kind of thing. Ends up being easier to not bother at all, to just treat the slip as a job or, as some other operatives do, something like a zoo.

But I wouldn't make a mistake with Lois. I know better than to talk to her about this Krezzler stuff. I just... I want to see my friend. Spend some time with someone real.

Shit, shit, shit! I'm stuck, ain't I? Stuck in this God damn city, with all these idiot fucking sceevers who think the most important thing they can do with their lives is be seen wearing the same fucking jeans as-

"Everything OK, sir?"

In The Slip

I look up. The whole restaurant's staring at me. There's a kid in a uniform standing over me, Adam's apple bobbing. My hand is a fist, burger smooshed beneath it. When did that happen?

"Yeah, sorry. I'm fine," I say, grabbing a serviette to clean my hand.

Kid glances around and then leans forward. "Only, this is a family restaurant, sir. I'm... my manager..."

"I get it. I'm going." Everyone watches me leave, kids filming me on their screens. By the time I make it out of the Mall, the footage of me punching my food is on the news feeds. On cue, my Holo pipes up.

Murdache: *My office. NOW.*

F. D. Lee

Loop 16.3

"You better have a good explanation, Kong."

So. Factor one: Murdache ain't mad about the burger joint incident, which was my initial worry. Factor two: it's a hell of a lot worse. Turns out I made the wrong choice, not following Krezzler in the slip. Factor three: I misread Murdache's want.

"I don't know what to say, ma'am," I reply, trying to keep myself formal for her. Every little helps. "I figured Clear2o was the priority."

Murdache fixes me with a stony expression. "For God's sake, Kong. The same woman who shot you turns up and intercepts your mark, and you do nothing – *nothing* – about it, potentially harming the One True Timeline."

I ain't got nothing useful I can say to that, so I keep my own counsel. I already explained my reasoning, which weren't exactly well-received the first time. Murdache keeps the evil eye going a while longer and then deflates. I ain't never seen her do that before. Nothing so real, so normal. She looks exhausted, and I'll own to the fact I feel sorry for her.

She takes her seat behind her desk and waves me into the one in front.

"Something happened... something unexpected. I sent agents after her – I had to do something," she adds, defensive, though I ain't said anything against her. "There was an incident. It's bad. We need to clean it up."

'We' is it? Something's going on, that's a clear bet, and it ain't to do with me, leastways not solely. Murdache is shaken – does that mean I should be, too? I guess so, but now I know I'm not the only one on the hook, all I feel is relief.

"What kind of incident?"

"It's easier if you see it for yourself."

Murdache sends me a wave, the date stamp appearing on my Holo. I activate it, the room fills with the tinny, metallic stink of the slip, and I find myself in what looks to be a Company holding zone.

In The Slip

Or used to be, anyway. The walls are riddled with bullet holes. The windows, too, are cracked and chipped – the glass is tempered, but it looks like it took a licking, nonetheless. Also, by way of confirmation that there was a ruckus, the floor is littered with dead operatives. Five of them sprawled on the beige carpet, holes in their heads weeping blood.

Skulled, each and every one.

With their heads blown open, the tanks won't be able to fix them. It's the only way to be sure, with an operative. Worse, it'll be damn near impossible to find out what happened. Leastways without sending someone back again, putting them in the middle of a firefight, which I'm thinking Murdache ain't gonna wanna do. Besides, whoever did this was professional – they won't have hung around presentimewise for someone to just pop back and catch them.

I poke around for about half an hour, looking for any factors ain't obvious on the first glance. The operatives are neatly killed, and judging from how they lie, they didn't get much warning. Seems they were probably in conversation when it happened, which leads to the conclusion whoever did this shaved time thin. Bullet holes speak to a slip gun and, sure as silver, when I find the casings, they confirm it. Not that it really needed confirming, but it's good to have an idea when the murderer came from. The One True doesn't rely on guns to put the fear of disobedience into people.

Factor one: someone knew the operatives were gonna be here and planned the hit accordingly. Someone good enough in the slip to get in and out quick. Good shot, too. Cool head and a strong stomach. Factor two: no way a tempo could've done this, not with the speed of the jump, the time pressure, the precision. Takes training, takes experience, takes chloros and a decent Holo. Factor three: this is Krezzler's work, I'd bet my life on it. But what is it she wants?

I punch the One True back into my Holo, appearing in Murdache's office about a minute after I left.

"Jesus Christ!" she exclaims, eyes wide.

I try not to grin at the implied compliment to my time shaving skills. This is a sombre moment, after all.

"You want me to find out who did it?"

"We know who did it."

Aha. Bean spilling time. "Krezzler?"

Murdache nods.

"How long have you known there's a rogue operative jumping the slip?"

Her mouth thins, but she don't ask me how I happened to guess so accurately. "Not long enough. Sit down."

"Right," she says once I'm sat. "Listen to me. I don't know what's happening. That's the truth of it. But I'll be damned if I'll get caught with my pants around my ankles, not with the new chloros about to go live."

I know what's about to happen. I can see it on her face. They're gonna ground me. I'm unreliable and there's a killer in the slip, someone who skulls. Murdache shouldn't have let me back on the job so quick. I screwed it up, folks got snuffed, and now she's on damage control. Looking for someone to blame.

I'll miss the chloros pilot. Six months in the tank having my gut repaired, then fouling up in the slip, losing Krezzler and them operatives getting skulled on account, plus losing my cool at the burger bar... None of it looks good for me. And that's without them knowing why I was at the dirt bar where I got shot in the first place, carrying on with Joe.

Joe?

No Lois. I went to see Lois.

Who's Joe? Why did-

There's a man with midnight hair and skin the colour of wet sand. Taller than me, heavier, handsomer. A scar on his chin and love in his eyes.

He puts his arms 'round me, grabs my hair, kisses me again and again and again. Frantic, quick kisses, not like the ones in the movies, but desperate and messy, like he's trying to leave a history of himself on my skin. My perfect skin, where no history ever shows.

I know him, I think.

Darkness slithers across his shoulders, up his legs, along his arms. Am I supposed to do something? It pools in his chest, contracts, expands, absorbs him.

In The Slip

Someone shoots me. The bullet ripping through my jaw, turning my teeth and tongue into so much gritty mush. And for a second, a second less than a second but long enough, I'm aware, awake. The bullet tears through my skin and muscle and bone, forcing itself into my brain, and I know that I want to die.

I know that I want to die.

I want to die.

"Jesus, Kong, what the hell?"

I'm doubled over in my chair, Murdache's hands on my shoulders, shaking me silly. My head pounding, the worse headache I've ever felt, ice growing inside my skull, my eyes about to pop out of my head, oh God, it hurts so bad.

I shrug Murdache off, grab the tub of chloros from my pocket, fumble a couple into my mouth and swallow. It takes too long, but the heat builds from my joints, finally reaching my head, melting away the pain and the terrible, freezing emptiness beneath it.

Joe. The guy I was with at the bar. The other tempo. Shit. There was another tempo the night I got shot? Why the hell did the tank take that away from me?

"Kong, what was that?"

I look up. Murdache has moved back to the safety of her desk. She looks shocked. Angry. Scared. Well, she ain't the only one.

"The tank," I say, trying to sound confident. "I'm still getting my thoughts back. It's nothing."

"Nothing? You had a God damn *seizure* in my office, Kong. I'm not insured for that kind of thing – how would I have explained it to the doctors?"

"It's fine. I'm fine. It's normal."

She shakes her head. "That wasn't normal. You've been working too long. I'm going to contact the lab. They'll look over you, get you fixed up."

"They'll put me back in the tank. That's all they ever do when things go wrong. And if they tank me again, I won't be able to get Krezzler. The woman who shot me and skulled those agents. Who was at the café."

"I know who she is," Murdache snaps. But her hand hovers above her screen. "Go on."

F. D. Lee

Here we go. Gamble time.

"I'm the best you got in the slip, and you know it. The time pressure don't get me so bad, and I can shave my jumps better than anyone. I can get into slips other folks can't, hell, I bet I can even jump my own slip, I'm that fucking fast. You need me to get Krezzler, and you need me for the trial. Sure as silver, ma'am, you ain't got no choice. Not this time."

A pause, a frown. Then she says, "No. You need to be tanked again."

"If we can bring Krezzler in, the bosses will be happy."

Fury on her face at that. Damn it. I pushed too hard. Murdache is a career woman, but she's proud. She don't like being manipulated, and I ain't good enough at corporate politicking to cover the fact that's what I'm doing. Fuuuuuuuck. Maybe the tank is still an option? Better than being fired. Should I tell Murdache about Joe, add some honey to the pot?

No. I can't give up Joe without also giving up Lois.

And, and, and.

And. And.

And I don't want to.

Murdache folds her arms. "How old are you?"

"Thirty-eight. You don't need to go through the questions with-"

"How long have you been working for the TTCP?"

"I joined up when I was fifteen. After Pop died."

"Do you remember how your Pop died?"

"It was an accident."

"What kind of accident?"

"I don't remember."

"What about shopping? Do you like to shop?"

"Sure, commerce is constancy."

"What colour's the-"

"Come on, Murdache – Nafre," I say, trying to sound reassuring and not wheedling. "You know I'm as good as I ever am. And who else have you got?"

We stare at each other a spell. Then she nods. "Fine. You can go into the slip, see what you can find out about this woman. Recon only. You understand?"

Shit. She went for it? "Yes, ma'am."

In The Slip

"Listen to me, Kong. We're under the microscope. Krezzler, the murders – the board is watching us both. That stunt in the burger bar hasn't won you any favours, and you know there's been complaints about you before. Your clothes, that voice you put on. It reflects badly on me. But if we can catch this woman... it would go a long way towards making some of that up."

"Yes, ma'am, that it would."

"This is an important period for the TTCP."

"I'm better in the slip than I am here."

"I'm not sure you're good anywhere, Kong."

I'd like to be able to counter that, but I reckon I've pushed my luck about as far as it'll go.

I check through the Company records, Murdache now approving me access to the dead operatives' TTCP files.

There ain't much to be had. The operatives were middle-of-the-road players, good enough in the more recent slips but nothing special. Joined the company young, like me. Orphans, too. They'd been tanked a few times, which goes with the job, but cleared and back on duty within a few weeks. One of them got a warning a while back for buying lottery tickets, but since she didn't do nothing with her winnings but spend it on clothes and drink and sex, the Company seemed happy to let her off with a short suspension. No changes, no babies, no murders. Just shopping.

Boring, empty people, right up to the point Murdache sent them after Krezzler and they became boring, empty corpses. Nothing to be had here. Still, I got access now... what else might I find? I try *Karen Krezzler* but come up short, the Company having no record of her whatsoever.

I try again, spelling the name different. Nothing. Try again; nothing. Pop a pill, rub away the headache building behind my eyes, try again. Nothing. Right. That's... unexpected. Krezzler ought to be in the system. She's a tempo and a murderer, not a ghost for Christ's sake.

Krezzler wanted something from that woman in the café on the Clear2o contract... I flick through a few screens 'til I get to the Clear2o records. I ain't entitled to see much, but what I get is still a

F. D. Lee

country mile better than what a cram school might teach, plus I don't have to plug my chip in to get it.

The Company have done a lot of work for Clear2o over the years; everyone wants water, right? Hardly a surprise tempos would target Clear2o. They worked on desalination first, after the seas rose. Seems like it was a government concern, back at the beginning. Strange, but stranger things have happened. The first station was an international endeavour out on the Antarctic slush plains, damn near on top of the actual Fracture.

Now *that* does surprise. Not the location – the Antarctic was higher and drier than the Arctic, which being an ocean suffered the same fate as the rest. The co-operation. The Antarctic was always the cause of squabbles between countries, and once it became clear it was the last, dwindling supply of potentially drinkable water – before Clear2o, anyways – the story goes everyone went coco over the place: governments, businesses, NGOs, charities, the lot. Hell, maybe they did. The records ain't history, not as such. They're corporate logs, kept in the Stasis Bank by the TTCP to make sure things stay as they should.

It's interesting. A new factor. Does that mean a new want, too? Or an old want I ain't accounted for? Something's tickling at me, that's for damn sure.

Water's the key. Once everyone that mattered accepted that the world wasn't salvageable, the domes went up pretty quick. Lotteries organised who got to live in one of the five, with those from the original countries getting priority, followed by the important folk from other countries, and then the remainder going to a lucky million or two regular folks. Those that lost got left in the world, poor slobs.

With the domes, we had a workaround for all the radiation from the sun, let loose without proper ozone. The Indian fans, once the weight issues were ironed out, were easily adapted to clean the air and keep it cool enough to counter the heating properties living inside a shell created, with the help of some black n' white paint on the outer sphere. Recycle tech already existed, ironical as that is. Food creation had been sorted, too, thanks to the food droughts meaning clever minds had to think of ways to feed 12 billion people without steady access to rice, grain, pulses, or vegetables.

In The Slip

It was the water that was the issue. What didn't join the rising seas got lost to the air. See, the heat burned a lot of what was drinkable into the atmosphere, leaving thick, salty sludge behind. Funny, ain't it? When the oceans first came up to swallow us, everyone thought that'd be the problem... drowning, erosion, that kind of thing. And it was, during the build-up to the Fracture, the cracking point. But, in the end, it was the lack of water that threatened the world.

Until Clear2o...

I sit for a while longer, running through what logs I got access to. At some point, the various governments pulled out of the Antarctic project, lacking funds and needing to deal with the mounting crises on their own doorsteps. And then, somehow, it was just Clear2o out there. There's even a picture on file: an old 32 mp, seven sceevers all lined up in fleeces and sunglasses, rubber wading boots sinking into the slush, grinning like chumps with a penguin sat in the middle of them.

Eight names are coded to the image, along with the sat nav and date stamp. Presumably one for each of the people in the picture and then whoever's holding the camera: *Kier Lore, David Snell, Aarvi Kaur, Kioshi Taiki, Barry Longsworth, Ivy Ivanova, Guilliam Bourdieu, Jiang Cheung. 2067.* The caption under the image reads '*Mission Accomplished*'. Nice boast, but I guess if they worked out the secret to the water, they got every right to it.

I cross-check the names on the image with the data stream, both general and TTCP, but I don't come up with anything. Whoever these people were, they ain't no one now. Just more dead faces floating in the slip, same as everyone else. Must have let the Clear2o patent fall from their fingers. Bad luck for them, worse luck for me.

None of this is any help working out what Krezzler's after, nor why she's skulling operatives to get it. Which means I gotta do something even I think is a damn fool idea.

F. D. Lee

Loop 16.4

New Delhi boils me in my skin, heat seeping through my grey overcoat and past my shirt to press up against me. The 60° heat should be a warning but, alltimewise, people been good at ignoring the signs of what's to come.

I can see the café my mark is waiting inside, no idea she's about to be accosted by either me or Krezzler. I ain't got a whole heap of time – if I'd known I needed to come back here, I wouldn't have arrived early. But that's the slip, ain't it? Even jumping in and out regular, you never know what's going to happen in your own timeline.

I've got roughly fifteen minutes before pasttimewise me will show, which is about an hour before Krezzler shakes up my mark. Can't be in the slip at the same time as myself; double DNA confuses the Holos, and you're as likely to be thrown out of the slip as you are to be squished up and flattened into a temporally uncertain pancake. This ain't the easiest of jumps, no sir, but it seems the most obvious place to start. At least Krezzler didn't shoot me here.

And while I might be too early to catch Krezzler, that doesn't mean I can't gather some factors in the meanwhile. Wherever she came in, it'll be close by, somewhere private, where she's unlikely to get stumbled on. Which is all well and good, but this ain't exactly a quiet place, even with the drop in population.

At this point in the slip, India is the heart of Industry, the place where the big bucks are made. There're skyscrapers all around me, interspersed occasionally by smaller buildings, more traditional to the area. It's not monotonous like the One True, each building still having something of its own personality, but glass, plastic and chrome are present in the newer constructions. Most of the big buildings are owned by Internationals, and the teasers are crass compared to what they'll achieve futuretimewise.

It's kinda quaint, to see the electric cars buzzing around, bikes weaving in and out of the traffic, the chipped pavements, the giant, ugly proto-hovers sucking all the dirty air up from the streets and off into the atmosphere. All the little touches here and there that let me know where I am, and that where I am is somewhere.

There's an alleyway about 10 metres away, people walking past it like it don't exist. Not unlike the one Krezzler shot me in. It's as good a bet as any that's where she'll be coming in. I'll be arriving soon, but at least I got a place to start. This presentime burned, I walk back into the Company owned office block, type the code into the door and, safely inside, I return sixty-seven minutes later, myself having come and gone in the time between.

First thing I do is head back to the alleyway. There's not much to see, not if you don't know what you're looking for. Me, I do know.

Factor one: there're scuff marks on the ground, sort of like a car took a turn too quick. Slip marks, but faint, easily missed or disregarded. Someone knew what they were doing. Factor two: a cat sits on a crate, its fur up, like the fine hairs on my arm. Factor three: along with the slip marks, there's a crackle to the air, indicating a temporal shift. Before the weather came under contract, you'd get the same sense during a thunderstorm, when the air tastes like rain and electricity. I like the rain, on account.

Seems open and closed that this is where Krezzler came and went from. Got to admire her skill. Even some operatives ain't so great at using their Holos, leaving more of a mess behind; darker slip marks, more atmosphere, sometimes even a few overturned items. She must have jumped just a few moments before I arrived, judging from the tingle in the air and the taste of rain.

Alone in the alley, I check my Holo – maybe there're some factors I can pull from the feed. The thing fritzes and flashes, the little dot that tells me where and when I am popping in and out of existence. Weird. Something stirs in my memory, a creature moving underwater causing ripples on the surface. And then it's gone, lost to the black. Damn tanks.

No matter, I'll check the feeds later. Take a closer look around and what do I see…? Factor four: there's a scrap of paper on the ground. Probably nothing, but I pick it up anyway, smooth it out, and am met with a name:

Barry Longsworth.

Same name from the photo? One of the sceevers in the Antarctic. A factor, right enough, just I got no clue what it signifies, what the want is.

I shove the paper into my pocket, my hand catching on a tub of chloros. Why not? Prevention is better than cure. Swallow one down and head over to the café. The mark's still there, nursing the cup of jasmine tea I bought her when I was pasttimewise me.

"Ma'am?"

"What – oh. Is... did you forget something?"

"Sure did." I pull up a chair. "Do you know anyone called Karen Krezzler?"

She frowns a bit. I let her take her time, not being in a hurry now that I'm not here anymore.

"No," she finally says, and I believe her. "But thousands of people work for us. We're one of the biggest firms in the region-"

"Do you mind if I borrow your screen?" I say, cutting off her boast.

"What for?"

"Bit late to be worrying about security, don't you think?"

She blushes at that but holds her ground. "Better late than never. Who are you, anyway? Who in Beijing do you report to? Your accent sounds American, but you speak strangely."

"I travel with the job."

She snorts. "We're an international company, and I've not met anyone like you. Almost American, but with a hint of Europe. Where are you from?"

Damn it. She's had time to think.

"I'm a consultant."

"I think I need to see some I.D. Just to confirm, you understand."

Shit. "Sure, sure. Or I could simply tell them that you just gave away corporate intel to a stranger in a café."

Her eyes narrow. "Who are you?"

I consider reaching over and hurting her again, but not for long. She's wary now, and the cafe is crowded.

"Do you wanna take a guess where I'm from? Or do you wanna give me your screen and hope to hell I don't report you for giving away intel *and* for waiting to meet an Intek headhunter? You changed your mind on prison in the last few minutes?"

In The Slip

She says a word I don't know but which I'm guessing is obscene, and hands over her screen. I open her VPN, go into the universal address list, looking for Karen Krezzler. I get nothing, but I ain't surprised by that. Didn't think Krezzler was from this part of the slip, but now I know it at least.

On a whim, I type in *Barry Longsworth.*

Nothing.

I close down the VPN and do a general web search for Barry Longsworth. This is even worse. Pages of results, links to socials, businesses, criminals, inventors, even a couple of celebrities. Who'd have thought there'd be so many folks out there prepared to name their kid Barry?

"Excuse me, sir, this lady says you're bothering her?"

There're three servers standing over me, my mark hovering behind them, looking smug and anxious all at once. I was too caught up in my searching to notice her getting help. Rookie mistake, but I can beat myself up over it later.

"Did she, now? Fine. Here's your screen, ma'am. Remember what I said about Intek. I really don't wanna have to see you again."

Time to leave. And there's only one other place left to try to find Krezzler.

I arrive in the alley outside the dirt bar about twenty minutes after I got shot.

My head starts screaming, my Holo vomiting a long, high pitch warning. Muscles tighten in my gut, the air collapsing, crushing me. My lungs struggle, spots of colour filling my vision.

The Company didn't clean me up properly.

I blink hard, pull my Holo up close to my eyes, trying to get a reading, but all I can see is warning lights. My brain feels like it's folding in on itself.

Keep calm. Can't be too much of me left here, or else I'd already be squashed out of existence, flattened, uncertain. The door there, the dumpster there. I got shot somewhere between the two. Moving my legs is like trying to lift a God damn car, but the closer I get, the more urgent the noise from my Holo becomes.

F. D. Lee

Follow the sound, each step harder, heavier... images flash in front of me – echoes, memories, timelines, all falling on top of me. The universe trying to right itself, to fix what I'm making wrong. I see myself standing, shaking, Krezzler coming up behind me, and then it's gone. I stagger closer to the spot, rainbows colours all around me, a smell like pine – no, burning sugar, sickly, cloying.

My Holo is frantic now, wailing its banshee scream. The smell of forests and sugar grows thicker, and I see myself falling, hand to my stomach, hitting the concrete.

There.

I crawl the last few feet, my insides tight like God himself is squeezing me dry, and spot it. A tiny piece of glistening, pink matter. A fragment of my gut, maybe; a chunk of flesh thrown loose. Doesn't matter. My head hits the ground with a crack, my ribs bands of burning heat, throat closing, tongue swelling.

My hand shakes as I pick up the forgotten, unnoticed piece of me and shove it in my mouth.

And, just like that, the pressure lifts, the colours fade, the smells disappear. I pull gasping breaths into my lungs, careful not to spit myself out accidental. My arms and legs ache like I've been running a marathon, my head pounding like I'm waking up after a week of cheap drinking. But I'm altogether now, and the universe seems happy with the hack.

Stumble over to the wall and rest against the bricks, my legs stretched out, aching. Gather myself. The little piece of me sits on my tongue. I almost want to laugh, but I hold it in. Instead, I concentrate on the feeling on my tongue, the weight of *me* there, balancing it the way people do with wine when they're pretending they know something about it. It's soft and still warm, and there's a bit of grit on it from the ground.

I'm conscious, in that way you sometimes are of what you're doing, of the fact I got a bit of myself in my mouth, an actual piece of myself that evidences I'm alive and real, and that I can feel it, feel it as close and personal as nothing I've felt before.

I chew it up and swallow it.

Hah. It don't taste of anything at all.

Guess that figures: blank inside and out.

In The Slip

Well, this ain't the time to worry about that. I haul myself onto my feet, take a look around. There are slip marks everywhere, which makes it impossible to tell if Krezzler's already jumped or if she's still here. Probably she jumped straight after shooting me. But I was hoping there might be something left behind. Something other than me, that is.

Damn it, those God damn sceever amateurs! When all this is done, I'm gonna find out who was responsible and break their legs. I mean, Jesus. Coming here was reckless even without those idiots leaving bits of me behind and ruining the scene, destroying the factors. I should have known better, right? And now I'm gonna have to go inside. Haven't got a choice, hands are tied.

Probably it'll be OK. I'm here with a reason, and Lois was absent the night I got shot. If Murdache or the Company get to asking questions, I reckon I can spin a tale. Besides, if they were going to, they'd have done it already, right? And I'm careful, making sure to keep myself irregular in Lois' slip, not spending too long with her at any fixed point. I keep it chronological from Lois' presenttimewise, to keep our friendship moving right for her... but I'm careful, like I said. See, I got a cover to explain the fact I might disappear for months at a time and if I do let something out which I shouldn't, well, my cover's good for that, too.

It ain't lying. It's caution.

Now, anyone with half a brain will work out that there's a canyon sized flaw in my friendship with Lois, and I've got more than half a brain. I know she'll age out, I just try not to think on it too much. Everything's got a sell-by date, you don't need no cram school to teach you that.

She won't be there, anyway. But Krezzler might. And yes, maybe the other tempo too. Joe. The mystery man, the seducer, the liar.

So I gotta go in. Ain't my fault. And I'm here now, ain't I? It's out of my hands.

F. D. Lee

Loop 16.5

The bar is God-awful.

Noisy, dark, sticky. Kind of place you don't wanna touch with your bare skin, on account of all the people previous who've touched it with theirs.

So, what's new?

Check my Holo first. It's still playing up, though whether that's on account of what happened outside or it's related to the fritzing in India, I got no idea. I ain't about to go confessing it's broken to the docs, not with Murdache on pins and needles about letting me in the slip at all. Not when I'm already pushing my luck being here.

I take my time looking around, eyes moving over the walls (still displaying paper teasers for local services; some electronic movers, but no 3D, not in this part of the slip), the pool table (same two women playing), the signs (still not multi-lingual). It's not changed, leastways, in no way I can see.

Factor: this bar was aberrant. I might have jumped back into this part of the slip, but this part of the slip shouldn't be the same as it was when I was here before, on account of the Company having fixed it. This timeline should have been pulled and tethered, sewn back into the history of the One True.

Which means...

It could mean...

Does it mean...?

I drag my gaze over to the bar, feeling like lead weights are pulling my pupils down. It's the same as I recall it being seven months ago, the same as it was thirty minutes ago, before I got shot. The robot serving up cheap beers, the teasers behind glowing with the promise of the future that's always, alltimewise, due to occur...

And sat on a barstool, drawing doodles in beer on the counter, blonde hair falling over her shoulders, is Lois.

Not Joe. Not Krezzler.

Lois.

In The Slip

Why is she here? Did she... did she come in after I went out back? What's going on? She wasn't here before – it was the guy, Joe. It was him I came here to, to... to confront. To haul back to the One True. Him and Krezzler.

He, no, *they* must have jumped the slip when they realised I was on to them. That'd be about right, tempo cowards. Sliming all over me, muddling my head, and then running away when his – *their* plans went south. But that don't account for what Lois is doing in his place.

Shit.

The air rushes out of my lungs, my gut knotting like I just took a punch.

I left Lois here with a pair of psycho tempos on the loose. No. It's fine. Krezzler and Joe ain't anywhere to be seen. I don't know what's going on, but at least they took the sensible option and jumped slip quick.

And Lois, my Lois, is alive and well, sat where she always does, no doubt waiting for me to pull up a stool and bitch and whine about the world being the way it is, why it's all going wrong, who's to blame. It's a topic she knows a lot about, and I like talking with her on it. It's good, right, to know you're not alone with your thoughts? Hell, sometimes I spend whole evenings drinking my beer and just listening to her rant and rave.

I swear I feel the air rushing back into my body as a grin stretches my face, the weight of my fears lifting.

I wanna go over and wrap my arms around her. Hug her 'til it all goes away: Murdache and the tanks and the pain of time. The memory of myself on my tongue, the gritty nothingness of it, proof that I ain't anything at all. Catherina and her anxiety addiction. My shitty neighbours who never leave their apartment. The stuckers on the sidewalk with their glassy eyes and outstretched arms. The cram schools, and the domes, and the teasers. Clear2o and the dirty, metallic water you get for free. All the choices, what to buy, what to wear, who to be...

I wanna hug her and bless her and thank her for being herself, for being here, for being alive and honest and angry, and for being my friend, trouble though the friendship is.

But I can't.

Besides, I ain't exactly sure what I'd say to her when she asks me what's wrong, as – sure as silver – she'll know there's something wrong. Well, something more wrong. Reckon she suspects already there's *something* wrong with me.

See, Lois and me ain't never lied to each other about the things that matter, just the little stuff like who I really am and what I really do. I got my cover, see. My way to not get caught out by the Company and to not get caught out by Lois, neither.

I told her I'm a ghostwriter for famous folk. If I don't see her for months or more, she thinks I'm working with some star on their latest novel or memoir or whatever shit they're trying to sell to make them look human. That allows me to keep irregular time in her slip which keeps the Company off my trail, on account of the fact I never seem too fixated on any one spot. As an added bonus, it also means that while Lois sometimes gets annoyed with my erratic visits in and out of her life, she don't ask too many questions.

More than that, though, it means I can talk about my life. If I say something that to her presenttime mind that seems strange or far-fetched or downright impossible, I can just tell her I'm working on a book. And because I'm a ghostwriter, I don't have to explain why she ain't never seen my name on any covers. Plus, I can say I've signed a load of contracts and such to protect my client's anonymity, should she ever wanna know any details about them.

One time, Lois even claimed she'd read one of 'my' books. Said the story matched a thing I'd been talking about. Out of curiosity, I bought the book she named. It was a dystopia.

All those evenings spent with Lois in this dismal place, talking about dismal things. Sharing it. And there she is, waiting for me. I imagine myself going over, striking up a conversation, talking in circles 'til I feel better again. Or worse, sometimes. Same as it ever is.

God, I am so...

So...

Just so...

I need to make sure Krezzler ain't still here.

Check the johns. No one in the ladies'; the men's also clear. Take a moment to breathe. Catch up with myself, that kind of thing. Got

In The Slip

the feeling like somehow I've missed out on something, which must be because of what happened outside. Seeing echoes of myself, almost getting made uncertain. No other way to account for this... disappointment.

Wash my hands and face, focusing on the silence of the slip. Catch my reflection in the mirror above the sink. Look away, eyes landing on the faucet. Study the water, pouring endlessly down the drain where it'll join the sewage, get to the sea, wherever that might be, and soon enough it'll be rain, then back to the reservoir and, eventually, come back out of a faucet somewhere. Maybe even back out of this one. 'round and 'round and 'round, with no idea at all that this is where it started from, just like-

F. D. Lee

Loop 16.6

I crack my eyes open, blinking in the light.
"Where am I?"
Someone snorts, dismissive. "Seriously? 'Where am I?'"
I snap my head up, dizzy for a moment. Lucky for me, I'm angry enough to push past it. Sitting opposite is the dark-haired woman, the tempo, the murderer. Before I know it, I'm trying to strangle her, but my arms are bound behind my back, and strain as I do against the rope, I ain't moving.
"Krezzler," I like to think I growl.
She crosses her legs, raises an eyebrow. "You remember me."
"You shot me, you dirty, chicken shit piece of-"
Krezzler jumps up, hits me across the head with the butt of her gun. "Let's get this started, then. How many times have I killed you?" she asks, settling back into her seat.
"What kind of question is that?"
"I'd have thought a pretty simple one."
She's lucky I'm tied up, that's a fact.
"Never. You ain't never killed me. But you wasted those operatives, I saw it. Why'd you skull them, huh? They get too close?"
A line appears between her eyebrows, gone in an instant. "I don't skull people."
"I suppose I just imagined it, then? You're a coward, right enough. You shot me in the gut and then skulled those sent to bring you in."
Krezzler starts thumbing the hammer of her gun, clicking it on and off. "Think what you like, sleepyhead, I don't care. So, you reckon I've shot you once, never killed you... But you remember the bar. Anything else?"
The bar, the bar and the toilets and...
"Lois – what did you do to her? I swear to God, if you've hurt her, I'll kill you with my bare hands."
"You're in no position to make threats."
"Where's Lois?"

"She's fine. I wasn't expecting you to come back to that moment in the bar. You've not done that before."

"Cut the crap, lady. Where's Lois? Why are you hunting operatives? What're you after?"

"Good grief. You don't remember anything."

She sounds bored, which ain't exactly inspiring. When you're tied up by someone who's already shot you once and seems to think they've killed you multiple times, you kind of want them interested. Leastways, that's what I'm thinking. Still, to my relief, Krezzler stops thumbing the hammer of her gun.

"Kong, Kong, Kong. Hah, Carrie Bagges, Joe King, Lois Pryce. And then there's King Kong, the terror of the timelines. They do like their little jokes, don't they?"

"Listen lady, it'll go easier for you if you tell me what the hell is going on. Why are you skulling operatives?"

Krezzler glances behind me. I try to turn to see what she's looking at, but she's got me tied up too tight.

"Sure, why not?" She smiles, sharp and cruel, eyes snapping back to me. "Sixteenth time's the charm, apparently. I'm using the slip to catch a killer, as a matter of fact, just like they set the TTCP up for, back in the day. But I guess you don't remember that, huh?"

"You're out of your mind."

"No, I don't think so. I'm not the one off my head on chloros, jumping through time with no mooring, no hope, no purpose. I'm not the one pretending not to see what's so clearly all around me."

"And what's that, then?"

"That it's all gone wrong. That we keep *letting* it go wrong. Back there, back in the One True, the only thing worse than being one of the working poor is being jobless, isn't that right? Not earning, not contributing. Nothing to show their value to the world. Fuck them, right?"

She leans forward, resting on her knees. Like we're having a sensible conversation.

"And then there's all the rest of you little worker bees, thinking you're free when all you've really got is the illusion of choice, and the terrible pain of spending your life pretending everything is exactly what you want it to be. Always looking for the next thing to choose from an array of identical things. How many types of chewing gum can you buy now, in the One True? How many different types of the exact same fizzy sugar water have they got in their vending machines?"

"What? So you're skulling folk because you can't decide between spearmint and peppermint?"

Krezzler's up, fast as a snake, the barrel of her gun to my forehead, her face up close to mine.

"I should kill you again. Hell, I'm doing you a favour each time I do." A smile settles on her face, worse than her boredom. "And killing you is satisfying, Kong. It relaxes me."

And then it's gone, her expression returning to something blank, calm. She pulls back, removes the gun. "You shouldn't forget that. Hey, here's a fun choice. You'll enjoy this, a One True Timeline man like you. If you were about to die, who'd you choose to spend your last moments with?"

I open my mouth to speak when someone else gets there first.

"Karen, for God's sake. This stops *now*."

Lois.

It's Lois.

I twist in my chair, frantic to see behind me, but to no avail. "Lois? Is that... you're here? Are you OK?"

She walks around the chair, resting her hand on my shoulder, squeezing it. But then she walks up to Krezzler, ignoring my questions.

"He doesn't understand," she says. "We need to reset."

"Fine by me, but you've got to admit this is the best he's been. Maybe we should let it play out."

Lois shakes her head. "No. We should start again."

"What the fuck are you talking about?" I demand. "Lois, what are you doing with her?"

They ignore me.

"Might work. Might not. He's a stubborn S.O.B.," Krezzler says, waving her gun in my direction like any normal person might wave a hand. "Up to you. I'm happy to try if you both-"

"What the fuck is going on!" I scream.

They finally turn to look at me. Krezzler rolls her eyes, folds her arms. Lois comes over to kneel in front of me.

In The Slip

"I'm sorry it's come to this, Kong. I didn't want it to," she says gently. "This must be very hard for you."

"Are you kidding me? No, it's peachy. I ain't never had such a nice time in all my life."

Lois smiles at that. She always did have a sense of humour.

"I aim to please," she says.

"Lois, what's going on?"

She looks over her shoulder at Krezzler, then at the wall behind me. I get Krezzler not being keen on looking at a person, eye contact being a human behaviour and all, but it stings that Lois is doing the same.

"I'm sorry," Lois says at last. "Can you give us a moment?"

"Fine." Krezzler slides her gun into the holster at her hip. "I need some fresh air, anyway."

Krezzler disappears from view. There's some shuffling behind me, a door opening and then, after a slight delay, slamming shut. Lois grabs the chair and sets it in front of me. She don't untie me, though.

"What do you remember?"

I tell her as much as I'm able, as much as I think will keep her talking. I wanna ask her so much more. I wanna know how Krezzler got her hands on her, and if she's safe – if she even understands the danger she's in. Does she know Krezzler can jump the slip, kill her before she even knows who Krezzler is? But I can't risk the mission, so I omit. Omission ain't lying.

"So, you've only met Karen those two times?" Lois asks once I'm done talking. "Before now, I mean?"

"That's what I said, ain't it? Lois, she's a murderer. You need to get out, now, before she comes back."

"That's not... How long have you known me?"

"Long enough to be thinking you should focus on the fact you're trapped with a killer."

Lois looks at me a long while, her lower lip caught in her teeth. "I know, Kong. Believe me."

"You know? What kind of game you playing, Lois? I thought... I thought we were friends." This last comes out higher than I intended, and I cough a bit to cover it.

F. D. Lee

"Oh, Kong," Lois says, leaning on her forearms. "We are friends. We're... we're family, in a way. But there's a lot you don't understand. I've been trying to help you see it correctly. I want to help you. I think you might be the only person who'll understand what I'm trying to accomplish."

"So tell me the truth, then."

"But what is the truth? How do you know when you find it – how can you help other people see it? I'm sorry this is happening this way. It's hard for me, too." She shakes her head. "Karen doesn't – she wouldn't understand. I don't think she can, not anymore. But you will, I'm sure of it. I'm counting on it."

"Nothing you're saying makes any kind of sense."

"Nothing makes sense, I thought we agreed on that?" She shoots me a smile. "How many times have we sat in that shitty bar, drinking until dawn, putting the world to rights?"

I get what she's trying to do but I ain't in the mood to be won over. Being knocked-out, kidnapped and tied to a chair does that to me. "Enough times for you to speak plain, I'm thinking."

"Yes," she sighs. "You're right. Ask me the question then."

I take a breath. Steel myself for what has to come next. What the factors are pointing towards. "You're a tempo?"

I want her to deny it. I want her to say I've got it all wrong, that she's, I don't know, working an undercover job, or that she really is someone from the slip and Krezzler's tricked her somehow. But the denial doesn't come.

"How long?" I ask.

Lois stands up, sighs. "I don't know where to start. How do you untangle something that's been knotted up so tight?"

"You could start the literal way, and untie me."

"I don't think I can do that."

"Then you might as well get the psycho back in here."

I say it, not thinking she will. Of course I don't think she will. But if there's one thing the slip teaches you, it's that you can always rely on people to be lying, cheating, no good, selfish sceevers, and it turns out Lois is no exception.

She makes to leave and, speaking plain, I'm tempted to let her go. What's the point of it all? I'm bound to a chair, locked away somewhere years from home, with the woman who shot me and the woman I thought was my friend letting her.

So, I'm pretty surprised when I say, "No, wait. Stay. Talk to me."

"I can't untie you. You're dangerous. You know that, don't you?"

"*I'm* dangerous? Can you hear yourself? I ain't never hurt anyone, leastways not in any way that lasts. And I'd never hurt you. That's the God's honest truth."

"You hurt people all the time, Kong."

"Bullshit."

"You're a killer, same as all of us."

"When have I ever killed anyone?"

Lois tilts her head. "In the slip, for starters. Every time you 'fix' an aberrant timeline, every time you ensure things stay the same, you kill a thousand possible futures, a million possible lives."

"Lives that ain't never happened. That's not murder."

"Maybe. But that's not how everyone sees it."

"Right, yes. I heard it before from you tempos – maybe, if we didn't keep the timeline in order, someone might come up with better tech, maybe someone might find a way to clean up the world. Maybe, maybe, maybe. Well, you know what? Even if there was some magical saviour of the little ball of death that used to be our planet, folk would fuck up the new world just the same as they already did the old one. But that woman, Krezzler, she's killed actual, real people."

"Killing those operatives... she, uh, Karen thinks it's the right thing to do – an acceptable means to a better end."

"I've seen a room full of dead bodies says otherwise. Your friend Karen did that. I'm just trying to set it right."

She shakes her head. "You don't care about them, Kong. We both know that. It's just a way for you to justify being angry." Lois returns to her seat. "It's hard for Karen. She's been awake too long. She was the first, you know? All alone, until Tyrone found her. She helped me wake up. Just like I want to help you."

She twists her lips, thinking. "When I was asleep, I knew something was wrong. I could sense it, but for a long time, I didn't want to see it. I'd go out on missions, do what was asked of me, and come home. Then I got shot, the Company brought me back, tanked me, standard procedure, but... well, that time I was awake for it. I... saw... understood. I'm awake."

Her eyes catch mine, bright and full of the type of belief only found in those that haven't realised there ain't nothing worth believing in. And it's right now, right at this moment, that I realise what an idiot I've been. The factors snap into focus.

Lois never took nothing as it seemed. She understood. Understood how fucked up it all is, alltimewise. I talked to her in a way I can't remember ever being able to talk to anyone. I thought she was my friend. And now she's looking at me, and I feel like I ain't never known her at all.

"You're not just a tempo. You're a God damn operative. A turncoat."

"I don't think of myself as a tempo, and I sure as hell don't think of myself as a TTCP traitor", she says softly. "It's worse than that."

"How can it possibly be worse than that?"

She sighs, exhausted and small and heartbroken.

"I'm going to save the world."

Loop 16.7

Well, I wasn't expecting that.

"Save the world? There ain't no way to save the world. If there's anything I've learnt from the slip, it's the world will always be what it is. That's the problem with you tempos. You think it can all be balanced and equal and fair, but it can't. It never was, and it never will be. It's a fantasy."

Lois runs her hands through her hair, probably trying to think of something that'll convince me all this B.S. has some merit. "You don't remember-"

I ain't having it. "Best thing you and your sceever friend can do is let me go. I don't know what damn fool game you're playing, but I'll tell you this, and you can have it for free: I'm gonna *remember* this."

Instead of trembling in fear and regret, Lois looks behind me, a question on her face I ain't able to intuit. She shakes her head once, pauses, then nods. I hear some movement behind me, a door opening and closing, and then hands on me, strong and professional.

Krezzler's back in the room, untying me. Perhaps I can get a hold of her, disarm her. But she's too clever to let that happen. Something cold locks around my right wrist and then, with a bit of allowance being made for my Holo, around the left. My hands are pushed away from each other, fixed in place so I can't bring them any closer. Company cuffs, keeping me from accessing my Holo.

Krezzler does a few checks, lifting one hand and making sure the other goes with it, that kind of thing. Only when she's satisfied my hands are useless does she untie the ropes.

I get up slowly, turning so I can see both women. Krezzler's leaning against the wall, a blank expression stuck to her face. Lois just looks wary. That tugs at me, but I push it aside, locking onto my anger.

"What's this, then? Trust issues?"

"Don't try to be clever, Kong. You haven't got the credibility for it," Krezzler says.

I glare at her. "You gonna skull me too? You'd better – only way I ain't gonna get you for this."

"Karen and I need to talk to... to our link," Lois says.

"Then I'll decide what to do with you," Krezzler adds, fingers twitching on her gun.

"And how long do you think all this will take?" I ask. "Only I got a favour to ask, if it's gonna be a while."

They look at bit surprised, and I'll own to the fact it's good to have the upper hand, even in such a miserable way.

"I don't know," Lois answers. "It takes us a while to set up the comms and-"

"It'll take as long as it takes," Krezzler interrupts. "You, go wait in that room." She gestures at a door I couldn't see before on account of being tied to the chair.

"What favour do you want?" Lois asks.

"In my jacket pocket, there are a couple of tubs of medicine. I need some."

"You mean your drugs?"

"I mean my medicine."

Lois doesn't move. It's Krezzler who goes over to my grey overcoat, checks the pockets and pulls out the chloros. She spends a moment reading the label before tipping a few into her palm. There's a faraway look on her face. She selects a pill and holds it up likes she's inspecting some rare and beautiful object.

Then she shakes her head, drops it back into her hand and closes her fist.

"Walk yourself into the room first," she instructs.

I do as I'm told. There ain't nothing else I can do anyway, all bound up with no access to my Holo. Inside, there're three beds, a real wooden night table between two of them with a lamp on it, a wardrobe, and a window with bars running across it.

"Sit on the bed – no, not that one, the other one," Krezzler says. I change direction and sit on the bed nearest the window. "Open your mouth. Tilt your head back and stick out your tongue. I'm not about to lose a couple of fingers."

I do as I'm told, and Krezzler drops two pills onto my tongue, and then, a split second later, two more.

"You're better off out of it," she says.

In The Slip

I swallow the pills, falling back on the bed to look at the ceiling. It's dirty, the paint peeling and cracked. The cracks are like branches of a tree, growing across the white sky ceiling, seeking the sun. My apartment ain't got any cracks in it. All the mess was brought in by myself, layered over the perfection the Company provides.

The door opens and closes, and I hear the click of a key turning.

I wriggle a bit, trying to find a way to lie comfortable with my hands caught underneath me, the bar digging into my back. I guess I could try to slip my hands under my ass and around my legs, but frankly, I can't be bothered. Seems like I'm stuck here whatever, and truth be told, I don't have the will to try.

The chloros are hitting quick, my elbows and knees warming up in that strange way they do just before the rest of me catches up. Four in one go is a hell of a hit, but I can't help thinking it's a shame I didn't ask for a beer to go with them. Who knows what the alcohol would add to the mix – might be I could drift off to a place where none of this is happening. Somewhere quiet... Somewhere that smells fresh, like trees or plants. Somewhere different from both the slip and the One True.

But then I guess I'd have had to ask for a straw to drink with, right? I get a picture of Krezzler offering me sips from the can, and I can't help but laugh.

I imagine telling that thought to Lois. She'd have laughed, too.

The cracks in the ceiling blur, like there's something fogging up the room. Must be the chloros. I force myself to blink a few times, and my eyesight clears. Bored of the ceiling. Pull myself upright and scoot across the bed, muscles warm and soft now from the chloros, so I can see out the window. We're high up, and I get a good view of the street.

There are folks on the sidewalks, staring into their screens, choosing to fill their faces with teasers. Idiots. Shops are still open, window displays flashing all colours onto the dirty street. Push my face against the glass, look up as best I can, and, sure as silver, there's a dome above us. Clunky, ugly; one of the first.

See, the thing is, I don't get these tempos. How do they think they'll ever change it? Stop the Fracture? Make it so we never hit the point of no return? But people are people, alltimewise. When you see things lain out across time, you get to realising what so many folks ain't got the balls to: *it don't mean nothing*. Everything all comes up the same, anyway.

And Lois... Lois is one of them.

How did I miss that? I'm a noticer, me. That's part of why the Company's held onto me for so long after my sell-by. That and the fact I'm good in the slip, dropping in and out without yet coming to forget that all these dead folks are still people.

And yeah, I guess Lois is right; I don't really care about those skulled operatives. Not in the sense that some might. But just because I ain't gonna cry over them, just because I see some use in their deaths, that don't mean I'm a bad man. Just cause I ain't gonna wring my hands over *possible* people dying and *potential* lives lost don't mean I don't give a shit about the folk who exist presenttimewise. Just cause I ain't moaning and complaining about things that can't be changed anyway...

Press my forehead against the glass, holding it there long enough that the chill starts to hurt, burning in that way being very cold can. The sensation smashes into the heat from the chloros, making me giddy. I close my eyes, focusing on the rising heat of the chloros, bringing me up.

The window's too cold. It hurts. Press my forehead harder against it. Sharp pain and sickness. Spinning out. The chloros should be keeping me fixed in the slip, but-

   I'm in the Mall, running through the swarm of
 want and need and greed and mindless desire...

      Press my hand to the glass as the gloop
    rises. How many times have I been tanked?

   Something's trying to push me out
 of myself.

Before that...

 Before that, I remember being in the dark, in the gloop, waiting. Waiting for them

In The Slip

to fix me up, and thinking, knowing, that it wasn't gonna work, not this time. Not now I'm dead... My Pop, helping me find my way back to the One True... I was thinking I was gonna lose something, something that wouldn't come back right. Pop told me it was all OK.

BAM!
She shoots me in the chest. I feel my blood pooling through my fingers as I try to stop the flow. I'll have a good scar now. They'll have no way to repair something so broken. A great big hole in my middle, that's gotta leave a mark.

I wanna open my shirt, check my chest, but my hands are caught behind my back.

BAM!
She shoots me five times, shoulder, chest, stomach. Messy. She ain't got time to make it neat.

The gunshot is hot and heavy, weird and distant, close and sticky. I start to shake. Shock. The bullets are inside me, I can tell from the way I can feel the edges of my flesh where there weren't no edges before.

In the black, the gloop crawls up my nostrils and into my eyes and mouth and ears. Into the bullet holes dotted over my torso.

Drains my blood, melts me down, dissolves me.

Makes me new, but the same. Time to upgrade, get the new model, update, repair, fix, improve, better, more value, less glitches, buy now, pay later, be real, fit in, get credit, trust us.

F. D. Lee

A woman speaks to me, soft, tender. Like she cares about me. She whispers secrets, tells me what the world means, what it all means. Tells me to remember.

Press my forehead against the glass, holding it there long enough that the chill starts to hurt, burning in that way being very cold can.

I look out the window, and I see all those folks walking down there, pulling their carts along the cobbles, kids staring at the occasional car as it rumbles slowly past.
There are soldiers in uniform, old and used up. Someone's shouting through a metal cylinder about reform, about voting, and making the world safe, about everyone having somewhere to go.

The sand beneath my feet, dry, scratchy.
The smell of wood.

BAM!
I can feel the muzzle of the gun against my chin, but I ain't sure if I hear the shot or if I imagine it. The gloop seeps into the crater in the back of my skull and gets to work dissolving my bones, my muscles, my brain.
I wanted to die.
I chose.

Burning in that way being very cold can. Outside there're all these women, marching with cigarettes in one hand, banners in the other.

In The Slip

Burning
sugar.

I warn them about the teasers. About the slip and the One True and what's coming that they ain't yet realised. But they can't hear me, even though I scream so loud I can't breathe.

I scrunch up my eyes. I got lights flashing in them, bright sparkles like dust caught in the space between my lids and my retinas. My head is falling out of my skull, I'm sure of it.

My chip is hot, burning in the gloop, and around it, my muscles untie and melt away.

Above me the stars flicker and wink, bright as anything, in a sky that swirls and spirals, dark blue, turquoise, purple, pink, like the universe being flushed down the drain. Trees rumble up from the soil, growing faster, faster, reaching higher, higher. The smell of fresh wood and rotting leaves. The air is cold and crisp. Clean.

A pine forest, the earth wet beneath my feet.

Burning sugar. A tent, and a man sitting by a fire.

My Pop's telling me it's all OK, reminding me about the time we went to the Mall and he bought me a new screen and some soda and a burger and a balloon, and told me all about the Fracture and the TTCP and how lucky we are to live free, that it's our duty to respect the freedom we have, and to keep the city alive and to keep looking our best and that we deserve it.

He buys me a go-kart and an action figure and a new musak player and he takes me to the shop, they put the chip in me, and we get milkshakes and a computer game and new trainers and a kite

F. D. Lee

and everything is so tidy and everyone has a job and everyone who's anyone earns their place. Misfortune is the burden of the unworthy.

    We don't travel outside the city, because beyond the city is the Fracture, the deserts and the food droughts and the skeletons of long-dead animals.
Pop gets me an ice cream and tells me he loves me.

    The chip flashes, *blipblipblipblipblip*, talking to the tank.
    My head dissolves in the gloop.
    But I chose to die.

    Alltimewise. I'd do the same again.

    I need to keep my head inside me.
These fucking cuffs. My shoulders scream at me as I pull, but I can't get my hands free. I twist my legs up, trying to pull my hands underneath me before my brain starts coming free. Hit the floor with a crash, my chin striking first in an explosion of pain that for a second is worse than the sense of my brain coming out of my eyes and ears and nose, but not by much and not for long. The world begins to change, the shape of it twisting and turning, the pounding in my head getting louder and louder.

    I'm losing my sense of alltimewise.

    I can't... I ain't so sure no more... My legs are wrong, too muscular, too heavy, they ain't mine... And there's blood on my shirt...
I thrash and kick and scream and tug, and my arms spring free from behind my back, my wrists bleeding against the cuffs, my Holo flashing lights like fireworks,

In The Slip

something spiny and metallic protruding from the skin underneath it.

My hands are covered in dark brown spots, my veins sticking out of skin that ain't my skin, paper thin and almost transparent.

"I need my medicine... It's coming for me... It's going to take me away..."
I'm screaming, my voice ain't mine, I ain't me, I ain't real, plastic poured man, I sound wrong, sound old, sound young, sound like a woman and a man, sound like nobody, like nothing.

"I need it. My medicine. Help me. Please."

I open my mouth and this, this, this *stuff*, thick like molasses, seeps in, slimy on my teeth, heavy on my tongue.
Someone's talking, but this gloop is blocking the sound. There's a light, distant, lost across a great ocean, a buoy blinking its presence in a space that don't care it's there and never has.
Blipblipblipblipblip.
There's something in the gloop, trying to get into my mouth. My tongue. My tongue.

My tongue is growing.

My tongue is being born inside my mouth, and I can feel my teeth now, wet and smooth except where they ain't, the little ridges where they meet, my tongue new and fleshy and now against my new teeth, and the chip, and my Pop reminding me of the time he bought me an ice cream and took me kite flying and helped me pass the big test.

My tongue, my head, my body...

...none of it's real.

Blink.

I'm on the floor, back in the room Krezzler put me in, my arms bleeding and bound in front of me. Don't know how they got there, but they're mine again. My head don't feel like it's running away from my skull no more, neither. I'm presenttimewise, the chloros bringing me back where I should be, above it all.

"What happened to you?" a man asks from the doorway, his face pinched, his hands grasping each other, dark eyes wide and worried.

Joe.

Loop 16.8

I'm on the floor, wrists raw and bloody, shoulder screaming murder at me. But my head is sitting right again, and I'm thankful for that.

He's in the room now, the door closed behind him, locks turned. Trapping us inside.

"Ah, right. The *homme fatale*." My voice sounds old and rotten, like wet, mouldering fruit. "Course you're part of this. They send you to finish me off?"

"You were screaming."

"Right," I say, getting to my feet. "I'm OK now, so you can skedaddle back."

He don't move, though. Just strokes the scar on his chin. "Do you want me to leave?"

"I don't want no help from a tempo sceever."

"I don't think of myself as a tempo."

"What are you, then?"

"What do you think I am?"

"I think you're a tempo sceever."

He leans his heavy frame against the door, watching me. It's weird. With Lois and Krezzler I felt... dunno, angry, betrayed. Stuff like that. With Joe, it's different. He seems easy with me, too, but there's tension in the air, electric like a fight about to boil over or something similar.

"In my timeline, you'd only been gone a few minutes before you came back," he says, still conversational. "I guess it's been longer for you. You don't remember me. It's OK."

"I remember you. In the bar."

I want to accuse him of manipulating me, pretending to be sweet on me, making me think we had a connection, but the thought of voicing those words makes my cheeks burn hot. Perhaps he sees them anyway, written on my face, because he says, "That's good. I've missed you, even though you haven't been gone long. Did you... have you miss me?"

My tongue pushes against the inside of my lip like it's got a mind of its own, brushing along the soft flesh, causing a rush of something hot and heady and unexpected.

Ain't nothing on my side, not even my own body.

Clamp my jaw shut, turn my back, fix on my hands, wait for the strange, sharp giddiness my tongue invited to fall away.

My wrist is pretty messed up. There's a wire sticking out from under my Holo which I don't imagine signals anything good. Another betrayal, though of the two, this one don't seem so bad. Truth be told, it's something of a relief to have it to focus on. Feels similar to standing on a thumbtack, the detailed pain of it and the sense there's something inside you that ought not be there. I can't pull at the wire on account of the cuffs keeping my hands apart. But then I guess I probably shouldn't do that, anyways.

A hand on my shoulder, gentle, urges me to turn. Urges, but doesn't move me. Still, I find myself following it. Joe picks up my hands and removes the cuffs. He's careful with them, and once they're off, he brings a wipe out of his pocket and cleans away the blood, mindful of the wire sticking out my wrist. Alcohol in the wipe stings, Joe's hands are gentle. I feel each press of his fingertips, even after his hand has moved on. For some reason I can't explain, it makes me think of clay. Makes me wonder what it would be like if he let his hands drift up my arm from my wrist.

His head is so close to mine, bent over, concentrating. I could lean forward and bite his ear off, tear his throat out. He's big but soft, easy to put down, I reckon. End it all, right here and now. Hero's welcome and a bonus.

I could run my tongue along his neck...

Shit. The chloros messed me up good. I close my eyes, think about things that ain't fingers touching my skin. Listen to Joe breathing. I ain't got no words to speak, ain't sure I could even if I had anything to say, so I keep my own counsel.

"I'll have to put the cuffs back on before I leave," Joe says.

I open my eyes. He's looking at me with an expression I don't think anyone's ever used on me before.

"You afraid I'll jump the slip before you can?"

"I guess I should be, but I don't think you will. Besides, that wire could be a problem." He gives a little shrug.

In The Slip

"Aw, shit," I say, more to myself than him. "I'm stuck here."

"Stuck with me? No. I'll fix your Holo for you."

"You want me to believe you can fix a Holo?"

A pause, and then he shoots me a smile. "Yeah, I learned how a while back. Why do you think I can't? Because I'm so pretty?"

"Hardly."

"Come and sit with me," Joe says, walking over to the bed by the window.

This don't seem like a good idea. I do it anyway.

"It's not your fault," Joe says, a distance to his voice that weren't there before. "Right now, you know something's wrong, and you're angry. You're just angry at the wrong things. But you'll choose right, eventually. I know you will."

"You mean when I 'wake up'?"

"Yes."

"I thought Lois was my friend." I scratch at my wrist, the one with the Holo on it. The wire itches, that's all. "But it's a lie, ain't it? She's been tricking me to, what, get secrets from the Company? Save the world?"

"Lois is your friend. You know that, deep down. That's why you keep coming back to her."

OK. He seems like he wants to talk, so let's make use of it. Get the factors. Yeah. Investigate. Ask the right questions – the most important questions.

"And what about... what about you? In the bar?"

Joe covers my hand with his, but he don't answer me. It looks right, his hand resting there. Doesn't seem odd or invasive. Familiar, almost.

"None of this makes any kind of sense," I say, staring at his hand. "I feel like I know you. Lois, she made me feel like I could talk to her because it never seemed like she was listening anyway. She was too focused on making everything right, on educating me. I don't know, something like that. But when I saw you in the bar... Who are you?"

"I'm family, in a sense."

"Huh. 'Brother'. That's the word the tempos use, right?"

"Brother, sister." Joe pulls his hand back. "We're all family. But I don't mean it in the way the tempos use it."

I look up at him. "So how do you mean it, then?"

"I just mean that you've been with me a long time, I suppose."

He's got beautiful eyes. Brown and soft and kind. Full of things he wants to say. I turn away, scan the room on the off-chance there's something in here that might help me out: a baseball bat or a gun. A bottle of liquor, a can of beer. But there ain't nothing. No escape.

"I met you before, then?" I ask. "Is that what you mean?"

He runs his hands through his hair. Dark hair, midnight hair. Fuck, Kong. Focus. What were the factors? Shit. I ain't been counting.

"You know all those stories you pretended to write, the ones you told Lois about?" he asks.

"What about them?"

"Imagine that a person gets killed. Again and again and again. But every time they die, they're brought back to life, only they can't remember what happened to them before they died. What do you think of that?"

"It's hack. Stuff like that's been written for thousands of years. Trust me."

He nods. "But what if one time they came back different? Like, if they came back but there was something buried deep down that they did remember? What then?"

"God. I don't know. You trying to say that's what's happened to me? Is that it?"

"What would happen to that person if they weren't ready for it? If they weren't ready to remember?"

This is nonsense. Why I am even speaking to him? I should punch his lights out, strangle him, break his arms and legs. Even if I can't hit the slip, even if I can't get to Lois or Krezzler, I could still deal with this tempo sceever. One less person to worry about, right?

"I guess, for that person, nothing would sit right," I answer. "They wouldn't know what's happening, but they'd know something's wrong."

"Right, exactly," he says. "So, what would they do?"

"Try to figure it out."

"Yes! Yes, they would try to solve it, wouldn't they? That's what I've been telling Lois and Karen. Where would they go to figure it out?"

"I don't know."

"Come on, Kong. You're smarter than this."

"I don't know," I say again, grit in my voice.

"OK. Sorry. Give it time, and you'll understand. Though you do look cute when you're embarrassed."

"I ain't embarrassed, I'm deciding how to take you out."

"Sure, I know that, too." The bed shifts as Joe moves to sit crossed-legged, facing me. "Do you believe Lois, about saving the world?"

"World can't be saved."

"Why not?"

"Well, where'd you begin? That's where you tempos get it wrong, see. You think the timeline's like an old sweater, where you can pull at a loose thread and somehow that'll make something new. Hell, maybe it was, once. But not any more. The One True's got it woven tight, leastways this close to their presenttime."

"But there has to be a moment, a point in the distant past, when all this began. If we could find that, then the One True would never happen anyway. There'd be possibilities again. The chance for change, for growth. Every time the TTCP 'clean up' the past, they stop any chance of changing the future. They keep everything just the way they need it. But if we can go back…"

I can't help but laugh. "Look, even if you tempos could get further back, how'd you know which thread to pull? It ain't possible. Like I told Lois, the world is what it is and always will be. Folk'll do what they always do, what they *did* do, and we'll be here again soon enough."

I'm half expecting him to make some snot-nosed comment having hope or seeing the best in humanity, but instead he says, "It sounds ridiculous. But it isn't, Kong. We're fighting a war. Yes, Karen might enjoy fighting it more than she should, but it doesn't change the fact the fight's needed. The TTCP won't ever stop creating their world. They don't care about freedom, not real freedom. They just want to keep you all busy, so you won't look out and see what you've lost. Won't try to get it back."

Joe looks at me, dark hair falling across his face. "You know it's true. I don't know what's holding you back, why you haven't woken up again, but there's something in you that knows I'm right, I know there is."

I'm up and standing, anger burning red hot.

"Wait a God damn minute. The One True ain't perfect, but it's a damn sight better than the alternatives. Say you get it wrong. Say you pull the wrong thread and we get the Fracture but lose the domes? You ever been outside, back in the One True? That's the world we got left with. No water, no plants, no animals. Air you can only breathe if you got masks on."

"That's not-"

"No, you listen to me. No one goes without in the One True. People got food, got medicine, got security. You look out there," I say, nodding at the window. "What have they got? You say the Company and all that don't give us real options, well, sure. You're right. But what choice are those folk out there given? Dirty air or dirty air. Dirty water or dirty water. Dirty lives or dirty deaths. The One True takes all that away."

Joe stands too. "You're right. It's not much better here, either. But at least here, there's a chance they can shape their future into something better. In the One True, the TTCP makes sure nothing ever changes and nothing ever will. Nothing *can*. They won't allow it."

"No. You're wrong. We're safe in the One True. Safe from ourselves. I need my medicine."

"No, you don't. You need to remember. We've done this before, Kong."

"Fuck you! I need it!"

"You need to listen to yourself. Listen to me."

"And who are you, anyway? Get the hell away from me!"

He steps towards me, hands up, palms out. Slow and careful.

"Kong. Kong. Listen to me. Put the lamp down and listen."

The what? I blink, refocus. I've grabbed the lamp from the night table and am holding it like a club.

I lower it, but I don't set it down.

"OK, it's OK," Joe soothes. "It's OK."

"How? How is any of this OK?" My anger evaporates, leaving me adrift. Lost. I don't know how I ended up here, and for the first time I can remember, I'm scared. "Lois, lying to me... and Krezzler shooting me... and you... I don't understand any of what's happening."

Joe shakes his head, drops his hands. His expression is a scream, silenced and bottled away. "We need you, Kong." He steps a bit closer. "Lois needs you. I need you."

"Ain't no one needs me."

He takes the lamp, sets it down. "Everyone needs everyone."

"How can that be true when I don't understand what's happening?" I whine, embarrassed at needful tone of my voice. I swallow, find my strength. "I need my God damn medicine."

"You do know what's happening, Kong. You've known all along, or else I wouldn't be here, explaining it to you." Joe searches my face, his eyes filled with something I ain't prepared to own to understanding. "Please, Kong. Think about all the tempos you've brought in and the reason you were given for it. Think about the people back in the One True. Don't you want to help them? Don't they deserve a chance at a future that's different from their present? If the Company keeps correcting the past, keeps closing the door against anyone who might challenge them, who might find a way to shake their stranglehold... I know you care about them, I know you do."

"I don't know, OK? I don't know! My head hurts!"

"Kong, the first time we met, you told me you saw a stucker on the street and everyone was just walking by her. She couldn't move, all the teasers flying around her, and she couldn't afford to get away from them. You said she was reaching out to the food teasers, grasping for something to eat, and you told me it made you cry. Right there in the street, in front of everyone."

"That never happened."

"I know you think that's true, but you told me that story, and I fell in love with you then. That was the moment I knew. It doesn't have to be like that, Kong. Life doesn't have to be so selfish, so callous."

"Who the fuck cares? People will always be selfish, dirty, no-good slack-jawed sceevers. Give me my God damn medicine!"

He puts his hands on my face, careful not to touch the part of my chin that's all mussed up from my fall. "Try, please. You have to wake up."

"I don't have to do anything. I'm a TTCP operative, God damn it, and you're nothing but a lying tempo sceever, trying to brainwash me."

"I love you."

"No you don't. You just want me to believe you."

Joe kisses my forehead. Gentle, quick. Pulls back. "No. I love you," he repeats. "OK?"

I have never been less OK in all my life.

Loop 16.9

I don't know what I'm thinking. To speak plain, I ain't even sure I care. He's staring me right in the eyes, the feel of his lips still lingering on skin. I'm more confused and angry and scared presenttimewise than I can ever recall being.

Factor one: nothing makes no sense. Factor two: I want to kiss him back and do it proper this time.

Want:

...I want to kiss him back and do it proper this time.

I grab Joe's arms, planting my mouth on his. He stiffens a moment, then presses back, his lips brushing mine, hesitant. What's he waiting for, anyhow? I don't wanna wait. Alltimewise, the slip takes everything, that's what you learn. Nothing's ever yours, it's all given on credit, and the bill comes due eventually. Get what you can when you can.

I deepen the kiss. Joe's stubble scratches at my face, stinging as it rubs against the cut on my chin. I run my right hand through his hair, following the fine threads to their roots. I can feel every follicle, clear and distinct, as they brush against the pads of my fingers. I ain't never felt nothing like it, the threads of his hair making their own impression on my skin, each one seeming to tickle and twist and behave as they like, rougher near his scalp, softer on my knuckles.

He moans into my mouth, ugly, unguarded. It hits me like a truck.

He ain't waiting no more. He's digging his hands into my arms and neck, kissing me back hard, hurting my chin something fierce. The pain mixes with the softness of his lips and the feel of his hair and the movement of his tongue, an ache growing heavier in my stomach.

When he pulls away, it's the same as waking up in the tank, lost in the darkness. I reach for him, utterances falling from my mouth I don't care to catch, needy and begging words I know will embarrass me later if I come to think on them.

"Shhh," Joe whispers, pushing me backwards, onto the bed.

He climbs on top of me, heavy, clumsy. He slips, his knee digging into my hip, his hand landing on my shoulder as he steadies himself. Untidy man with his eager, frantic, joyous lust, so unlike the skilful performances of the One True, where everything is a show, a tease, a chance to be better than the rest, to be seen and valued. Auctioned. Joe don't seem to care what he looks like nor how ungainly he is.

He just wants to... just like all he wants is... like the only thing in the whole world is...

The thought falls from my mind, the beginning of an idea too big, too abstract, to comprehend. A thread lost to the tangle.

Joe presses his thighs along mine to keep him balanced and rocks forward on his hips, once, twice, three times. Stinging shocks, threads of a different sort, run through my nerve endings as he brushes against me, grinning all the while, knowing the effect he's causing. He does it again, slow, torturous. Tempo sceever that he is.

"OK?" he asks again, killer smile in place, riding slow and steady above my clothes, pressing himself against me.

Pull him down, his forehead pressed to mine. More nonsense babbles out of me, my cheeks burning at the hearing of it: pitiful, exposing, trusting words, telling him to carry on, to give me more, to take me, to love me and make me real. Not to buy me, but to own me, nonetheless. Words I ain't never said to no one. Words I didn't know were inside me.

He takes my chin and turns my head, exposing my neck to trail wet kisses along my collarbone and up to my jaw. I tilt, stretching my throat, encouraging him. Some part of me that's still thinking can't make head nor tail of what I'm doing. Everything feels so natural. A dance with moves I memorised long ago. He said I forgot him. How could I forget this?

Oh, God. Will I forget it again?

How many times have we been here – how many times have I had the weight of him on top of me?

"Kong? Are you OK?"

Don't speak, don't speak. I pull him back, grab him hard, press his mouth to my skin. Ignore the factors, focus on the want building inside me and the cold air on my skin as his lips press

In The Slip

softness against my empty, unreal body, his spare hand pushing up my shirt, his hips rocking slow.

Stay in the slip, don't lose this. Don't forget.

Stay here.

Stay.

"My God," Joe breathes. "Look at you."

I take a moment to see straight, to realise he's undone my shirt, exposing my chest. My never-been-lived-in, off the peg, standard issue chest, no marks, nor scars, nor spots, nor moles, nor nothing, laying out for him to stare at. My mannequin-plastic torso, box-fresh from the tank. My perfect, pristine body that reminds the world I ain't anything. That I don't belong.

Ugly for its lack of ugliness.

Exposed.

Empty.

His eyes widen as he runs his gaze over me, taking in the horror of my unbody. He actually touches me, like he can't believe what he's seeing. A black hole opens inside me, a gravity well like the pull of the slip, sucking up my insides and leaving this, this, this *shell* behind. Waveforms roll, spreading faster than light, a second less than a second and it's all the same, one giant swell of my own stupidity, my shame.

My guilt.

"Shit, look, no, don't – shit," I croak, my voice dried out from the heat inside me. I shift and wiggle and try to get out from underneath him, but he's got me pinned on this cheap mattress. I grab my shirt, pull it closed. My eyes sting, blink it away, hot wetness on my skin.

"Get off me."

"Kong, please, I'm sorry, it's not-"

"Get off me! Now!"

He pulls back, releasing me. I'm up at the other end of the bed before I even know I moved, my shirt caught in my fist, the wire from my Holo pulling at my skin, catching against the material. Pain, wonderful, glorious, focusing.

"Kong, listen, I didn't mean-"

"Get out. Or I swear to God you'll be wishing it was the lamp I hit you with."

He swallows, his throat working fast. Looks down at the bed.

"I need to fix your Holo," he says. "And... and put the cuffs back on. Karen won't... she needs to be the one to take them off."

"...Fine."

I swing my legs over the bed, grab my shirt with my right hand, keeping it closed, and hold my left arm out. I know he's looking at me, now. I can feel his eyes. I know what he's thinking, too. Thinking how foul and unreal I am. Thinking I'm like everything else in the One True. Plastic and chrome, bought out of a catalogue. Hell, even my wires are showing.

Too clean. Too new. Same as everything else.

He takes my hand, pulls back my sleeve. Begins repairing me.

Factor one: the night table is in front of me. Factor two: there're knots in the wood, chips, scratches in the varnish. Factor three: it's a pretty nice table. Factor four: the legs are tapered, the table itself a block of darkly varnished wood with two draws. Factor five: minimalist, Europhile design.

Factor six: I could fix it up if I got it back to my apartment. Sand it down, fill in the chips, re-varnish it...

Fuck this fucking table. Let it sit here in the slip and rot 'til someone comes by to throw it in the trash and buy a better one, shiny new. Fuck it. Let the table die.

"This is going to hurt," Joe says, off to my side. "Do you want some of your, uh, medicine? Before I take the Holo off?"

"Yes."

He drops my hand, moves around. I catch glimpses of him out of the corner of my eye. Close my eyes. Hear the door open, close, and open again a few minutes later. The mattress dips, and my hand gets picked up again. Two pills drop into my palm. I swallow the chloros dry. Offer my hand back. Joe sets to work removing the Holo from my chip.

The pain ain't no different from when the doc stuck the damn thing on me, all them pasts ago, but it ain't nearly so satisfying this time around. This time, it just fucking hurts, leastways 'til I start getting that nice warm feeling in my joints that signals the chloros hitting.

Factor seven... wonder which bit of the night table will rot first? Legs, probably. The damp'll get to them, and then it'll spread.

Factor eight: wood rots quite pretty. Prettier than meat. Wood separates first and then just sort of crumbles. If that table was never moved nor thrown away, it'd be dust, eventually. Factor nine: there's a smell to rotting wood. You don't get it back home, but you do in the slip, sometimes. Earthy, warm kind of smell. Sort of like when-

"Can you flex your fingers?"

I do so. My pinky and ring finger are stiffer than they should be.

"Right, I see," Joe mutters. "Hold on."

More pain follows, but it ain't so bad now. Nothing seems so bad now, not sure why I let this tempo get me so worked up. Rookie mistake. I ain't no rookie. I'm a professional. Sure as silver, good as gold.

"Kong?"

"What?"

"Can you, look, can you just look at me a moment. Please?"

"...fine."

My arm's resting along his thigh, my hand in his palm. You ever look at a part of yourself, but it don't feel connected? Like you could move it, but it don't belong to you anymore? That's what my arm looks like, sitting in his lap. My Holo's off, and I can see he's tidied the wire away, back into my skin, back to the chip. Or maybe it's just gone. It don't seem to matter all that much.

"What?" I say, finding a spot just above his right ear to look at.

"Do you want me to put your Holo back on? I don't have to. You could... We could stay here." His fingers close around my hand. "What do you think?"

"No."

"Kong, you don't understand. I love you. I know what you're thinking, but you're wrong. Please. You have to believe me."

I meet his eyes. "Just get on with it. Make me good as new."

Sometime later, long after the chloros have worn away and I'm back down in the cold and the dark, Krezzler comes into the room. There's no gun in her hand, but I ain't in the mood to think on what that signifies.

"Someone have a tantrum?" she asks, looking at the overturned beds, the pieces of lamp, the night table smashed up. "Impressive, with the cuffs on."

"What do you want?"

"Follow me."

We go through to the next room. Lois is standing in the centre, looking fretful, brushing her golden hair from one shoulder to the other. Joe ain't here.

"So, you gonna shoot me again?"

"There's been some disagreement on the matter," Krezzler replies.

"Shame."

"You've got no idea."

Lois glares at us, tugging at her hair. "Not funny."

"I wasn't trying to be," Krezzler answers.

"Kong," Lois says, ignoring the sceever, "We've been talking, and I think we have an idea about what to do with you."

"Yeah, well, I've been thinking, too. Who's Barry Longsworth?"

It's a delight to see their expressions, and that's the God's honest truth. A gun appears in Krezzler's hand, no idea where from. Probably pulled it out her ass. She aims it at me.

"How do you know about him?" Lois asks. I note she doesn't tell Krezzler to put her gun away.

"I knew it." See, these sceevers ain't the only ones who can make a plan. "Knew that name was to do with you. So, who is he?"

"I told you," Krezzler says. "He's starting to-"

"We've discussed this," Lois cuts across her. She steps towards me. "We don't know who Barry is. He seems to be from before the Fracture. We'd hoped you'd help us find out."

Her brown eyes are wide, sincere. The woman has a face built for convincing, and she's using it full force.

"Go to hell. I'd rather die than help a pile of lying, skulling sceevers like you."

Something like satisfaction passes over Lois' face, gone in an instant. She throws a glance at Krezzler, who shrugs. "Fine. We'll do it your way."

Lois moves behind me and begins typing a destination into my Holo.

In The Slip

"There, done. Ten seconds," she says, stepping to the side.
Krezzler takes position in front of me. "See you later, alligator."
And then she shoots me.
Again.

F. D. Lee

Reset

Murdache is here. She's asking me questions, skin all puckered up between her new diamond-studded eyebrows. I can't hear her. Something between us – glass. Glass, and the gloop filling the tank.

Use the fucking microphone, woman. Ain't you ever seen a tank before? I try to gesture towards the mic, but my head won't move. Press my chin to my neck, as much as I can, and yes, there's a hole in me, in my shoulder.

"Kong, can you hear me?" She's found the mic.

I nod. The gloop is rising fast, washing over my middle.

"She shot you again."

No shit.

"What did you find out?"

"She's a tempo. I think she's gone rogue. Ex-TTCP."

Murdache scrunches her face up even more. What a trick! She turns off the mic and shouts something at the docs.

The drugs in the gloop are lovely. Delicious. I've got a hole in my shoulder between my collarbone and my heart and I can't even feel it, except to know it's there.

"Do you know what she wants?" Murdache again, her voice crackly with urgency over the speakers. "These idiots won't alter the code. You need to tell me now."

"Mmm. Yes. She wants to save the world."

Murdache stares at me. Clearly that wasn't the answer she was looking for. She turns back to the docs, forgetting to turn the mic off. God, that woman's got a mouth on her! I ain't seen that side of her before. Glad I ain't one of the docs.

Murdache, back to me. "How?"

The gloop is at my shoulders now. Thick like molasses or oil. Sweet and toxic. I should tell her about Lois and Joe. Tell her now, in case I forget.

"I want to keep my scar," I say.

"What?"

"My scar. On my chin. I want to keep it."

In The Slip

Murdache slams her fist against the glass and the gloop shudders, too thick to roll or wave. Quick words with the docs, then back to me.

"Fine."

"Barry Longsworth. She's looking for Barry Longsworth."

The gloop hits my scar, and then I'm sunk into the black, the tank melting away my wonderings over why I gave that name and not the others.

F. D. Lee

Loop 17.0

"Where'd you get that thing on your face?"

An operative is standing over me. Curious, not meaning to be rude. I rub at the raised skin, a sharp line that runs from the curve of my chin up to my lower lip. I don't know why, but it makes me happy to feel it there.

"I had an accident when I was a kid, my Pop took me walking on the Sky Rail and I lost my footing."

The other operative takes a seat on the bench next to me. Is he new? He's Europhile, sandy hair and blue eyes, dull and average and unremarkable... except he's got a slight tan to his skin that tugs at something inside me, keeping me more civil than I might be inclined to be, otherwise.

"Why don't you get it fixed?" he asks. "The Company would do it for you."

"Yeah."

"I'm surprised they let you work the slip, looking like that."

"Yeah."

"No one else has a scar. And you sound weird, too."

"Listen, friend, no offence, but ain't you got somewhere else to be?"

He smiles at me. "I can recommend someone if you like. Maybe sometime you and I could get a drink together? I'd, uh, I'd really appreciate some advice on the slip. You know. Before the new chloros are brought to trial."

Ahh. Kid's a climber. Probably Murdache put him up to it – she used to have this notion I could teach others to be as good in the slip as I am. It's odd she should be trying it again.

I finish dressing, ignoring the guy until he goes away.

I'm outside the Company soon enough. Watch the teasers a spell before paying to be left alone, take a cab home. Sit in my apartment, enjoying a couple of glasses of whiskey, chloros washed down with it. No books, no sewing, no repair jobs, and no voksac. Just the big screen on for the company.

In The Slip

My Holo itches, like it ain't sitting right on my skin, as if the wires ain't connecting as they should. Got this notion that the damn thing might disconnect itself and fall off like an old scab. I'll ask the Company docs about it.

Bored. Check on my neighbour, Catherina. She's angry with me because I forgot her after my last tank. Anyways, I drop off her medicine and she slams the door in my face. I'm asleep before the sky turns pink and yellow and blue and green.

"What do you mean, there's nothing wrong with it? You hardly looked at it."

The Company nurse shakes his head, bored. "Nothing at all."

"No loose wires? Only it itches something fierce."

"Look, I checked the connections *and* rebooted it. You want more than that, you'll have to get clearance to open it up," he says. "Is there anything else?"

"No – wait, yes. Chloros. I need some more medicine."

He fills in the form on his screen and gets me a couple of tubs. He doesn't say goodbye when I leave.

Work a case. Work another, and another. Good jobs, too. Difficult jumps. But for whatever reason, the challenge of it don't excite me the way it ought to.

The company start running tests, too. Getting ready for the chloros pilot. Take some blood, run scans, check my vitals before and after each jump. Ticking boxes, seems to me. Probably for insurance purposes, making sure that, if I do die, their payout will be worth the trouble.

Either way, I reckon all this means I'm a shoe in for the actual test run – the pre-Fracture jump.

That don't excite me like it should, neither.

What's wrong with me?

Love Across Time hits the floor with a dull sound that still, somehow, shatters the silence in the room.

I turned the big screen off, bored, fidgety. Unsettled. Don't know why, but I decided to read through the inlay card that came with the voksac disc, studying the lyrics. Most of it's trash. Then, right at the end... this, this song, this poem, this *thing* just... I don't know, it's like it bit me.

And that's when I dropped the case. Just dropped it. You know, in surprise. I ain't getting spooked by some stupid song words.

The case stares back at me, the dancing prick playing his stupid flute while all the animals pretend such a thing is normal, the tree-hag grinning inanely at him. It's just a crappy old piece of nonsense I must have pulled from the slip for some joke I can't even remember. It's nothing. A curiosity, at best. There's no reason for it to have spooked me. Especially the last song.

I shove the case onto my top shelf, turn on my big screen and buy a new set of chopsticks, some toothpaste, 70cl of vodka, and some tampons on account of them being on sale and the teaser swearing that *real men know what their friends need*.

The tempo bursts into tears when I catch her. She's maybe sixteen or seventeen, much younger than I'm used to.

"Please, I'm sorry. I just... I don't want to... I just want to make it better for me and my family, that's all. I wasn't going to make a change. Please. It's only a few years back."

I ignore her, pull up the TnCs.

"Please, you've got to listen to me. My brother invented this new air purification system. He was just seeing if it could be done. And then they took him away. They stole it. Please, mister, please. They'll take me away too, and then my mom will be alone."

She starts sobbing louder, so much so I'm thinking she might be about to throw up. Shit. I grab her arm and drag her out of the office block I found her in and into a tea room. Buy her a cup. Don't ask me why.

She sips the drink, coughs, takes another sip. "I wasn't going to change anything, I was just going to take my brother's name off the project. That's all. That way, they won't take him away."

"Listen, kid, everyone knows the rules. Where'd you even get hold of a Holo?"

In The Slip

She shakes her head. "I can't tell you. I won't."

Her Holo's the real deal, meaning the tempos got a supply line into the company. Worrying, what with the new chloros trial coming up. I could press the matter, should press, but I don't have the energy. Instead, I let her finish her drink and then I ask her, "So what was it your brother made?"

"Purification machine. He found a way to clean up the air outside the dome. The water, too, eventually."

"Can't be done."

She glares at me. "Yes, it can. My brother did it. And then they took him away and stole it."

"And why would they do that?"

"Are you for real?" She looks like she thinks I'm joking, but I guess my expression tells her otherwise. "Because he was going to make it for free. He wanted to give it away."

"Oh right, sure he was. Save the world, huh? Grow up, kid."

She makes an obscene gesture that, I gotta say, I try hard not to laugh at. Good for her, right? But she don't say nothing else 'til I book her. She won't accept the TnCs, even though I explain the Company don't like it when people don't. That they got lawyers and such coming out of their assholes. She tells me she doesn't care, that it don't matter what happens to her now, that all us operatives are the same and we all deserve to die, and that she hopes that one day someone I love will be taken away from me, except that no one will ever love me, anyway.

Alltimewise, I don't think I've agreed with anyone more than I do with this kid.

Water, water, water. Something tickles the back of my head long after the girl's gone to processing.

I try to recall her brother, the one she claims started all this, but no bells ring. Could be another operative got the job. Could be I'm yet to remember it; my last tank screwed me up pretty bad.

Water, water, water. The kid said her brother had found a way to clean up the air, maybe even the water, too. I was working a case for Clear2o before I got tanked. Looking for some woman in the slip. Debrief just said the case went sideways and Murdache was ordered to pull it. Word from on high, apparently. It's odd for a case to get cancelled halfway done, but I guess not unprecedented. We do what we're paid to do. We ain't the police, following grand notions. We're a business, same as the rest: the client pulls the brief, we stop the work.

And yet, I can't stop this tickle, this itch, like the one on my God damn arm, under my Holo.

Neither of them will let me scratch them away.

Loop 17.1

My big screen buzzes. Grab my HomeSuiteHome and open the wave, an invitation from some other operatives to go shopping tomorrow at the new Mall.

I send back a wave, *fuck off, fuck off and die, you dirty, brain-dead no good sceevers*, but somehow it comes out nicer on the screen. They reply with an insistence I come, saying they're looking forward to seeing me, especially Rob.

My tongue darts outside my lip, pressing against the top of my scar.

Robin, the operative from the changing room. He followed me around the Company whenever I was there, asking for my help, my insights, and then, eventually, just making a fuss about spending some time together. I tried reporting it to Murdache, but she didn't see the problem.

Anyways, I agreed to a drink about a week ago just to get him off my case. We talked a spell, and then he stuck his hand down my pants. His passion played out like in the teasers, all pretty looks and tidy hair and minimal mess or friction, and I replied in kind. Two plastic people, pretending to be real for an audience that's always and never there. The next morning, he bought me breakfast and declared himself my boyfriend. I didn't pay it much attention, beyond the fact it gave me something to do at the time.

There's a lot of time, recently, but I don't seem to be doing so well keeping up with it.

My fingers dig around the edges of my Holo, trying to ease the itch. The Company nurses don't know shit, that's for sure. Maybe I should go to a private clinic.

Grab a bottle of whiskey and take a walk down the hallway. Catherina considers slamming her door in my face – four weeks and she's still pissy. But either her deep affection for me or the bottle in my hand changes her mind.

"He's probably spying on you," she says, once she's had a bit of medicine, the drinks are poured, and I've done my explaining about Rob.

"Don't know why. I ain't particularly interesting."

She presses her nose to her glass, sniffs the muddy-brown liquid. Looks up at me, alarmed.

"It was a new bottle," I remind her. "You undid the seal."

Calmed, she goes back to Rob. "He works for the TTCP, and you've been in trouble recently. How do you know he's on the level? You said you didn't recognise him."

"I don't recognise any of them, truth be told. What trouble?"

"It's not right, you people. The things they do to you. It's all wrong." For a moment, her face hardens, and she's full of anger. "Why did you forget me? You're no better than the rest of them."

"I know it. But I always find my way to your door sooner or later, right? What kind of trouble?"

"Oh, Kong," she sighs, sad now. "How did I end up like this?"

I refrain from casting an eye on the powder scattered across her table. "Catherina, what trouble?"

"You were on some case about a woman, Karen something. A made-up sounding name, like yours. You had a man in a suit visit you, important looking, and then you went away again. Went into the tank. I think they've hacked my privacy. I was in my reading room and the windows opened. All the noise came in. That's how they get you. Sneak up, change everything."

Great, she's too far gone. I listen to her ramble for an hour or so, enjoying the privacy and, I confess, her ravings, then put some food on a timer and make her drink a glass of Clear2o. I forget about the itch, leastways 'til I stumble home and find myself staring at my reflection in my bathroom mirror, blood under my fingernails. Wash my hands and head to bed, but the sunlight's coming on and I'm too hot to sleep. Infection. Must be I've got an infection from scratching at my skin.

Breakfast. Take some chloros. Busy myself around the apartment, re-arranging all my odds and ends, nick-nacks and collections. Sewing machines and magazines and posters and books and crockery. Then I scroll through the shops on the big screen, order myself a new chair, a couple of portable screens, a coffee machine, some clothes, a teddy bear, toothpaste, more whiskey, condoms, and, just for the hell of it, a black beret. A new message from Rob, reminding me about the trip to the Mall, flashes in the corner of my screen.

I open the data stream and type '*Robin Banks*', my shiny new boyfriend, into the search bar. I get a link to the TTCP HR information stream, nothing else. I search my own name, get the same HR page and some video, redacted, of an incident in a burger bar.

Wonder what Catherina was talking about. Probably just her madness. Still, I type '*Karen*' into the search bar. It's obviously a useless search term, but I spend a few hours on it anyway, looking at pictures of faces, seeing if something jogs. Drink some more, expand my search, typing in anything that comes to mind. I'm not even paying all that much attention, whisky hot in my throat and the world drifting by in dirty hours, leastways not 'til my eye catches the most recent name I've typed in, '*Barry Longsworth*'.

Weird name. Not weird like mine, sure enough, but still. Wonder where it came from, but then it ain't the first time something's bubbled up from the darkness the tanks create. I put my glass down, try out a few additional search criteria, aiming to get fewer results. Nothing interesting, leastways as far as I can tell. Weird. Maybe he's someone I-

A new wave comes through, flooding the screen. Says I'm late to meet Rob and the others. There's a shindig later, a big Company affair to celebrate the kid I brought in, and I'm told I need something new to wear. I never agreed to meet them, I'm sure of it. Maybe Catherina's right. Maybe he is spying on me.

Fuck it. Send back a wave, *be there in twenty*. Besides, I got my own reasons for wanting to visit one of the Malls, and Rob is as good a cover as any.

"I want to go to a doctor," I say, once the others have left us alone.

Relief washes over Rob's face. "Really? For your accent?"

No, you stupid, slack-jawed sceever, because I'm broken, there's something wrong with me and you're too dumb to see it. "Just a check-up. For the new chloros. I want to make sure I'm top of the pile when they choose who gets to test them."

He rolls his baby blues, puts his arms around me and squeezes. "The Company are doing that, aren't they? Besides, why are you worrying? Murdache loves you."

"We're here now."

"Well, yeah. OK. There's a clinic on the 34th floor. We could go there and then maybe get some food?"

He leads me up the escalators, picking up a new watch on the way. The clinic is busy; we take a number and wait. I tell him he can go on without me, but he laughs and pulls up a catalogue on his screen, comparing his watch to the others. He buys a second strap and then, ten minutes later, returns to the base screen and buys a new watch face, too. Same brand.

Eventually, my name is called. Rob stands with me, but I insist he waits.

Inside his office, the doc explains the charges, which I accept. Way too much, but then I'm asking him to run a diagnostic on Company tech, which is risky on account of the shit storm that would rain down on him if he broke it. He picks up my wrist and examines the Holo, making small talk, asking what it's like to work for the TTCP, where I've been that day, what I've been buying. I offer answers he don't really listen to.

"There's nothing wrong with it," he says at last, having run his scans and checked his screens.

"Course there is. It itches – look at my skin. Run the tests again."

He starts to shake his head, and then his hair is in my free hand, his face pressed against his desk, and I'm putting all my weight on him, screaming at him to run the tests again. He changes his mind, sensible man that he is. I let him up and he rubs his face, which is bruising something fierce.

"You're a fucking psycho," the doc tells me, which I reckon might be the most honest diagnosis he's made all day. "Look here." He turns his screen around, showing me lines of code.

"I don't know what I'm looking at."

"That's your chip. It's all normal, from what I can see. If you want something more detailed, you need to see a specialist. I'd recommend going back to the TTCP and speaking to the person who designed it, one... here, Tossenberger, T."

"How do you know that?"

"Because I'm a doctor. How else do you think we know what you've had done?"

"Tell me who this Tossenberger is."

"I don't know who he is." The doc glares at me. "Listen, I've done what you paid me to do, and I won't charge you for the assault. Get out."

"But I-"

"If you don't leave now, I'll call the... I'll call..." He falters here, because who can he call? I'm a TTCP operative. He's bitten off more than he can chew, and he knows it. But seems like he's told me all he can about my chip, and leastways now I've got a name.

I leave, Rob running behind me, shouting my name. I lose him somewhere around the 23rd floor, though by the time I get home there's a series of increasingly angsty waves waiting for me. He's worried about me, he wants to see me, wants to break up, wants me to know he's there for me, wants to buy us a holiday, wants to know what the fuck my problem is.

Me: *You are.*

Robin: *They told me you weren't worth the trouble.*

Me: *I'm not worth much, don't need anyone to tell me that.*

I look at what I've written, consider the manner in which Rob might reply. I backspace and replace it with *then you're better off without me.* Stare some more at the little screen floating above my arm. Backspace again. Block him without replying.

Wander around the apartment, not sure what to do. I wanna drink, but I gotta be presentable for the party since it's being thrown for me. I take half a chloros, open my big screen. I'm about to enter the name '*Tossenberger, T*'. into the search, but something changes my mind. I spin in my chair, stare a while at the wall.

Then, I don't know why, I go to the top shelf of my musak library and pull out a plastic case. *Love Across Time.* It's weird. I don't even need to look, really, to know where it is.

I put it in the machine and watch as my finger presses the button to skip the tracks forward, all the way to the final song. It starts soft, sparkly guitar and some other instruments I don't know. The skin on my arms crackles and tingles, a sharp pain in my chest that feels wonderful and terrible all at the same time, growing as the music builds. A woman's voice comes in, sharp like a blade, quick and keen. It surrounds me. And still I listen.

'*Remember me to the man...*'

Each word and line cuts, leaving me shaking, stumbling backwards, landing heavily in my chair. Some strange noise joins the woman's voice, a deep, brutish, blunt thing that only makes her knifework all the more elegant, all the more devastating.

It takes a moment to realise the bludgeoning, feral noise is coming from me. I'm crying, ugly and animalistic.

'*He once was a true love...*'

The music swells, her voice slicing faster, deeper, right into the centre of me. Tears the skin from my bones, letting the lyrics slide into the wounds, into my blood, into my chest, my centre, myself.

'*...and he shall be a true love of mine."*

The song ends, the disc whirling to a stop inside the machine. I can't say how long I sit, but eventually I manage to get up, pour myself a drink, and then another. Soon, the bottle is resting on the table next to my chair, and I've programmed the machine to play the song on repeat.

I settle back, refresh my drink, and restart the music. My eyes sting, drops of warm salt water rolling down my cheeks and dropping onto my collar bone as I sob, shaking with each razor-edged note, waiting for the future to become the present and then, God willing, the past.

Loop 17.2

"I'm hearing good things about you at last, Kong," Murdache tells me, guiding me through the partygoers.

"Ma'am."

"These last few months, you've really been... driven. It's remarkable, considering."

"Ma'am?"

"I shouldn't be telling you this, but, well, it's a feather in both our caps. You got the chloros trial. You're going back, before the Fracture."

"That's good."

"Good? Look around – all of this is for us. I knew you were worth the effort, Kong."

Murdache grins like she's just found a gold coin in a pile of shit, which I guess is factual. Alltimewise, I don't reckon I've ever felt so dirty in my life. I take a slug of the sweet, fizzy wine being offered around. Celebrating my find.

Apparently, the girl I brought in was one of the worst tempos the Company's seen in years, a deadly little sneak thief with designs on destabilizing the Fresh Air company, confusingly written as one word, FRESHAIR, which reads to me as 'fre-shair'. Sounds somewhat like 'free share', right? Makes me feel happy and hot and sad and angry all at once. Makes me think of earlier, back in my apartment, and the way my face feels tight and strange from the crying, like the salt water's dried it out somehow. Makes me damn sure glad of the sickly drink in my hand and gladder still for the chloros hidden safe in my suit, ruining the line.

There're more suits than operatives at this shindig, which is fine by me. The boardroom is clean and long, and the carpet's thick, and the air tastes of cotton candy, which is the hot new flavour. Ice statues of the TTCP penguin logo decorate the tables, clear as crystal. Waste of water, but then I guess the Company ain't paying. Outside the glass wall, the city blinks and flashes, the teasers too far down to read, but always there, like stars. Only right now they're below us, so I guess that means we're Gods.

Murdache leads me round different groups of brightly coloured people, talking twenty to the dozen, answering questions for me so she don't have to explain my accent. It don't bother me none; recently it feels like people ain't hearing what I'm saying, or I ain't speaking it plain. I hold my empty glass out and a robot whizzes over, exchanging it for a full one. There doesn't seem to be a limit, which also suits me just fi-

I'm at a party, filled with suits and money and boorish jokes and cigar smoke. Black oil seeps into the corner of the room, a slimy crawl, moving closer. A man in a suit, his skin dark like wet sand, warmed by candlelight. The black laps at his feet but he keeps on talking, unaware of me or it.
I can't hear a word he's saying, don't know who he's talking to.
The black slime climbs up his legs, tentacles of viscous horror.
I let it take him.

"Kong? Kong?" Murdache hisses at me from the corner of her yellow-painted mouth. "Don't make a scene, for God's sake. Are you OK?"

"What? Yeah. I just... had a thought."

"Hell of a thought. It's not... you're not-"

"I'm fine," I say, unknotting my hands from my hair. Try to keep hold of whatever the hell it was that just happened, but it's drifting back into the darkness already. Another little thing lost to time, lost to the tank. "Can I leave now?"

She gives me a look somewhere between concern and annoyance. "No. You've only been here an hour. They want to meet you. They want to meet me. Just behave yourself."

"I'm going to the bathroom."

Murdache's eyes dart around the room at all the bigwigs, her mouth pinched, but she don't try to stop me. For all her saying these suits wanna meet me, none of them collar me on my way to the john. I lock myself in a cubicle, take a pill, and sit on the seat, my head against the wall while I wait to warm up. Dig my fingers into the skin around the Holo, scratch, scratch, scratch, trying to find whatever it was I just had. I can taste it almost, if thoughts had a taste.

In The Slip

I had a banana once, in the slip. Paid a fortune for it, freeze-dried, at an auction when I was done on a job. Only now, see, I can't quite figure out what the real ones must have been like – the proper, fresh ones, I mean, from before disease wiped them out. Somewhere between what we manufacture in the One True and that odd, sweet, dry thing I bought. I know I got the factors to figure out the taste, but it never quite settles right in my mind what it should be.

Bananas! Why am I thinking about bananas? What the hell is wrong with me?

Factor/Want: I can't be here. I can't... I can't do it. I gotta be somewhere else. Fuck it. I type random coordinates into my Holo and open the slip.

The bar is... different.

I peer in through the window. No suits, no carpet, no cotton candy air nor robots buzzing around, filling me up with alcoholic sugar syrup.

It's dirty, cheap, used up. Nothing like the One True. I reckon if I were to touch anything I'd probably get some pasttime disease, except I've been inoculated against them all.

Factor one: there's a robot behind the bar, signs in Chinese, Spanish and English, musak playing through crackling speakers. Factor two: it's dark and warm, and the windows are narrow, looking out onto an alleyway. Factor three: the stars are back in the sky again, real stars, only a handful through the smog, but stars all the same. Factor four: I don't know why I'm here specifically, but it seems like the kind of place no one will come looking for me, and that's exactly the kind of place I wanna be.

I go in, order a beer, and spin my stool around to watch the game being played on the pool table. The couple playing are drunk, giggling their heads off as they miss shot after shot. The woman, young, happy, starts cheating, but the guy she's with, handsome in a preppy way, doesn't mind. She starts making a show of it, dropping balls into the pockets with more and more obvious abandon, him pretending not to notice nothing 'til she finally acts so brazen he ain't got no choice but to kiss her.

It's the kind of story they'd tell in a teaser, except I'm not quite sure what it'd be selling. Clothes? Make-up? Confidence, maybe? Phetes or bliss, something like that.

Shit, I'm dumb.

Pool tables.

That's the teaser, right there.

I order another beer and ask the robot if there's a screen I can use. It points to the corner behind the pool table where an old upright is standing. I slide past the couple making out, drop some coins in the slot, and load up the data stream. Look at the world as it is presenttimewise, skim through the stuff that matters to the here and now. Try to convince myself it matters to me, too. Drink more beers. Ignore the couple.

Two, maybe three hours later, I figure it's time to go. What exactly am I doing here, anyhow? I could be back at the party, celebrating my success. Should be happy. I am happy. Just drunk – drunk and bored. That's all. Pay my tab and stumble out the bar. The air hits me cold and hard, smashing into the alcohol and chloros, dizzying.

I wander over to the dumpster, scuff my shoes against the concrete. My arms feel heavy. I can't go back. I can't. The thought makes my chest tight, heaviness pulling me inwards. I'm going mad, ain't I? Shit.

The bar door opens and the couple tumble out, arms wrapped around each other, kissing and trying to walk at the same time. She trips and he catches her. They laugh and kiss. I watch them all the way to the corner of the alleyway, and then I keep on staring long after they've gone, my tongue running across my lower lip, catching on my scar, arms wrapped tight around me, fighting the cold.

I wash my hands, splashing water on my pants, and rejoin the party three minutes after I left, shaving time nice and neat so no one will know I ain't been here all night. I'm the best there *fucking* is. Like to see these slack jaws do it so tidy, jumping into such a small space, so soon after I left, no slip marks nor nothing to give me away.

In The Slip

Hell, I reckon I could do a jump futuretimewise. Yeah. That'd be a fun thing to try out. Future ain't writ, see. Even the Company can't control that. Dangerous to jump it. Could be you land inside a wall that weren't there before. Could be you land in the middle of a war or, worse, you end up outside the dome, in the real world.

…could just go outside. Take a trip to the edge, past the Dirt Malls and the working poor. Find a crack to fall through and never come back again. Hah. Funny joke. Grab a drink from a robot. Back to work.

Murdache is chatting up a circle of people. She looks happy, which is a sight I don't think I ever thought I'd see and almost makes all this worthwhile. Take a gulp of fizz, which sits uneasy on top of the cheap beers from the bar. I knock it back quick, get another. Murdache calls me over.

"This is the operative," she says, ushering me into the circle. She frowns when I stumble, but she can't say nothing in front of all these rich, important folks. Besides, it's my party. If a man can't travel back in time, sink cheap beers for hours, take a couple of chloros and then jump back a few minutes later at his own God damn party, what can he do?

"Ahh, this is the famous King Kong?" asks an old man with a vivid orange beard and yellow lips, both of which clash against his flushed skin.

"Kong," I say. The wine bubbles itch my throat. Finish the glass anyway.

"Love the name," he says to Murdache. "I understand this one's been on more operations than any of the others. Very impressive. Strong, too, I'd wager. How long has he been active?"

Murdache looks a little uneasy but mumbles an answer I don't catch. I do, however, catch the attention of the nearest booze-bot.

"What a very special man you are, Kong." He looks me up and down. "I can see bright things in your future. Why the scar?"

"It's a variation we're trying out," Murdache answers, her hand finding my arm and squeezing; a warning or a show of familiarity, I can't rightly tell. I feel giddy. The air smells awful.

"He's attractive," the orange-beard man says. "Good skin, even with the scar."

Murdache fields this one, too. "We always aim to employ attractive operatives – not too attractive, of course, ahahaha."

"Why not?" the man asks.

Murdache starts to answer, but I cut across her. Spill my drink as I gesture. "On account of ugly and beautiful stand out. We gotta blend in."

The circle looks at me with a mixture of interest and surprise. Murdache's grip ain't uncertain no more; she's aiming to hurt me.

"We gotta look like what everyone thinks people look like, back in the slip. Not like here," I continue, ignoring her. "Here... here is all colours. You lot hide it better, right? Hide it where it shows – people look at me, and they see what we left behind." I raise my glass to toast, but it's empty. Shame. "Jokes on them. Nothing survived the Fracture."

"What Kong means is-" Murdache begins, but she's interrupted again, this time by a woman.

"I'd pay a fortune to look as good as you do," this new woman laughs, sharing a joke with the group. "I mean, look at me – I'm sure I look dreadful."

A chorus of disagreement meets this, and she smiles and dips her head and titters like a bird. The edges of the room have gone all weird, distant and blurry. My glass is still empty, my suit sticky and damp.

"Is that why you have that accent?" the man with the beard asks. "To fit into the slip?"

"Hah. I don't reckon so. Leastways, everyone keeps telling me I ain't supposed to have my own way of speaking." I grab another drink from a passing robot. Murdache is liable to rip my arm off, but no one else seems bothered. The woman who made the joke reaches up and touches my face, her fingers dancing like spider legs on my scar.

"I like the position. I might get one." She turns to Murdache, her hand still pawing me. "Do you keep them here?"

"No, we lease apartments to our operatives," Murdache replies, a line to her mouth which makes me think she ain't too happy with that question. "Kong, in fact, has one of our best spaces, to reflect his time with us. City views. Isn't that right, Kong?"

In The Slip

I pull away from the woman's hand, take a big swig of my drink. "Sure is! City views and nothing to look at. Pasttimewise, cities look different. They've got areas."

"I think it's time for Kong and I to mingle," Murdache announces, fingers digging into me.

"I'm thinking I might get a few stuckers in," I continue, shaking Murdache off. All these women trying to touch me. My glass is empty again. The robots have disappeared... I take the drink off of the woman who was so interested in my face. "I ain't hardly there, anyway. Help a few stuckers out, get them off the teasers. Ain't right, having folks stuck to the sidewalk."

"There's no helping them," orange beard man informs us. "If they had anything to offer, they'd have jobs instead of cluttering up the place. In the future, I hope we'll have resolved such problems."

"What's your job then?" I ask him. Murdache has gone silent, but there's an angry red flush growing on her cheeks.

"I'm on the board for Clear2o." He indicates the handsy woman. "So is my daughter."

"Ain't that a thing? I reckon your water's the best there is."

Hearty laugh. "I'm glad you think so well of us, Kong, truly."

"Yeah, yeah, yeah. I like a nice tall glass of it. See me, I'm a good citizen. Clear2o. Really hits the spot. It's a good thing the water's so dirty, ain't it? Elsewise we wouldn't get to enjoy Clear2o. I did a job once... Yeah! I did a job for Clear2o. You should give me free water. Hah. Or one of them ice penguins. Why's the TTCP logo a penguin, anyway? Any of you fancy folk know?"

I don't get an answer due to Murdache grabbing me and steering me away from the group, offering apologies over her shoulder. She herds me to a corner, eyes bright with humiliation.

"What the hell do you think you're doing? Do you know who those people are? How important they are?"

"I didn't do nothing wrong. I drink his water. Sometimes."

"If you've damaged my reputation, you ungrateful little shit, I'll make sure you never work the slip again, you understand?"

I open my mouth to tell her I don't understand nothing no more, but instead I throw up. Murdache's face falls, her mouth hanging open, eyes wide, like she ain't never seen nothing so disgusting in her entire life, which is probably true on account of people in the One True rarely getting sick. I knew I was ill. Damn docs ain't worth the money you pay them.

Murdache pulls herself together, and, whether for my benefit or her own, I don't know, puts her arm around me, shielding me from the room, and rubs my shoulders.

"S'rry."

"...it's fine," she says, though she don't sound like she means it. "Oh, shit." She grabs my shoulders, tries to haul me up. "Kong, pull yourself together, oh my God, it's on your shoes! Stand behind me, no, not like that, can't you do anything right – hello sir, how are you?"

She's talking to some tall, black guy in a suit, nice eyes. He's painted his nails orange, his hair flecked with yellow. Think purple would suit him better. When did purple go out of fashion, anyway? He holds out his hand, but when I go to shake it, Murdache pushes in front of me.

"Please accept my apologies, sir. We don't usually... They aren't used to... I mean..." She gives up, her words run dry.

"So, this is the famous operative, is it?" the new man says. His hands twitch. "Our most valuable asset, so I'm told. He looks a little worse for wear."

"Sir, I'm so sorry. I don't know what to say. I didn't know you were... I'm very sorry, sir."

"It's not your fault. Go on. Enjoy the party."

Murdache looks between me and this new man, torn between her fear of leaving me unsupervised and her fear of having to explain me.

"Kong, we'll speak later," she settles on, before offering up another apology and making good her escape.

"Right then," this new guy says once she's out of earshot. "I've heard interesting things about you, Mr Ki- Mr Kong. A lot of cases solved recently. That was quite a show," he adds, waving over a robot and handing me a glass of water. "How are you feeling now?"

"I wanna go home."

"Yes, I think that would be best. Drink that first, and we'll put you in a car."

"Do you think she'll fire me?" My throat hurts, tight and dry all of a sudden. "Take away the slip?"

"No. Don't worry." He says this with a level of certainty that makes me think he might be crazier than me, but I'll own to the fact it's comforting to be mollycoddled. "Come on."

He takes me down the eighty floors in the elevator, his hand on my back the whole way, his fingers tapping against my shoulder blades. At the lobby, he waits 'til the car pulls up and opens the door for me.

"Thanks."

"You're welcome. Have hope, Mr Kong," he smiles, closing the car door. I watch him through the window as he turns and heads back into the TTCP building, wondering who he is.

And then I grab my bottle of pills and swallow down two more.

F. D. Lee

Loop 17.3

The chloros stink me up pretty bad. I ain't so sure how many I took in the end, but when I cool down, I'm naked, covered in sweat and vomit, and thirstier than I think I've ever been, alltimewise. The emptiness is back, but it's the calmer sort now. Not the absence of pain, but the universal, background taint of it that bleeds so neatly into everything else that I don't even notice the stain.

  I wrangle myself into something resembling an upright position and drag myself to the kitchen, wave my wrist across the faucet. I pay the extra for Clear2o, vague memories of an orange beard floating around my head, and drink a pint of the stuff without even tasting it.

  I get myself another glass and try to drink it more slow, ignoring the jingle from my sink that thanks me for my purchase and asks if I wanna share my shopping choice with my friends. Damn fool thing don't realise I ain't got none.

  I take half a pill and then shower, using the free stuff this time, which comes out like pale rust and stinking of sulphur, and then get the worst of the destruction around the apartment cleaned up. *Clean and fresh, clean and fresh, buy it new and be the best.*

  I'm halfway through sorting out the apartment, halfway to convincing myself I'm back on my feet and settled, finally, into the One True, when I realise my tongue's stroking the inside of my lip, behind my scar. Aware of it now, I can't seem to stop, can't focus or think on nothing else. And just like that, I'm hard. Like I'm some idiot teenager who ain't learnt how to control himself.

  Well, shit. What now? I got a sore spot in my memory of the night before which I ain't in a mood to examine, but I *can* remember turning my voksac on before the party and letting it flay me raw. And now here I am, not even a full day later, hungover in my apartment, debris all around, with a tentpole rising up to greet me. But then, I'm on my own time, if time is ever my own, so… well, it's easier to go with the flow, ain't that right? Besides, I might even enjoy it. Stranger things have happened, or so I'm told.

In The Slip

I get to work, my tongue pressing against the back of my lower lip, tracing the scar. Giddy heat. The taste of beer and good health coming to mind, the warmth of the chloros, and the sensation, almost like a memory, of cold sand underneath me. It begins to hurt, my hand moving faster, enticing the pain into one place, ready to expel it all, the whole God damn mess of my life, get it out of me, out, out, out. Cramp in my legs, my tongue running against the inside of my lower lip, tingling, my hips stuttering, body tensing, and a face, a face I don't know, never seen before, dark skin, heavy body, pain, and-

I'm sat on my chair, sweaty, sticky, panting like a dog, my factory setting stomach quickly growing cold. I don't feel any better for it, just sticky and weirdly embarrassed. Not by the act, but by the realisation I'd hope it might make me feel less alone, somehow. I don't know. Do these things ever make sense to anyone? I shower again, the scar on my chin throbbing a touch from the hot, dirty water. I hold my face under the heat longer than I need to.

I'm dressing when there's a knock at my door. I open it to find the suit guy who got me home from the party, his charming smile curdling as he looks me up and down. He glances over my shoulder at my apartment, then whistles through his teeth.

"Well, Mr Kong. It seems you really do have it bad."

I ain't sure what it is he thinks I got, but in the face of the evidence, I find it hard to deny that whatever it is, it's bad. I let him in.

"What are you doing here?"

"I wanted to check up on you. You seemed, ah, vulnerable, last night."

Oh, shit. Yeah. I threw up. Fuck. Murdache is gonna kill me. She'll take the chloros trial away from me. Why is this guy here? I need to get on the wave to Murdache, try to make my apologies – Oh, God. I said all that stuff to the guy who owns Clear2o. Fuck, fuck, fuck. I slump down in my armchair. There's a plastic bottle of chloros on my table. I fumble with the lid, grab one of the white, chalky little pills and swallow.

"I know someone who was addicted, you know," the suit guy says, big brown eyes full of concern. "You can get off them."

"I ain't addicted. I need them for work."

"Oh. Right."

We're silent a while, him embarrassed and me waiting for the warm up, horror-filled memories of the previous night whirling around my head. While I'm trying to ignore my recollections, he makes himself busy in the kitchen, paying for Clear2o and the high-voltage electric, moving with the ease of one who's done it before and knows where to find what they're looking for. He puts a big cup of green tea down in front of me and then takes his own seat on the couch.

"What do you remember?"

"From last night? Not much. You helped me into a car?"

He crosses his legs, his foot dancing up and down. "And that's all?"

"Well, I haven't exactly been my best self these last twenty-four hours." Not my most hospitable, but I don't even know who this guy is or why he's at my door. "You wanna tell me why you're here? Only I got some brown nosing to do."

He takes another look around my apartment. "HomeSuiteHome?"

I grunt and wave at the apartment's control device, lying on a dark, wet stain on the carpet. He gives it a distrustful look and raises an eyebrow at me.

"Whiskey. Probably."

He looks none too convinced, but he picks it up anyways, opening windows on the big screen I ain't never seen before, lines of code whizzing by under his finger-tips. He alters a few. Next, he goes to my window, pulls the drapes closed.

"There, we've got some privacy now. Ten minutes shouldn't be noticed."

"I can't afford any God damn privacy – what the hell are you doing?"

"You're not paying. I've jacked it from your neighbour. Now tell me: how many times have you died?"

"What the fuck?"

"Let me rephrase. In the slip, how many times have you been shot?"

In The Slip

I consider what I should own to. But this guy was at the party last night, and I've got a vague memory of Murdache nearly wetting herself when she saw him. Probably should try to be more polite, now I think on it. I take a sip of my tea. "You get hurt, they tank you. It all bleeds into one."

"How old are you?"

"Thirty-eight."

"How long have you been working for the TTCP?"

"Since I was about fifteen, after my Pop died."

"Do you remember how your Pop died?"

"In an accident."

"What kind of accident?"

"I don't remember."

"Do you like shopping?"

"What?"

"Do you like shopping?"

"It's a person's responsibility to shop."

"But do you *like* shopping?"

"I do what I must."

"What colour's the sky?"

"Blue, black, grey, orange. No, wait. Whatever's fashionable."

"Have you ever seen me before?"

"Sure, last night." I pause. "And a few months back...?"

"Ok. That's enough," he says. "Murdache will keep you on the chloros trial."

"Fuck off. You can't know that."

Another flash of that smile, which is fast evolving from charming to obnoxious. "What did I tell you last night? Have hope. Just make sure you use your chance."

I won't deny that he has me on the hook, but I ain't no idiot sceever, taking on debt I can't repay.

"Just who the hell are you?"

"My name's Tyrone. Tyrone Tossenberger."

"No way. You designed my chip?"

"I've got the copyright, yes." He leans forward. "There's a lot going on, and we're running out of privacy."

"Oh, no. No way. You don't get to come into my life and drop clues and give me instructions. I don't care what you own, I want to know what's going on. Right now."

Tossenberger stands up suddenly. "I understand. And I will explain. But Murdache is going to be looking for you soon. I don't know what to say to you to make you trust me. We've never had... well, let's just say I don't think I'm the right person. Listen, when the time comes to choose where you go, trust your instinct. I'll take care of the rest."

Murdache summons me to her office that same afternoon. She don't mention the party, but there's a change in the way she looks at me. A film of something greasy like wax between us which, now it's there, I find myself mournful for not appreciating it when it wasn't. Not appreciating the fact that, though she surely hates me, she didn't used to be disgusted by me.

She talks to me about the mega chloros, just as Tossenberger predicted she would. The jump is going ahead, she says. I'm still the test case, she says. I'm expected to arrive bright-eyed and bushy-tailed the next day. I nod and 'yes ma'am' and try to pretend everything is the same as it was. She goes on about some admin crap and then, just when I think I free to go home, Murdache finally looks at me proper. For the first time since I arrived, she sounds like she's actually talking to me.

"Why do you want this jump so badly, Kong? You obviously don't care about the TTCP."

"I'm a good citizen. I do what I must for the One True."

She shakes her head, annoyed at my pat answer. "Fine. I'll send you the details on the wave and-"

"I want it because I can do it," I say, surprising myself. "I ain't got anything else. I don't belong anywhere else, and even if I did, no one wants me. But I'm good in the slip – *that's* what I am."

"But you don't believe in the work?"

"I don't think it matters what I believe in. We all got choice, ain't that the line? But what choice do I have? I don't belong here or there. At least in the slip, it ain't so obvious."

In The Slip

She pauses, lower lip caught in her teeth. Then she comes around her desk and perches on the edge, in front of where I'm sitting.

"None of us belong here, Kong. We should be outside, in the world."

"So why bother at all?"

"I think about it as a moral problem, when I think about it at all."

"Moral?"

She nods. "We gave away our choice, back then. We passed it off to everyone else, let everyone and no one deal with the destruction we were creating. People blamed governments, companies… companies blamed governments and people… around and around. But now, you see, we don't have that responsibility any more. The TTCP and the other companies have taken on the burden for us." She reaches down and puts her hand, briefly, on my knee. "What we do here is the only possible moral choice left. We protect everyone from themselves. We give them the freedom not to have to bear the burden of it."

I don't think she's ever spoken to me like this before; the way she's looking at me, the tone of her voice, makes me think this is real and new. And I'm hungry for it, a gnawing, feral hunger that catches me unexpected and urges me to reach out to her, to dive into her arms and let her tell me it all makes sense. That everything is right and proper and that I am, too.

"But nothing ever changes," I say, ignoring the grouching ache inside me. "And what about them that live out by the edge? What about the Dirt Malls and the stuckers? What about the tempos?"

Murdache pulls away. Stands. "That's their choice, their moral failing. If they want to kill us all a second time, I can't stop that. But I *can* stop them achieving it, and I expect you to do your job to help me, understood?"

"…Yes, ma'am. Understood."

"We're going to send you to a point just before the Fracture, monitor you, and then bring you back." A pause. "They've told me to let you choose where you jump. You'll be there for an hour."

"An hour? And if the pressure gets me?"

"Then it gets you," she says, which seems fair, considering.

F. D. Lee

Loop 17.4

I'm in Paris. I think I've always wanted to see Paris. Or at least, I answered quick enough when the question was put to me.

Don't know why I bothered, to be honest. I'm about ten years prior to Fracture, the moment when the planet finally realises that nothing can be reversed, nothing can be saved, and it fucking stinks – literally and metaphorically.

Factor one: there's a dirty haze to everything. Scum on the Seine. Sand in the atmosphere from the desert storms, scratching at my skin. I can just about make out the line of the Eiffel Tower in the distance, wavering in the miasma, its lights barely making a dent in the soupy air. Factor two: the folks in this part of the slip must have been the sorriest sack of slack-jaws ever birthed not to realise it's all rotten. That it's already too late. That's life, though, ain't it? Factor three: the new-fangled chloros ain't exactly fool-proof. This far back in the slip, the time pressure weighs heavy, breathing is hard, and I've only been here twenty minutes.

I take another pill, sand getting in my mouth as I do so. The pain in my chest eases. Forty minutes to go. Right then. Paris, the city of love. Hah. Let's see what's on offer. I find a patisserie, order a coffee, take a seat at the window while I wait for my drink. Or for my heart to pop and my lungs collapse. Either or.

One cup of coffee later and I'm still alive and kicking. There might well be a lot of things going south with me presenttimewise, but I'm good in the slip, hell yes I am. Halfway through my hour, time to check in. The café's busy, so I make my way to the john. Funny how all those rich folks at that party were so interested in my job, but I reckon if they knew how much of it was hiding in toilets so no one sees me accessing my Holo, they might think differently.

Locked away in a cubicle, I pull up a screen and send a wave. The message takes almost five minutes to be received. Can't control the future, sure enough, but if the Company wants to get its hands on the past, they're gonna need to up their tech.

In The Slip

The Company updated, there's one more thing I fancy doing while I'm here. Pay the check and head back into the sandy smog, pulling my collar up and squinting. I can't see hardly anything in all this, so it stands to reason no one can see me, right? Fuck it, that's what I'll say to Murdache if it turns out I create an aberrant slip.

The Holo glows green, but as I can only just see it, I doubt any of the locals will notice I'm using future tech. Anyways, they're clearly God damn morons back here – people are still driving petrol cars, even now. Some folk, see, they're just destined to keep making the same mistakes. Good thing I ain't one of those types.

I look at the map, make my way to the Eiffel Tower. It ain't a long walk but the roads are wide and the storm rages down them, so it's hard. The sand gets in my face, scratching up my skin and forcing me to walk with my eyes closed, only to open them again briefly to check the map on my Holo, but I make it.

I ain't so sure what I expected, but what I get is... spectacular. Even in the smog and the sand, it takes my breath away.

The legs are thick and wide, and the metalwork that looks wholly practical in photos is, in real life, stunning and intricate and alive. The whole tower takes on the same aspect, the sense it ain't a static thing, but something birthed, created, *grown* from the minds and hopes and aspirations of those that dreamed it up. The stink from the fetid river, the rows and rows of weatherproof tents in the shanty town on the grass boulevard, the sand on my tongue as my jaw hangs slack so I can tilt my head up and try to see the spire through the smog... none of it matters.

Here's something that ain't rotten, that ain't meant to make you feel like you need more or deserve more or even want more. It just *is*. A structure made by people for people, no teasers dancing off it, no charge to look. A sense of time in the metalwork, different from the slip. Time spent creating something. Time invested, not an investment in time.

My Holo starts beeping – the alarm, probably, warning me I need to get back to the One True. I go to shut it off, and that's when I notice it's playing up. There should be one spot on the map, me. But there's two, each one flashing. I look up and I see him, the only other person idiotic enough to risk the storm standing out here in the open.

He's staring straight at me.

I shield my eyes, try to get a better look. Taller than me, heavier. His face is covered in a cloth mask, his eyes hidden behind thick goggles. I take a step towards him, and he wakes from whatever spell he was under, turns and runs, and the next thing I know, I'm running after him, my hand protecting my eyes best it can. He knows the area, that's for damn sure, but for all his advantages in clothing, he ain't as fit as me. I keep him in my sights, focusing on the factors that define him, almost knowing without knowing the shape of him.

He makes it across the grass, over the wide road and onto the sidewalk on the other side. I'm halfway over when lights appear out of the sand, moving towards me at about thirty k an hour – not fast enough to kill me, but there's no warning, and the hood wings me, sending me skidding into the next lane. I see the shadow of the runner hop on a tram, lit bright with some kind of horn blowing low blasts every other second. Scramble to my feet, lungs full of sand and heat. Ignore it, pursue.

I can see the lights of the tram, moving slow through the storm, its horn like a siren's call, leading me on. It's barely a jog, but the sand gets in everywhere and more than once I have to close my eyes and follow my ears, my feet occasionally picking up the hard metal of the tram line through my soles. The rhythm sets, the tram keeping beat as I follow behind. Restful, almost. Just running, running, running. Chasing, chasing, chasing.

A long, low blast and the tram slows to a stop. A shadow emerges, silhouetted by the lights. My guy, unmistakable, sure as silver. He hops down. I stop maybe four and a half metres from him but, I'm guessing, hidden in the storm because he doesn't run. For a moment he stands there, his head down and his shoulders slumped. Almost like he's sad, which don't make a lick of sense considering, from his understanding, he's just escaped a man chasing him down. Probably he's ducking his head from the storm. Except he's wearing protection, ain't he?

He heads down a narrow street, tall buildings with lights blazing, sending weird shafts of yellow through the orange, like fingers reaching down from on high. I keep away from the beams of light. Creeping up on him, my throat no longer sore and scratchy, the ache in my hip from the car reduced to a gentle burn. It takes a minute to realise I'm excited, eager in fact, to catch up with him.

I'm maybe half a street behind him, hidden in sand and shadow, when my God damn Holo starts buzzing against my wrist, panicking because it can't locate me, the little dot spasming and jumping around the map. I disable it quick, before it lights up the whole alleyway. When I look up, he's gone.

Shit.

OK. Factor one: the sand is thick, but he wasn't paying much attention before, so he must know where he is and where he's going. Factor two: He's out of shape, so he ain't gone far. Factor three: straight ahead seems clear, though it's hard to tell. But it's lit up better than the alleyway to the left. Factor four: if he saw the Holo, he'd have run, right? A guy like him, I'd see him running, even in this soup. Factor five: if he didn't see it, if he's not running, he's reached his destination.

I take the side street, mostly on account of it's where I'd hole up if I needed somewhere to be. Not my best work, I'll own, but sometimes you just gotta make a choice. It's empty and dark, the sand swirling and dancing across the paving stones. The alleyway opens out at the other end onto a wide road, the wind racing down it, caught in the vector. Worse than the street I came off, which bent and wound and blocked its flow, but not as bad as it was by the Eiffel Tower.

The guy ain't anywhere to be seen.

I should go back to base – why'd I run after him, anyway? This is supposed to be a recon mission. But my Holo went crazy, and he was looking straight at me, and then he ran. Say what you like about my professionalism, but if someone's that keen to get away from me, my figuring is there's a reason. And now I've lost him.

A dry lump forms in my throat, my chest hurting like I've had the air knocked out of me. Time pressure coming on sudden, must be. Swallow another pill. Too many, even for me; too strong, even for me. Time to go back – well past time. There ain't no angry waves on my Holo, but that don't mean they ain't on their way, what with the delay and my Holo fritzing. I should open the slip, get back to the sand-free, coconut air of the One True.

There's a door set into the building on the right. I pull at the handle, not surprised to find it's locked. Shit. Smash my fist into it, *bang bang bang*.

I'm just about to wave back to base to let them know I'm coming home when the door opens.

"Oui? Bonjour? Oh..."

There's a blonde woman in front of me. I knocked and she answered. Ain't that a thing?

I answer in French but she just stares at me, so I try again in English.

"Hello, ma'am. I'm sorry to come knocking unannounced. I... uh..." Shit. What the hell do I say? I followed this man who was staring at me, and now I'm banging on your door? "I'm lost – the storm, y'know? I was wondering if you could help me?"

Her features are set rigid, a sheen of sweat on her skin. She looks sick as a dog, now I come to notice it.

"Help you?"

"Uh. Yeah?"

"I... no. I'm sorry. My family and I are just visiting, so..." She makes to shut the door, and that's when I see it on her arm. She's wearing a God damn Holo.

"You're a tempo?"

"What? No – shit!"

"Lois, what's going on down there?" a woman's voice calls from inside.

She – Lois? – pushes her weight against the door, trying to slam it closed. Quick, I pull it forward so she stumbles, then slam it back. Her head cracks against the inner wall with a thud. I step over her body and into the building.

It smells of old wood, sweet and musty that way it gets when trees start to rot. There's a smell to rotten wood. You don't get it back home, but you do in the slip, sometimes. Earthy. Warm kind of-

A screeching wail, painful like needles pushed into my brain, breath hissing between my teeth, fire in my temples, chest tight.

Dig my hands into my hair, fingers pressing against my skull, and then it's gone. Just like that.

Slam my back against the wall, jab out a wave to base with my coordinates: *Found tempos. Help needed.* Get my bearings. I'm in a short corridor, a double staircase with a small landing ahead, hallways left and right, the blonde woman's body behind me, the front door slamming open and closed, the sand storm outside.

A noise from the top of the stairwell, not a scream but something akin to it, full of pain held tight, bottled and lidded quick, smoke in a jar. On the landing between the two stairwells stands a second woman, dark hair, white skin with a sweaty film to it, breathing hard.

The brickwork above my head explodes in a cloudy storm. She missed the shot. I duck back, rifle through the blonde's clothes and, sure as silver, find a small gun at her waist. I take it, send a warning shot up into the air.

"You ain't getting out of this. If I don't get you, the time pressure will." That's a question, ain't it? How long have I got, and is it longer than the gunner? Shit, where's the guy? How many tempos are here? Keep calm, work the slip. "Best come down, give up. I ain't looking to see any more folk get hurt."

I slide along the wall, duck my head around the corner, no one there, duck back. If I move to the opposite wall to check the right-hand hallway, I won't have a shot up the stairs. If I stay here, I'm easy pickings, being as I am clearly visible to anyone coming in from the right. Forward or back? Are there any more tempos? Where's the guy?

"You still up there?" I shout.

Silence.

Dust showers from the floorboards above. Wipe it out my eyes. The door behind me thumps against the jamb, the wind rattling it something fierce. Check my Holo: *Message sending.* Shit, it's taking too long. Too far back in the slip.

"They're on their way," I shout. "Don't make them bring you in by force."

The storm's getting up behind me, door banging loud, a crash from outside. "Your friend's in trouble down here, reckon she's gonna need some help. Her head's bleeding pretty bad. Don't you wanna help her? Throw down your gun."

One second, two, three, four, five – her gun clatters down the stairs, slides to a stop in the open hallway between me and the bottom of the staircase.

"OK. Now you come down, slow and steady, hands on your head."

She makes her way down the steps, hands on her head, feet beneath her struggling some, her Europhile complexion waxy, sweat-shiny, her eyes bright with fiery rage.

"You're a real piece of shit, Kong."

What?

"How do you know my name?"

She stumbles to the foot of the stairs, her hands tight at her scalp, a marionette doll keeping itself up.

"Every time, every God damn time we give you a chance, you fuck us up," she wheezes. "Every. Fucking. Time."

"What're you talking about?"

Message sending.

"If she's dead, I'll kill you, and I'll do it right," the woman continues. "I swear to God. I'll rip out your Holo, and then I'll put my gun to your head, pull the trigger, and watch your brains splatter across the world. No miraculous rescue, no tank. Not for you, not this time, Kong."

I take a step forward, the only sounds are the door banging, the wind, and her voice, splintered, as she sways at the foot of the stairs.

"What are you talking about? Who are you?"

"I guess you wanted it, huh? You coward."

"Wanted what? How do you know my name?"

She's right up against the barrel of my gun, pushing into it. My Holo beeps: *Message received.* We both see it.

The woman collapses, shouting, "Now!"

I spin. Standing right behind me, gun wavering at my head, is a man dressed in an old grey overcoat – my coat! That's my coat! – with goggles pushed up onto his head and a thick scarf around his neck, and he's got a scar on his chin like mine-

In The Slip

Blackness all around him, bubbles of it like water on hot tin, boiling off him. He steps towards me, arms open, a smile stretched wide across his face.

I try to back away but I can't, and now he's got me. Holding my arms, stroking me gently, calming me, and it works. I feel my breathing even out. The black rears and strikes, but it can't touch him, not now. His hand on my face, thumb stroking away the tears.

I push him away, and the darkness envelops him.

He's gone. He's gone.

Joe's gone.

I stare at him, ignoring the gun pointed at my head.

"Joe?"

A flash outside and the burning stink of ozone.

"Shit," he says, his voice raw and thin, chest working fast. "Shit, shit, shit. I can't, Karen, I can't."

"Now! Do it now!" the woman screams.

The door behind him crashes open, three other operatives storm in, guns raised. I put my hand up at them, waving like a lunatic. "Wait!"

"Take the shot," shouts one. "Now!"

"No!"

BANG, louder than thunder, as thunder ain't never gone off right next to my head. Heat and sand all around me, the hallway filled with operatives.

Burning ozone, the dark-haired woman disappears.

Bullets fly past my face to land in the wooden stairs in a shower of splinters.

It's over in less than a second. A second less than a second. Joe is on the floor, dying. Ain't no other way to read it, on account of the bullet hole right above his heart, blood mixing with the sand, the light draining from his eyes. I fumble my own chest, checking for holes, heat in my leg like chloros but sticky and sickly instead of relaxing.

No holes in my torso. One in my thigh, my clothes turning dark.

I reach out for Joe, his eyes empty now, my hand cold, shaking-

F. D. Lee

Sand everywhere but no water, and above us no sky. We pretend it's a beach at midnight, anyways. We pretend a lot of things, him and me. The endless storm above our heads covering the sun, the moon, the stars, and below, our little fire burning green at the edges. He looks warm and relaxed, skin like wet sand, hair dark as midnight, eyes brown like mine, but flecked with amber.

Joe leans against me, my arm around him, his head on my chest, his fingers dancing at buttons of my shirt. Nothing, nothing, nothing, and then a quick brush against my skin, followed by a kiss dropped on the material, above my nipple, on the hard muscle of my pectoral.

Time washes, drifts, ebbs, disappears.

Fall backwards and hit the hard sand, his hand creeping under my shirt. It don't make much sense to me why he'd want to touch my skin as it must feel strange, abhorrent, unreal, but still he explores, and to my surprise I press myself to his hand, encouraging this intrusion into the horror show of my body. His fingers brush across the centre of my chest, no attempt to wander lower nor higher, just dancing on the smoothness of me.

"I know this isn't the most romantic spot, Bai, but I'm glad we're here, together.," he says, laughing, his breath hot, soft and real. "I hope you'll know how wonderful I think you are?"

Reset

In the darkness, strange sounds, strange voices. Calm silk with steel scissors of anger cutting through it, ripping it, edges frayed. Blunt scissors. You have to keep your scissors sharp when you're cutting silk, or it'll fray and once it starts, it's the very devil to stop it. They always cut it wrong.

The trick, I wanna tell them but I can't on account of the gloop sticking itself to my tongue and teeth, sliding down my throat, but I wanna tell them that the trick to cutting silk is to hold it firm between paper. But they don't got no paper, just the thick, sticky oil of the tank, and the little tiny robots inside it, and the invit chemicals. Invit is a clever thing, a marvel of the One True, the catalogue to end all catalogues, but it ain't no good for cutting silk, nor for masking anger.

My brain throws up images from the slip.

The woman on the floor, blonde hair like the sun, only there's blood matted in it now from the knock she took when I slammed her into the wall. That don't sit right with me. I ain't the kind of person who would hurt someone, I ain't. I do things... I do things I guess which ain't what you might call exactly wholesome, but I ain't never been a hurtful man, ain't happy to see her there, bleeding on my account.

Darkness swirls around her, gloop slithering over her prone body. I bend down and wipe it off, but it creeps back soon as my hands ain't there. There's a candle in her hand, and a lighter. I light the candle; a pool of warmth surrounds her, and the snakes slither away.

Joe next. He's dead, that's for damn sure. Not by me. I ain't no murderer. So why does my stomach knot and my head pound and my chest heave when I look on him? Everyone's dead anyway, ain't that what being in the slip means? Moving through ghosts, people long dead and done, adding to the dust bowl.

I'm dead, too.

No. No, I'm in the tank. I can't see anything, my eyes are welded shut, but if I concentrate... if I push past the pain in my head and the high, screaming noise all around me, I can feel myself being made. I didn't know that before.

Huh. It seems so obvious now.

Joe's almost covered in the thick, tarry snakes, his legs and arms turned liquid and losing their shape. Leave the woman – LOIS! – leave Lois in her cocoon of candlelight, head over to Joe.

I'm twelve or thirteen years old, and the camp is dark. Stars above me, scattered confetti, bright like I've never seen them before. The air smells weird, like the pine scent that was popular a few years back but softer, somehow. Earthier. My hand reaches out and grabs a handful of mulch and leaves. I bring it to my face and breathe it in.

The darkness surrounds Joe, worming over his body.

There's not much of him left, but I clean off what I can, saving his face and most of his torso. Why didn't I save him first? I was afraid. I understand it, in this old, sweet-smelling forest, in this dead building, in the tank. Sooner or later, all things die, and I'm dead already. I died, I died and I wanted to die.

I pick up what's left of Joe, near weightless now he's half dissolved, bring him back to the light. Cradle him in my arms, drop kisses on him, beg him to forgive me.

Black snakes rear back, dart forward, but the light keeps them away, keeps me awake in the darkness.

There was another one. The woman. Krezzler. She ain't here... Did she jump, did the gloop get her? No, wait. She's in the light too, long as I think on her. Joe, Lois and Krezzler and me. In a puddle of light.

The snakes hiss and squirm. They're speaking to me. Hissing words I remember my Pop telling me when I was a kid, but it doesn't sound like him anymore. Sounds sibilant, sinister, sickly.

Do I remember when we went to the park and saw the animals? What about that time he took me walking on the Sky Rail and I fell and nearly cut my face open, but he caught me? Do I remember my languages? Who owns the patents, the big test is tomorrow, son. Do I remember that boy, the one Pop caught me with? The bad boy who was leading me astray until Pop chased him off. How about playing catch in the backyard? Pop bought me a big screen. Rising mechanical horses, watching plastic animals running by on tracks.

Animals. Zoos. Mall. Kites. Catch. Screens. Teasers. Horses. Soccer. Boys. Razor. Mandarin. Spanish. French. English. German. Italian. Portuguese. Japanese. Korean. Punjabi. Hindi. Arabic. Museum. Patent holders. Big Test. Cake. Dog. Sky Rail-

No.

No, I remember running around the backyard, building forts and fighting and digging up the trees and throwing rocks and burning bins and stealing, and how it was that Mom and Pop were so angry with me.

My Pop is off to save the world, Mom smiling at us from the doorway. Me crying and promising to never be bad again. How old am I? When did I join the TTCP? What do I like the most?

How did my Pop die?

I know what happened.

Screens and teasers and people, everyone eating the animals and giving the animals the forests to eat. Chemicals in the air and the water and the earth. Little wriggly creatures in our blood that can't be killed on account of we bred them to be better than us, bred them to kill us and we *knew it too,* and still we bred them strong. Companies taking money from governments for sea walls but refusing to cease their productions, to stop the oceans rising. The storms as the currents change. 2.5° and rising. Enough plastic toys washing over the world that if you melted them down, they'd encase the Earth five times over. Tax breaks. Famine. Drought. A conspiracy, they say. Other planets survive, they say; but not ours. Trickle, trickle, *trick.*

Mom and Pop. Talk of moving house, moving somewhere new, but there ain't no time for that...

The slip is nothing but time so that can't be right, can it?

Weren't no money, then. Mom and Pop arguing, that's what I remember. I was there, the good old days that weren't never good. I heard them argue over how to pay for it, with Pop promising that if we give him more money now, he'd double it back to us soon. If we loosen the regulations, untie his hands, he could save us. But it never came. We got the domes instead, and the teasers, and choice. So many choices to think about. So much to keep up with.

Pop went off to buy a packet of cigarettes and a new car and dioxin and a side of beef, and when he came back, Mom was dead.

F. D. Lee

Loop 18.0

Joe.

I remember Joe. I remember Lois. I remember Krezzler. My head hurts when I think on them, but I can stand it. Stand it better than this feeling I'm left with. This sense I've been broken up and stuck back together, that my whole self is made up of thoughts and ideas I don't recognise and yet I know, sure as silver, belong to me.

There are versions of me who have been everywhen and done things I ain't never want to think on doing. Things that shame me, make my chest hurt worse than any time pressure ever could. Things that confound me for their viciousness, their stupidity and cowardice. Worse, though, are the things I did that made me happy; that made other people happy, too. The things I can remember now that tell me that, at some point in my broken life, I was something approaching a real, decent person.

How could I do that to Joe? To myself? All those times in the tank, I had the chance to rescue him, revive him from the blackness, and I let him go. I didn't choose him. I buried him, stuck him away on the sidewalks in the frozen parts of myself, surrounded him with teasers and noise and darkness and *I left him there*.

I have to get him back. And if that means I have to save the whole fucking world as well, so be it.

I'm taken to a medi, as per regulations. Look in the mirror, the one I smashed two, three, twenty timelines ago. They took my scar away. My chin is new, smooth, no stubble. No lines around my mouth. I press my tongue in front of my lower teeth, making a face.

It looks a fright. But it's relaxing in a way, watching my face distend, the lump of skin my tongue creates rolling in the reflection. I follow the line of Joe's scar, my scar, our scar, left side of my mouth, where it used to be. Push, push, push my tongue

In The Slip

against the wet, warm flesh, my mouth hanging open, head tipped slightly back so I can get at it even harder.

"They're sending you home."

"Huh?"

Nurse rolls her eyes. I hadn't even clocked her coming in.

"Sending you home – well, after the briefing, anyway. I need to check you over. Here, take a couple of these." She hands me some chloros, regular kind, then goes back to her work, switching me off. I thumb open the tub, bring it to my mouth, tip, let the pill sit on my tongue.

The nurse taps away at my screen, asking the de-tanking questions. Nothing ever changes, except when it does.

How old am I? *Too old to be so young and stupid and selfish.*

"Thirty-eight."

How long have I been with the TTCP? *Feels like I ain't never not been here.*

"Since I was fifteen."

What about my Pop?

"He died." *He never lived.*

How did he die?

"I don't remember." *He lied and then he left.*

Do I like shopping?

"Yes, of course." *No. No. I hate it because it ain't real. It's busy work. It's a lie. It's false hope. Hope that this next thing, this newest thing, this latest thing, will make me happier, make me valuable and important and better than anyone that don't have it, and just as good as those that do.*

No, I don't like shopping.

I like Joe.

I love Joe.

I killed Joe.

The room fills with the siren screech of alarms, like the universe warning of something coming. Ice crackling across my brain, so sharp I can feel it in between the folds, cutting its way through me. Tighten my hands, try to push the pain somewhere else, but it won't... it won't stop...

The chloros is still in my mouth, wedged under my tongue, so I swallow it. The sirens stop, and the tightness across my crown gives way, that nice warm feeling, the deft fingers of the drug easing the pain.

The nurse closes down her screen, oblivious.

"Hey," I say as she stands.

"Yes?"

"What happened to the tempos? The one... the one who died? And the other one?"

The nurse frowns at me, pulls a torch from her pocket and shines it in my eyes.

"Open your mouth," she instructs.

She lifts my tongue with a little plastic stick, swishes it around my mouth, poking hard but not nearly as satisfying as my own tongue. Nods. Taps out something on her chip, pulls up another screen, opaque so I can't see it, and does some typing. I hold myself still, ignore the impulse to break her arm and read her screen.

"I'm sorry, Kong," she says. "I just need to run a couple more – I'm going to check your chip again. OK? Take another chloros. I'll be as quick as I can."

I pop another pill into my mouth, hold it under my tongue, watch her typing, my Holo flashing up all sorts of lights as she does so.

"Kong, can you tell me about the mission you went on?" the nurse asks from behind my screen.

I think on the dream I had in the tank, cradling Joe's torso in my arms. "I went back before the Fracture, road testing the new chloros. I found some tempos. There was trouble. One of them got away, one was injured, and one was... one was terminated."

The pain in my head returns, hollering for attention. Pain, see, it tries what it can to get you to listen. Pain is a warning, the alarm to end all alarms: get out, get help, stop this or you're gonna be in trouble. Nerves like little soldiers running messages across the battlefield back to command, screaming that retreat is the only option. But this time the General ain't listening. Too late, little soldier, the war is lost.

Nurse nods. "Anything else?"

Yeah, the Company took Joe away and I let them. Every single time. And now I'm gonna fuck them up, real, real, bad. "Nope. I guess the time pressure got me? I only remember being there and then getting detanked."

The nurse leaves. I'm on my Holo quick as the door slides closed, scanning through screens trying to find out what happened to Joe and Lois. The Company keeps records like, hah, like a bad clock keeps time, adding seconds and minutes and hours. If I can find Joe's body, maybe I can get him in a tank somehow. Lois said she woke up in a tank – shit, that means she was an operative. How am I only realising this now, or did I know it and forget?

I let myself forget.

No time for that. Keep thinking, keep looking, before the nurse comes back. If Lois was an agent, it stands to reason Joe was, too. So, they'd have records of them both. Yes, yes, yes. The tank could work! If I can get his body into a tank, the invit gloop might know who he is, which means it should be able to rebuild him. Chest shot, not head. Body and soul, both ready for repair. I'll need a doctor. Easy. I'll find one, force them to fix it. It's all possible. Have hope, right?

I can get Joe back, we'll find Lois, and then we can all get the hell out of here and... and then I can work how I'm ever gonna apologise enough to him. To them both. But I can do it. A second less than a second. There's always enough time in the slip. Yes! I can get him back and make it all good and-

The Company incinerated him.

Running through the back alleys of a city made of stone, operatives on our tail. They're gaining on us and Joe ain't running so good, his leg injured from the fall he took getting out of the souk. He stumbles against the brickwork, scraping his face, his mouth and chin leaking blood.

I haul him up, try to get him to see reason. See what has to happen.

"You gotta shoot me," I tell him.

"No. Karen will find us. She always finds us. Come on! We have to move."

"Joe, you listen to me. You have to shoot me. They don't know I'm with you. They'll take me back to base, and you can get to the meeting point, find Lois, get your Holo fixed."

"No! I can fix it now – I've been getting better at it and-"

"There isn't time, love. Besides, you're too pretty to be a techie."

"Fuck you." The words are undermined by the break in his voice. His eyes shine, pain and anger mixing. "I can't lose you. Please. Let me try,"

I kiss him, arm slipping around his waist, pressing his body to mine. My hand lands on something hard and cold.

"I promise I won't get lost," I tell him. "I promise. I'll find you."

"You won't – you can't." His expression changes. "They'll trace us anyway, they'll have your feed. See? It won't matter if you go back. It won't matter. Please. Listen to me-"

"They won't find you." I pull the gun from his waistband.

"Wait, no, what are you doing-"

"I'm choosing you. I'll always choose you."

"No - !"

I shoot myself in the head.

"Do you think they should tank him again?" the nurse asks. "I've never seen one have a fit like that before."

The suit guy is in the room. From the party, from my apartment. Only now he ain't wearing a suit, he's dressed up in a white coat, his screen up, my wrist in his hand.

They incinerated Joe.

I think the search is still up on my screen... No, the man – suit man, doctor man, whatever man – has turned it off.

They incinerated Joe.

"No tanks," suit man, Tossenberger, tells the nurse. "His chip is working."

"Oh. Sorry, sir. I just thought... what with everything..."

Tossenberger turns to the nurse, offers her a big smile. "No need to apologise. You were right to alert me." He turns to me. "There's nothing wrong with you. I expect that's a relief. If you don't mind, though, I'd like to run a couple of quick tests? Since I'm here and so are you?"

"Who the fuck cares?"

"Well, I do, for one." Back to the nurse. "Please can you look at the other operatives? Thank you."

She hesitates a moment then nods, leaves the room.

"They incinerated him."

"One moment, please."

Tossenberger opens his screen, tap tap tap. "Now then. You've made something of a mess of things, and I need you to answer me honestly. I know you lied to that nurse. If you don't answer me honestly, I'll put you back in the tank. Understand?"

"Good. I want to go back in the tank."

He shakes his head, his hands flexing on his knees. "No, you don't. Now, will you please stop behaving like a child and listen?"

"Fine. Whatever. Ask your questions."

"How old are you?"

"Forty, no, thirty-eight."

"Forty or thirty-eight?"

"I'm not sure."

Tossenberger nods. "How long have you been working for the TTCP?"

"Since I was about fifteen, after my Pop died."

"Do you remember how your Pop died?"

"My Pop died in an accident."

"What kind of accident?"

"Does it matter? What are you doing here, anyway?"

He reaches out, gentle, and lowers my hand, placing the tub of chloros next to the sink. "You can take some, just wait a few minutes. Your head hurts, is that it? It's perfectly normal. Just a few more minutes. Have you ever seen me before?"

"Yes, obviously. At the party, at my flat. Why the hell are – no, I don't care. They *burned* him up into nothing. Tank me. Take it away from me."

"Do you like shopping?"

"No, I fucking don't. We done? You gonna tank me now?"

Tossenberger settles back in his chair, looking at me with those handsome brown eyes of his all encouraging and kind, but I got the feeling this ain't kind at all. My head hurts. I wanna go back in the tank. I want to forget again. Go back to sleep. He's not much built. I could smash his skull into the glass...

But folks been smashing their heads into shit...

It don't make any...

Messy and needful...

Alltimewise, the same...

"OK. That's enough," Tossenberger says, lacing his fingers together, his knuckles pressing against his dark skin. "You can take your pills now if you want them."

I reckon I got a chloros in my mouth before he even finishes the sentence. Swallow. Heat. Better.

The doc gets to his feet, picks up my wrist, pulls up my screen. "I owe you an apology. We pushed you, instead of letting it happen on its own. But time *is* running out. Do you want to save Joe or not?"

"What are you talking about? They incinerated him. There ain't nothing to save."

"Well, yes and no. But you'll need Krezzler if you're going to get him and Lois back."

I stare at him.

"How the hell do you know about Krezzler?"

"Because I was the one who woke her up." He's got his own screen up now, tapping away. "I need to fix something first, and then you're going to have some explaining to do. This isn't... But we are where we are. Go to the briefing, then head home. Do not talk to anyone."

And then he's out the door, and I got this sense that this isn't the first time this white-coated sceever has walked out on me.

Loop 18.1

All fifteen of us sit in the debriefing room, them upright and eager, me at the back, slumped into my coat, hands in my pockets, tub of chloros weighing in my palm.

My mind keeps fixing on Joe, on the memories flooding my brain, and it burns. My whole body reacts each time my mind touches it, a violent shudder that draws the attention of the other operatives. I gotta hold it together. Find out what Tossenberger is talking about. Find out if there is a way I can save Joe and Lois.

The door slides open and Rob walks in, little flushed. He looks around for a place to sit, catches my eye and looks away. Not angry, not ignoring me, just his gaze moving over the room, natural as you might when you're late and looking to slide in. He spots a seat near the front, sits downs, leans over to say a few words to his neighbour. Like he ain't never known me. Guess I ain't the only person tanked recently.

The big screen at the top of the room flashes up the penguin TTCP logo, before Murdache's face appears. She welcomes us all to the room, then sets about briefing us on the events of the slip. She kicks off with an account of the new chloros and how I lasted over an hour pre-Fracture, bringing in two tempos while I was at it. Everyone cheers. I think I'm gonna throw up.

"Clearly, the mission was a success," Murdache says. "Now we have a viable means of travelling a decade or so before the Fracture and – who knows – perhaps to even more exciting parts of the slip. Imagine it: for the first time since the TTCP's inception, we can finally and completely protect the One True Timeline. We can keep everyone safe from temporal terrorism, from those who would steal our freedom, our way of life. We have a chance to fix the slip so that there's no way any tempo, ever, will put it at risk again. The war, my friends, is about to be won."

There's even more cheering at this, which I join in with because it seems like the thing to do. Murdache lets it last a full minute before shushing everyone down again.

"More tests are needed. Our success was great, but the time pressure is still an issue. An hour is a long time in the slip – you don't need me to tell you that, ahaha – but if you can't function properly, an hour might as well be a second. Nevertheless, this is a seminal day for us, for the TTCP, for humanity, and for the One True Timeline. Still, we cannot rest. We must be ever vigilant." Her voice rises, her eyes shining. "Temporal terrorism never sleeps, and neither can we. While our scientists work on new avenues to maintain our victory, we will continue to do our job. We are the line in the sands of time, the creators of the future, the protectors of the status quo. New missions will be posted to you as they come in, but for now... For now, I would like to suggest you all go buy yourselves something nice to celebrate!"

All the Holos in the room light up, mine included, as a bonus is added to our accounts. The biggest cheer of all meets this. Murdache is grinning on the screen, looking genuinely happy, rosy-cheeked and bright-eyed. Shit, she's crying even, a couple of tears that are and wiped quickly away. Folk are up on their feet, hugging each other, conversation growing from a buzz to a roar. Murdache cuts her comms link, and the penguin appears again before the screen goes blank.

But all I'm thinking on is Joe's body, his blood, his ashes. The wailing in my head gets louder, blasting out over the ruckus of the other operatives' celebrations. Lift my thoughts from the blood and the sand, my fingers digging into my scalp, trying to match the pain coming from inside me. I get out the briefing room, ignoring Rob and the others, and find myself on the outside steps, making a point to scuff my boots on that stupid penguin's stupid beak.

Factor one: penguins were black and white so's they couldn't be seen from above or below. See, the creatures in the sky, they wanted to eat the penguins, and the creatures in the sea, they also fancied themselves a bit of penguin meat, so these little critters fixed a loophole by designing themselves a white belly and a black back, so that from above they were hidden in the darkness of the sea, and seen from below, they blended in with the brightness of the sun.

Course, presenttimewise, if there was a penguin and he wanted to hide his fat ass, he'd have to design himself a reddy-orange belly and a beige and grey back. Mind you, he'd also have to find some ocean to swim in, so I guess there ain't all that much going for penguins no more, which is probably why the TTCP penguin went into the private sector.

I burst out laughing, tears pouring down my face. A nearby stucker drags his attention from the teasers swarming around him just long enough to grin at me, and then goes back to the neon and the noise.

I drop him my entire bonus as I walk past.

I mill around my apartment, waiting for Tossenberger. Sky changes colour a couple of times. I buy some Clear2o to mix with my whiskey. Stand outside in the hallway, come back in again. Look around for something to do, find myself standing in front of my musak player. The *Love Across Time* case rests on top of the black box. Flip it over, read the song list.

My gaze hones in on song fourteen, the one that broke me into pieces the day of the party. '*Scarborough Fair* – an old English folk song about a couple who must perform a series of impossible tasks to prove their love'.

Joe was my love, and I failed him.

Throw the case across the room. It hits the wall and shatters, already cracked from some past mishap I don't even remember. Pick up the pieces, put them in the trash. Look at the inlay card. Hold it over the recycle, ready to drop.

Instead, I pull the disc from the machine, find a new case, and put it and the inlay card back together. Grab a chair, set it front of my shelves, and shove the case, disc and all, as far up and back as I can reach.

Fix myself another drink. Wait, staring at the blank big screen, sipping hot, earthy firewater.

Hours pass until there's a buzz at the door and Tossenberger is in my flat. He's even more fidgety than I remember him being, which I own don't mean he's never been fidgetier, just not as far as I know or, frankly, care.

"How do I get Joe back?"

He shoots me a sympathetic look before grabbing my HomeSuiteHome and tinkering with it like he did before, stealing us some privacy. When he's happy we're alone, he answers.

"Joe King was an operative, like you. So was Lois Pryce and Karen Krezzler – Carrie Bagges, then. You four were among the earliest operatives we trained, the best of them, too." His fingers dance against his trouser legs. "There's no time to explain it all now. Look, you've trusted me before. Can you do it again?"

That's a damn good question, but I don't see anyone else trying to help me. "OK. So... what do you need me to do?"

"Well, the first thing is-"

The air picks up, sending my magazines dancing in spinning reels. The room fills with crackling ozone, the slip opens, and Krezzler appears in the middle of my living room.

"-we need to make a plan," Tossenberger finishes.

Krezzler blinks a moment, adjusting the new now. Then she spots me. Her hands clench, fury taking control of her face. I tense for a fight, my body working on auto. She takes a step forward-

Tossenberger steps in between us. "We don't have time for this. We need to get the other two out and all four of you back in the slip. I could only siphon off a few minutes of privacy; your neighbour pays attention."

Krezzler spits on my rug. "Fine. You know where they are?"

"I do," Tossenberger replies, pulling up his screen and showing it to her. "Lois is being held in the detention centre, you remember the one?"

Krezzler nods. "Hard to forget."

"Right, yes. Of course. So, considering you know the layout and where to jump to, you go there. I'm going to get Kong into the Bank, which means you'll be on your own. You go in first, get their attention away from the upper floors. I've managed to reroute some people, but it'll still be, uh, busy. Hopefully... hopefully, they won't have had time to finish their interrogation."

His voice catches. Krezzler reaches out and squeezes his shoulder. "If they have, I'll get her the other way. Don't worry."

A moment passes between them that I wouldn't have thought Krezzler capable of, to be truthful. Tossenberger swallows, gathers himself. "Thank you. Well then. Kong can get Joe from the Bank

In The Slip

while you're doing... that... and then you two can rendezvous here," he points at his screen, "Get Joe and then get to one of the safe houses. I'll give you the location, Karen, and you can get in touch with me when you've all had a moment to, uh, to catch up?"

"Sounds like a plan." Krezzler hits a command on her Holo and vanishes in a whirl of air and ozone.

Tossenberger wrings his hands, looks over at me. Sighs.

"We've got about two minutes left before we lose privacy and the TTCP can pick up us again. Any questions?"

F. D. Lee

Loop 18.2

Tossenberger puts me in a car and sends me to the Company, where I have to wait until Krezzler sends me a wave saying to go in, and I gotta go in calm. They don't know I'm not on the team yet, see, and Krezzler's about to make her entrance wherever it is they're holding Lois.

Plan is, I walk in, get in the elevator and ride up nice and quiet to the rendezvous point, where they're keeping Joe. Don't draw attention to myself, let the guards distract themselves dealing with Krezzler.

I walk over the penguin, glaring at anyone who looks at me, daring them to get in my way. Lucky for me, I guess my reputation precedes me as no one bothers with any hellos or how've you beens. Score one for social misanthropy.

I enter the elevator, wave my Holo across the pad, and the door slides closed – Tossenberger's hack, hastily done as he explained the plan, holds up. Still, my stomach flips as the elevator begins its ascent. This is the part I would have appreciated more guidance on, but the privacy ticked away, so I settled for listening to Tossenberger's instructions. Trust, see.

He's sending me to the Stasis Bank on floor 75. Apparently, that's where I'll find Joe. I'm stepping into the belly of the beast – the place where the Company keeps track, where they can spot aberrant timelines before they get a chance to become permanent. Got me directions and a series of codes, which Tossenberger says I'm to enter into some machine they got up there and it'll do the rest.

None this makes a whole heap of sense to me, but as long as Joe's there, and Krezzler manages her side of things, that's all that matters.

The floors count up as the elevator rises. Past Murdache's, past the executive boardroom where they held that shindig for me, higher than I ever been. Another belly flip as the elevators comes to a stop at the 75th. So far, so good, the plan's working with no issues.

In The Slip

The doors slide open, and the issues begin.

Two guards on either side of me, one standing to attention, the other with her chip to her ear, probably listening to the comms as the folk downstairs realise they're under attack. They startle when they see me, too focused on whatever the hell Krezzler is up to. Their shock is what does for them.

I slam the first guard's head against the wall, dazing him. The second pulls her gun, but I'm already shoving guard one at her, and she shoots him in the shoulder instead of me in the head. He falls, screaming, to the floor, and I'm down and kicking out with my leg, ready to swipe her off her feet. She sees it coming, jumps back.

She's quick, practised in some kinda fancy fighting. Lands with her feet planted, her gun already taking aim at me. But she ain't an operative, and she ain't never faced anyone as good in the slip as me. I roll, come up kneeling at her feet, her gun aimed square at my face. She's in control now, can see it in her expression. She'll call it through, she won't shoot. If she does, the bullet will travel straight forward, hitting me between the eyes and painting the elevator doors with mush and bone. If she moves, she'll shoot wide.

Right? Right. OK.

Deep breath.

Either this is gonna work, or I'm about to jump myself into the path of a bullet.

I jump two seconds into the future, arriving on her left, shaving time like a barber on 'phetes. No bullet in me, so I guess I judged it right. Jumping futuretimewise in a God damn gun fight... Knew I was good in the slip.

The guard's confusion is writ large as my fist slams into her face, once, twice, three times, and then she's on the floor, joining guard no. 1. A new head appears around a door, takes one terrified look at the mess I've made and darts back, the door hissing closed, red light signalling it's locked.

OK then. More guards on the way soon enough.

I pull up Tossenberger's directions, type a few new settings into my Holo, and head down the corridor. Two turns on, a troop of guards appear, hut-hut-hutting their way towards me, guns raised.

The bullets leave their weapons in the past and shoot the wall in the future.

Too slow.

I'm in the middle of the pack of guards, relief flooding me that no one had time to move. Don't much fancy landing *inside* a person. Punch the nearest one in the balls, crack his head on my knee and he goes down. Spin around and uppercut the one behind me, nice crack as his jaw snaps shut, my elbow slamming into the nose of the next one, followed up with a fist in her face.

Fucking future jumping! Seconds only, but a second is enough, long as I don't wind up landing in the same space-time as a bullet or a fist. I guess if I do, I won't know it.

One behind me gets a kick in, right on the small of my back. I stagger forward, hit the slip, arrive behind him three seconds later. He's looking around for me. Well, he's found me, right enough – his head's in my hands, my knee rising up to meet it. Slam him onto it a few times, squelchy, and then back in the slip to come up for the last one. She blinks, her gun aimed at where I was. Punch her in the gut, snap her arm back, twisting it just so. The gun falls to the floor, and her head goes into the wall.

Catch my breath. Check my Holo. My timeline's jumpy, a host of warning lights flashing. Shaving time close is risky as sin, increasing the chances of there being two of me in the same spot – but jumping the future is worse. At least in the past, you got a sense of what you might be jumping into. Balance the bad on the bad and hope the whole thing don't come falling down.

Next problem is that the warning will be making its way to the white coats in the lab. I've had it easy so far. Guards up here weren't expecting much on account of security being so tight. But more will come, and they'll be better prepared.

I run down the next few corridors until I arrive at a big, shiny silver door. Footsteps clattering somewhere behind me. Heavier sounding. Guess the Company worked out they need to send some harder nuts. Wonder how Krezzler's getting on; she'd have been faced with the hard nuts from the start.

Type in the code Tossenberger gave me, door slides open, I slide through, slam the red button on the inside as bullets start whizzing through the gap. The door closes, *whoosh*, and there's a tinny

In The Slip

sound as the bullets hit the other side. Spin around, type in another code, the door locks.

Take a breath, look around.

Room's long, like the boardroom down below. There ain't no tables nor waiters nor ice penguins here though. Lines of tanks run down the walls, cool glass cages with bars of shiny chrome nestled in white plastic casings. Bigger than the ones the docs use, heavier, like the difference between a coffin and a tomb. In the middle of the room, the Stasis Bank rears out of the marble floor like some kinda black obelisk folks way back in the slip might have worshipped. Mind you, I reckon it ain't over-stating too much to say the damn thing is probably worshipped just as devoutly presenttimewise as ever such a thing were back in the slip.

The Stasis Bank.

I set myself up at the keyboard and type in the codes Tossenberger gave me, opening a menu. There's a VDR port like the one in the cram school, designed to hook my chip into the machine. Tossenberger's notes don't say anything about that, though. In fact, he's very clear that I'm to use the keyboard to work the machine. OK, then. Old fashioned it is.

I rummage around in the files, looking for the one holding the tempo information. A list of names pops up, tiny font, four columns, a catalogue number under each entry. There sure is a lot of them. I guess I shouldn't be so shook by it – me of all people, right? – but it's unsettling to see the tempos' names all lined up neat like that, I don't mind owning it.

It's a wonder so many people managed to jump the slip, speaking plain. Even knock-off Holos are hard to get hold of, expensive on the black market and about as reliable as a one-legged horse in an ass-kicking contest. I've been running the slip for damn-near my whole life and I sure as hell wouldn't have thought so many tempos were out there, and I sure as silver ain't crediting the other operatives with even a tenth of my productivity. Where did they all come from... where did they all go?

The Incinerator. Right, yeah. Think on that little girl making obscenities at me as she tells me I ain't worth nothing, my throat burning like I'm swallowing hot sand. Push her aside, concentrate on the present.

Find Joe.

I type in the number Tossenberger gave me, expecting to find Joe's entry, but it brings me up Krezzler's. There's no name, no date of birth, just serial numbers and a list of the operations she went on, detanking protocol, that kind of thing. But there is a picture, and it is her. Not Joe. Type in the number again, same result.

My fist hits the Stasis Bank with a satisfying, tinny thump. That fucking suit-wearing sceever played me? Double-crossed me? Led me up here on the promise of getting Joe and Lois back just so's he could-

Could what? I'm locked in here. What could he want with me locked in here? Take a breath, work the factors, find the want.

Factor one: Tossenberger knows a lot more than what he lets on. He's important in the Company. Rich. Good with the tech. Says he designed the chips. Factor two: he's called on me twice I can remember, and he was ready with a helping hand both times. Factor three: Tossenberger's working with Joe, Lois and Krezzler. Factor four: he's risking his shit to get me in here.

Want: he wants them back just as much as I do.

OK. So then, there's something I'm not seeing, something I'm getting wrong. Krezzler comes up where Joe should be. Perhaps Tossenberger made a mistake with the numbers. He was writing awful fast, privacy disappearing. Could be.

I pull up my screen from my Holo, load my ident number, and type it into the search bar.

Lois' records come up. I scan through them. She was a good operative in her time. Lots of catches. Lots of time in the slip – near enough on my record, probably would have eclipsed it if she hadn't gone rogue. So, I get Lois, Joe gets Krezzler. I go back to Krezzler's screen, scanning through the notes.

Fuck me, but she's got a history to her. Hard to tell how long she's been around, her records are patchy at best, but I'll say this: she ain't no spring chicken, not by a mile. Pull up a vid file, watch a dark-haired figure cut her way out a Company safe house. The shot is long, details lost, but it's enough to see her slice through what must be twenty souls, methodical in a way that's worse than

In The Slip

anger. The camera goes dead on the image of the figure wiping her hands on her thighs.

Right. I ain't opening no more vids on her. I dig around Krezzler's files until I find a serial number that resembles those I've been typing in. Try it in the search bar.

My own self comes up on the screen. There are vids on my file, too. I don't open them. Scroll through the text instead, my finger pressing down on the cursor, watching pages of my life go by. Years and years and years of it. More years than I can account for. More slips. More tempos. More tanks. More, more, more, all in front of me, evidenced and catalogued.

A sharp, sudden pain in my head, my skull squeezing small, crushing my brain and sending white flashes of searing electric across my vision. Got the chloros on my tongue before I register the action, my hands moving to my forehead and pressing hard as I can, almost as if I could push the pain back inside me.

I don't know how long I'm standing there, leaning against the Stasis Bank, my head caught between my hands while I wait for the warmth of the chloros to bring me back up. But up I come, sure as silver. I look at the data, my head no longer trying to crumple itself as I do. I've been jumping the slip for... shit, maybe two hundred years.

Not important. Where's Joe?

Check through my data, looking for the next serial number. Find it hidden in some gumph about a tempo I brought in pasttimewise, maybe... yeah... maybe seventy years back? Fuck me. Anyway, I got the number, type it in.

There's Joe.

My Joe.

Like the ones previous, it's mostly numbers and a list of operations. Everything he did while he was an operative. I open a few sub-folders. Service records, detanking questions, shopping habits, housing, lovers, fashion sense, tempo stats, disciplines, languages, commendations, debts. I start reading and then stop. I don't want to know. I don't want to learn it from this screen, from vid files and reports and lines of temporal latitudes and longitudes. I wanna hear it from him, and a lot more besides.

F. D. Lee

I follow the next set of instructions on Tossenberger's list, entering a long line of what might as well be gibberish, but the tech seems to recognise it. One of the giant tanks lights up, blue fluorescent with a greenish tint, like the moon. Tossenberger's instructions warn me of this, and then, below, they say **DON'T TOUCH ANYTHING.** This last bit is underlined six times.

I pull up a chair next to the tank and try to do as I'm told. Which, honestly, I'm reckoning on being easy enough, until the room starts filling with the rainy, ozone scent of time.

Someone's coming.

Loop 18.3

I'm on my feet, my fingers dancing over my Holo, eyes darting left and right, expecting some sceever to jump into the room.

Nothing, no one.

The time is inside the tank.

The God damn *slip* is opening inside the tank.

I peer through the glass. A crackle of atmosphere, the taste of tin, and there's a boy in there, fourteen or fifteen years old. He looks like Joe, I reckon, but not quite, neither. Same Latin heritage, but the face ain't right. Too hard, somehow.

Then the boy's gone, replaced by a man in his late sixties or early seventies, long torso, slender but muscled for such an old sceever, a scar on his chin, paler skin, though not pink like a Europhile. Handsome face, but not too handsome. Sino.

This new guy... it's me.

It's me older and with a scar, but it's me. What the hell is going on? I reach out to the tank, to do what I don't know, but then I remember my orders and sit back down again, my hands stinging with the want to do something.

Older me vanishes. The stench of time fills the room.

A woman comes up next, one I don't recognise, and she's gone almost as quick as she arrives. Three more bodies come and go, all male, various ages, various heritages, but each one getting closer to how I remember Joe being. The changes get smaller, but noticeable if you're looking for them. The set of his shoulders, the curve of his mouth, the bend of his fingers.

I have no idea what the hell is going on, I'll own. But I see enough to give me some ideas:

Clones.

It's got to be clones. The Company's been cloning us, the dirty, slack-jawed, no-good cheating sceevers that they are. What else answer is there? It'd go some way to explaining my pristine, show-nothing know-nothing body, wouldn't it? And the fact all us operatives got such a similar bearing. We're different, sure, but all the same when you get underneath the veneer. Handsome, healthy, of a good height, of an average weight, fit enough and strong enough to work the hard cases but nothing monstrous – leastways, not to look at. No scars, no marks, no creases or folds or moles. Looking real, looking like we might have some culture, some history, something remarkable to hide our absence of marks.

My headache roars back into life. The screamer. *Waaaaah, waaaaah, waaaah*. The tub of chloros reanimates in my hand, and I bite off half a pill, dulling the alarm but not turning it off. Hitting the snooze button.

Another body appears, almost exactly like Joe except there's no expression to his face. Just a mannequin, waiting to be put in the storefront window. The tank fills with black sludge, the goop I know so well. Guess it must have settled on the model I want. The Stasis Bank behind me hums, the giant fan on its flat top whirring into life. Lights flash. I scoot my chair back over to it, watching code run across the screen.

A hand lands on my shoulder.

I spin on instinct, reaching up to grab the wrist of whoever has me, but before I know it my hand's bent up behind my back at an angle that hurts something fierce, my face smooshed into the smooth wall of the Stasis Bank.

"Kong," Krezzler says into my ear, a low note in her voice that is either a warning or an invitation. Might well be both.

"Krezzler," I reply, trying to match her menace. I'm not aided by the fact I'm all but making out with the cool metal of the Stasis Bank, she's got me pressed against it so hard.

"I'm going to let you go," Krezzler says. "Don't make me do something I'll enjoy."

The pressure drops from my arm, though the pain remains in my wrist and bicep. I turn to face her and-

"Holy shit."

I let out a low whistle, unsure exactly whether I'm scared witless or impressed. Working the slip, it's rare you see something new and, well, what I'm seeing right now sure as silver ain't nothing I've seen before.

Krezzler's covered in blood, most of it dried but, and this is evidence of how thickly she's smothered in the stuff, some of it still wet. Head to toe, there's more red on her than I ever seen on a person outside of a... Hell, I ain't never seen someone so completely bathed in the stuff, and that's a fact. There's no way all of it's hers. No chance a person could survive having that much blood on the outside.

Her eyes, dark brown, sparkle from the gore. When she smiles, little flakes of it fall from her cheeks. She reaches towards me and wipes her hand across my chin, leaving cooling, sticky plasma behind.

"You had a smudge," she says, her eyes laughing at me. "Tough fight, baby?"

"Smug-ass sceever. Where's Lois?"

Krezzler walks over to another tank, so I follow. There on the floor is Lois, back resting against the wall of the tank. She's out cold, dressed in some kind of thin, papery jumpsuit, but she doesn't seem badly hurt.

"They took it gentle with her? That don't seem... don't seem like the way the Company does things?"

"Guess I got to her before they had a chance to apply the thumbscrews." Krezzler marches back to the Stasis Bank, reads the screen. "Joe'll be another few minutes. Better hope they don't crack the door before he's ready. We won't get a chance to do this again any time soon."

"How'd you get in here, anyway? Tossenberger said you can't jump into this room."

She smirks, I think. Might be a sneer. Hard to judge the subtleties under the blood. "I jumped Lois and I to the door about twenty minutes ago, before you'd even got up here. We're time travellers, Kong. Keep up. I was going to say hello when you came in, but it was such fun watching your little face as you tried to understand it all."

My fist is up quick, but she's got me twisted over quicker.

"Now, now. Let's not fight. We're family, after all."

"You ain't no family to me," I snap, but I lift my hands in surrender mainly because I suspect she's right, what with seeing my clone in the tank, and also because Krezzler is fucking terrifying right now. Not the blood or the easy way she grappled me; the way she's so still underneath the devastation, the violence, covering her body.

Outside the dome, the storms rage and swell and press up against the outer shell – hell, more than once I've been on the Sky Rail when the wind has thrown the skeleton of some long dead animal against the poly. The storms are normal, violent, and futile.

But when I was younger, every now and again, for whatever reason, the atmosphere outside the dome would flatten. The storms fell and the sand dropped, and suddenly you could see it all. The world, flat and pale and dead, stretching for miles. And it's then it was horrifying, when you could see what we did to ourselves. What we did to our home. What we stole from every living creature, including ourselves.

Krezzler's like that right now: cold and quiet and terrifying.

They don't let us see it anymore – the real world, that is. They make the domes pearlescent when the storms drop. Humanity lives inside the domes, near ten million of us in each one, most with no idea what the world's like on the outside. The domes *are* the world, which sounds depressing, I guess, but then you got to think people've always been making the world smaller than it really is. My country, my city, my street, my backyard... their problem.

"You've done this before?" I ask Krezzler. "Broken into the Company?"

She leans against the Stasis Bank. "Not like this. But something similar happened to me, way back when. Tossenberger woke me up in this room. Seeing it all as it really is. He woke you up here, too. Guess you don't remember. Good for you." She closes her eyes, a deep breath filling her chest. A moment passes, and then she opens her eyes again, staring at Joe's tank. "I did Lois differently, the first time I got a chance. Let her come to it on her own."

It's the second time I've seen Krezzler express an emotion that ain't somewhere on the scale of fury. She seems almost wistful, sad in that way you can get when you wish the world were different.

"Anyway, what's done is done," she says, turning to look at me at last. "How's your head?"

I take the hint. "I... yeah. It hurts. A touch."

"Fuck off. I know what it feels like. It'll get better with time, now you're finally awake again. Now you know the truth."

In The Slip

"The truth... Jesus. I ain't sure I'd have believed it, if I ain't seen it, here, with my own two eyes. I thought they gave up on all this junk when those sheep started getting brain cancer."

Krezzler cocks her head, the dried blood on her forehead flaking as she frowns. "What are you blabbering about?"

"We're clones, right?"

She bursts out laughing, her glee hitting me right in the ego and echoing back off the walls to hit me again.

"Clones? My God. What the hell have you done to that head of yours? I know you ate a bullet, but still..." She laughs again. "Clones. Wow."

I feel myself bristle and try to calm down, not wanting my blood to join the mess covering her.

"What's so funny about that?"

"Lift up your shirt."

"No."

She puts her hands together like she's praying. "Oh, pretty please, handsome Kong who I love so much, let me see your tits. Urgh. Just lift your shirt up."

"Fine."

I lift my shirt, ignoring the heat in my face. Krezzler jabs me in the gut, leaving a spot of sticky, coagulating blood behind her.

"What the-?"

"Belly button," Krezzler says, wiping her hand on her pants – a gesture I take to heart, considering she ain't exactly clean. "If you were a clone, you wouldn't have a belly button."

"Oh." Shit. "So, we're..." What can I say that won't sound dumb? "So, we're robots, then? Is that it?"

"Oh my God," she laughs at me afresh. "No, of course not. A robot would be easier if you ask me, but the Company isn't going to send metal people back in the slip. Can you imagine the trouble a time travelling robot might cause if anyone pasttime were to discover it? No, you're human. We're human."

"Well, what then? What the fuck is going on?"

Krezzler pushes herself off the Stasis Bank and wanders over to Joe's tank. "We're family," she says, pushing buttons on the side of Joe's tank, leaving little red fingerprints behind. "You'd better come here."

I walk over to the spot she points to, at the foot of the tank. It tilts upwards, so it's standing straight.

"Arms out, Kong," Krezzler instructs, pushing more buttons. I ain't got a clue what's going on, but I do as I'm told. The tank lid opens, and Joe stumbles forward, naked and covered in black gloop. I catch him.

Krezzler grins at me, the blood caking on her cheeks. "They used to say to thine own self be true, I think? In a teaser?"

I hold Joe in one arm, wiping the gunk from his face with my free hand. He blinks at me, confused.

"Yeah. Body spray," I reply vaguely, my eyes fixed on Joe's, looking for the flecks of amber. They ain't there though. Not anymore. His eyes are dark brown, so dark it's hard to see exactly where his pupils begin and end. Just like mine.

Joe reaches up, frowning, and touches my face. "Buy?"

"Er... Shop?" I look up at Krezzler, begging her for some kind of insight into what's happening.

"Not 'buy', dummy," she says. "*Bai*. Bai Yu. Not one of their best, I'll grant, but at least it works both ways. That was your name, a long time ago. His head's screwed up, that's all."

The alarm I feel must show on my face because Krezzler softens a touch – which is to say, she don't sound quite so much like she'd rather smash my face in than talk to me.

"When we die, we reset. Our feeds, you get it? When they tank us, they overlay our experiences – the ones they want, anyway. Being awake means you remember what *you* want to remember, not what they give you. That's why getting skulled is such a big deal – nothing left to upload, to bring back. You're the first and only one they've managed to reset, special boy. It's why you've been such a massive pain in the arse to wake up. Why the Company value you so much, too."

I look up at her, my heart beating so fast I think I'm gonna puke. "Will Joe – will Joe go wrong? Will he be like me?"

"Nah. He'll be OK."

"Will he-"

"Sure. He'll remember you. He always does."

Joe leans against me, heavy, unsteady. One hand on my shoulder, the other on my face. Krezzler goes to Lois, still unconscious, and lifts her up. Pats her face, gentle, to wake her.

"This has happened to him before?"

"Not this. We've all been reset a few times. The best way to wake someone up is via a reset in a regular tank. This the hard way."

"What *is* this?"

"Full rebuild. Nasty way to come into the world. The Company tries to avoid it – takes a lot of energy, especially from the Stasis Bank." Lois stirs, blinks. Krezzler watches her intently. "Plus it's harder from them to control what they get, though God knows they try."

"So what's the, uh, the right way, then?"

"We think it's better to let people reset themselves, if they can. Kill them a few times – not skull them, obviously – and let them work it out in the tank. We've been trying the gentle way with you for years after you skulled yourself, but you always were a difficult son of a bitch."

I think about the tanks and the memories that come and go. The flashbacks and the seizures and the screaming headaches. Is she making sense? I guess so, leastways as much as anything makes sense anymore. I look down at Joe. "His eyes are different."

"Tossenberger probably just gave you a version closer to the original source. It's not like he had a lot of time for nuance." She chuckles. "Joe had a scar last time, you remember that? Then you had it, which struck me as disgustingly self-reverential, even for you. But this'll work, it'll be him, don't worry. You can trust Tossenberger." She pauses. "And Joe's tough. He'll make it back."

"Krezzler," I say, trying to sound calm for Joe's benefit, "I wanna know right now what the fuck is going on. I remember Lois, and being with Joe, and shooting myself in the head... But I don't have a fucking clue what you're talking about. All I know, know sure as silver, alltimewise, is that I love Joe, and I forgot him. So you'd better clue me up nice and quick, OK?"

"Fine – but only because I get to see your face when you find out, and the other two would insist on telling you gently." She puts her arms around Lois, helping her stand. "You're the same person."

I have no idea what face I'm making, but I reckon my jaw's hanging open on account of all the cold air suddenly in my mouth. That and the fact Joe reaches up and pokes my tongue with his finger.

"Stuph h'up." I pull the intrusive digit from my mouth, rest Joe's hand on my shoulder. "Ain't no way that's true."

"And yet, it is." Krezzler is clearly enjoying herself. "You and Joe. Me and Lois, too. All of us, in fact. We're all the same person, originally at least. The use the Stasis Bank to run us through various 'molding' scenarios in the slip, and then, with a bit of invit tech and so on, the tanks implant us with the memories they want us to have, overlaying them on our previous lives. Hey presto, operative. There, see? Easy." She chuckles. "Robots and clones. Good Lord."

Lois mutters something I don't catch, but she's waking up quicker than Joe. Krezzler still keeps her supported, holding her gentle enough but not, I'm bound to note, with the same feral intensity I'm holding onto Joe nor he to me.

He to me. Me to him. He's me? We're all each other. Not clones nor robots nor nothing like that...

Oh.

Oh, shit.

"You mean I've spent my entire life fucking *myself*?"

Krezzler grins at me. "You betcha, sunshine. How's that for ego?"

Loop 18.4

Krezzler's got two other Holos which she sets to work attaching to Lois and Joe. Lois is groggy as all hell, but she's pretty much conscious now. Joe is... dreamy. Distant. He's talking in a language from way back in the slip and keeps calling me Bai.

Krezzler concentrates on her work. I'll be damned if she knows what she's doing – I sure as hell don't – but when she's done, their arms are stained red from her hands and the Holos look to be attached.

"Now for the fun part," she says to me.

I'm pretty sure that's irony. "What could be more fun than this?"

She ignores me, putting her arms on Lois' shoulders and talking to her softly. "We're going to have to do some fighting. You handle that?"

Lois blinks, confused. "Why?"

"We're in the Stasis Bank."

"Oh."

"Yup."

Lois pinches the bridge of her nose. "OK. Give me a minute, I'll be fine. What about Joe?"

The two women turn their attention back to us. Joe is leaning heavily on me, babbling away in his dead language, covered in sticky gloop. He don't seem aware of anything, though he has taken a keen interest in the buttons on my coat.

"What's the problem?" I ask, knowing there is one.

"This is a Stasis Bank," Lois says, noticing her paper jumpsuit and tutting. "A time safe. That's why they keep the base files here. Whatever changes in the slip, it doesn't change here. Or not as easily, anyway. It's complicated. The main thing right now is that you can't jump from in here, not in or out. Stasis."

We all three turn to the locked doors.

"I'm betting there's a fair few folk on the other side of them doors who'd like to see us," I say. "And by see, I mean shoot full of holes."

Krezzler grunts an affirmative.

"What about the tanks – the slip opened up in there?" I ask. "Can't we use them somehow?"

"No," Lois answers. "The tanks aren't designed for that. They're not Holos, not doorways. They're more like... more like windows. Light passes through glass but nothing else can, not without causing some serious damage, anyway. It's the door or nothing. Hell."

I've known Lois longest, or leastways I remember knowing her longest. But in all that time, I ain't never seen her look how she does right now. She seems angry, which is fair enough given the circumstance, but that's the thing: she don't seem angry in the right way. There's something off, like she's pissed at the boat for having holes in it rather than at the person who made them.

"Alright," I say, pushing the thought aside. "So let's go through the doors. Krezzler, you got a gun hidden somewhere under that blood, right? Lois, you take Joe and jump him and you out quick. Krezzler, you do some shooting."

Krezzler nods. "Suits me. What'll you be doing?"

Finally, there's something I understand in this whole sideshow.

"What I do best," I say.

The door slides open.

Factor one: there's a brassle of guards in the corridor. Factor two: the narrow space ain't working to their advantage, and they're stacked up. Factor three: the front eight are the main threat.

Krezzler opens fire.

Two guards fire off their weapons, the bullets hitting Krezzler in the head and shoulder.

I hit the slip, jumping three seconds back, into the middle of the cluster of guards. The door starts to open. Two seconds. Smash my elbow in the neck of one guard, shove her sideways into another. One second. Swing round, fist into the face of a third, knee to his chin as he topples forward.

The door slides open.

I see myself standing in the doorway, hand on my Holo. Vomit fills my mouth, swallow it. Yellow spots and thin shapes as for a fraction of a fraction of a second I'm in the same place I am.

In The Slip

Jump 00.021 forward.

I land in the moment I jump back, a feeling of distortion and thinness. Close... Too close. Shave time, Kong, don't cut your own throat.

Krezzler opens fire.

The two guards in front of her shoot wide, their colleagues behind them toppling to the ground. It worked. Lois and Joe jump. Metal hits metal as more bullets land in the doors behind where they were, but Krezzler was already aiming at the firing guards, shouting "Left, le-!"

I jump, landing in time to see the first two guards begin to stumble and Krezzler shouting "-ft, left!"

I grab the head of the guard to my left, pull him backwards, shove him at the rest of them with all my strength, no time for anything fancy, and jump back-

Misjudge it.

I'm there and so is me. Krezzler's gone. The guards are a smear of stretched-out faces, wrapped around us like the walls of a barrel.

The world cracks, taking my skull with it. We both fall to our knees as time seeps from our pores and turns our skin to mush, burning like acid, and I can see it all, past, present and future, everything that went wrong and will always go wrong, but it's too late because now I'm uncertain in a certain world, an impossibility, a tear on the silkscreen of life.

This is it, this is what time is and death within it, but all I can think is how I at least managed to save Joe. I laugh and laugh and laugh, my other self self laughing too, because what else can you do? Time beats harder, pressing me into nothingness, a slice of impossible, thinner and thinner, faster and faster.

The space above me bursts open, stars scattered across the sky like rice after a wedding. The smeared faces of the guards blur and fade into the brush strokes of the night, not black, not neon, not fluorescent white, but blue and purple and grey, a swash of pink and yellow running across the firmament, more beautiful than anything I ever seen. Roots split through the ground, shifting and

F. D. Lee

changing in nanoseconds to saplings and then huge, strong trees, filling the world with the heady scent of nature.

A man's voice, indistinct, and the smell of burning sugar cutting across my sense.

The other me screams, disappears.

Krezzler grabs my hand and pulls me into the slip.

Loop 19.0

Krezzler and me appear in a hotel bedroom. Tossenberger's safe house. It's pretty flash, all told. It's also totally soulless – prints on the walls are blotches of colour and the window is plastered with a plastic scene of a beach at sunset. For some reason, the image of a nighttime sky filled with stars and the smell of trees swamps my mind. Don't know why, as I sure as hell ain't never seen nothing like that. Even Paris pre-Fracture was a reddy-orange bruise.

The image dissipates, leaving me with the memory of the memory. In addition to the fake scenery, there's also a coffee machine which Krezzler fills from the sink in the john and turns on.

"That was some shit-hot jumping, Kong. Really shit-hot." For a moment, she seems about able to tolerate me. "But that last bullet almost got you, so don't get cocky."

She sets about making coffee, so I guess that's all the recognition I'm getting from her. Lois, however, don't say nothing at all. She grabs a chair from the vanity and sits, staring at the wall. It ain't like her to be distant. I should think on that, but I got the strangest unsettlement about me, so I ain't in the right mood to consider her problems just now.

Joe's asleep on one of the twin beds, his big naked body shiny with residue goop. He looks like a conker. I grab the duvet, cover him, noting that it *is* a duvet, not a comforter or eiderdown or throw. Material and stitching give it away; most would just see a blanket.

OK, then. Factors. First things first, where's Krezzler brought us to? Could be Australia, but it's doubtful as we must be decades post-Fracture for the time pressure to be so light, and Australia got hit bad. Alice Springs cooked first, then the rest of the continent, the world following quick behind. Australia was the trendsetter, I guess.

I stand, causing Joe to murmur something mournful. Krezzler looks up from the coffee machine, winks at me. I pretend I don't see it.

Factors. Right.

Flick through the magazines the hotel provided. They're about seventy per-cent teasers and the rest stories about people I assume to be famous. All written in the Finnish-Norwegian hybrid that took up in mainland Europe when it became clear Scandinavia was the safest place to be, and everybody wanted in.

I can speak it so-so but reading it's a different game; the words on the page might as well be alienese for all the sense I can make of them. The language didn't last long. Too severe, too quick a change in a world that had already changed more than anyone ever wished it to. For a lucky few, it was a way to blend in if they got across the borders. For the majority, it came to be symbolic. A middle finger, a quick, reflexive show of anger to the systems and structures that had failed. A 'fuck you Pop, I'll do what I want' type of thing, before they all realised Daddy still owned the roof over their heads.

Krezzler looks around for a spoon. Seeing none, she stirs the coffee with her bloody finger and then hands me a cup and one to Lois. It tastes metallic. I drink it anyway.

The coffee seems to wake Lois up. She sips it slow, her eyes refocusing. "Hey," she says.

"Hey," I reply.

"So, are you going to be trouble?"

"I don't know." I figure that's the truth. "But I guess I'm gonna make an effort not to be." Figure that's the truth as well.

Lois and Krezzler share a look. Krezzler shrugs her eyebrows, tilts her head: *he helped me get you and Joe.*

Lois looks down then up again. Not as happy about things as I'd hoped for.

"Sit down again, will you?" she says. "You're making me nervous."

The bed dips beneath me, Joe fidgets, sighs. Dreaming, maybe. Tank dreams – is he remembering me? Keeping me in the light? Could be I'm disappearing right now...

"So, you're me?" I ask Lois.

"No, you're me. How awake are you?"

Joe stirs, digs his heel into my flank. It'd be nice to think he meant it to reassure me, but even I ain't that dumb. And yet, an ache in my shoulders I wasn't aware of eases. My hand cups his foot, thumb brushing against the bone in his ankle. The gloop is thick and cold like hair gel, but underneath he's warm.

Shit. That's pretty weird, ain't it? I ain't taken my gaze from Lois or Krezzler, so I see it when they both glance at my hand, Lois looking annoyed, Krezzler wearing that smirk she likes so much.

"Awake enough to know I probably need my head shrunk," I answer, aiming to make light of it.

Krezzler snorts. "Yeah. It's pretty gross."

"Says the woman covered in blood," I reply, but there ain't no sting in it. She offers me a lazy salute in acknowledgement, and I smile in return.

"Not gross... just... complicated," Lois says, apparently not seeing the funny side.

"So, either one of you gonna explain this properly?"

"What was wrong with my explanation?" Krezzler asks.

"Nothing except it made as much sense as a bag full of frogs in a laundromat."

Krezzler laughs at that. "Sure. How's that foot massage going?"

"Jesus, guys, cool it," Lois snaps, glaring at us both. Definitely not seeing the funny side. "Right, Kong, let me try to explain, OK?"

Krezzler mutters something that might have been *'good luck'*. Joe flexes his foot under my hand and sighs; my fingers drift from the bone of his ankle to the arch of his foot, softer and, somehow, more intimate.

Lois crosses her legs, her paper jumpsuit rustling, refocusing me. "When the TTCP send you back, your job is to fix aberrant timelines, correct?"

"Sure, bring it all in line so the One True happens right."

"Good, OK. But when they do that, they stop all other possibilities from happening. When we make a choice, it should offer potential. A thousand, million, billion choices being made all the time, shaping the world. Shaping people."

I nod. "Yeah, that's the tempo line, right? That there might be timeline where the Fracture didn't happen, or one where we develop better technology to deal with its aftermath, but we just need to make it happen, make it real. It's nonsense."

I expect her to tell me I'm wrong. Instead, she says, "Yes, largely it is. Besides, who knows if there is anything better? Maybe this really is the best timeline."

"So why bother?"

"Because the TTCP are stopping things from changing *at all*," Krezzler says. "They keep the present in a chokehold, stopping anyone from challenging them. The past is dead, but the future shouldn't be. So, if we could get pre-Fracture, we might be able to do something that would stop the Company before they even begin to begin."

I pause a moment. Never been one for the tempos line, but there's some sense to what Krezzler said. That girl I brought in, she wasn't going far back. She just wanted to get her brother's name off the paperwork. And her brother, he didn't want nothing to do with the past. He was trying to improve the present, the One True. Make better air filters, give them away free. Water, too.

"Yeah, OK. Maybe. But what does any of this have to do with us being the same person?"

"We're from aberrant timelines, the ones the Company erase," Lois says, taking the lead again. "Somewhere in the past, we were the same person. There's a single point, way back when, that we share. None of us know when or where, not even Tyrone."

"Come again?"

"Karen? Little help?" Lois looks over at Krezzler, who's turned her attention to one of the magazines.

"You wanted to explain it to him," Krezzler says, not bothering to look up.

Lois turns back to me. "They use the Stasis Bank to do it. There's an original person, somewhere in the slip. The Company lets time play out for them.. us… lets them have a certain life, then pulls them out and erases that timeline. Then they do it again, and again, and again, adjusting things to make sure they get what they need. Then the tanks and the invit blend it all together and… well, that makes us. The same person, but also different. Think of it like having the same great-great-great-great-great-great-grandmother."

A long breath hisses through my teeth. Not sure exactly if I'm more relieved or more confused, but either way it's good to know we ain't *exactly* all the same person. "So that's why my Holo acted weird all those times?"

"Yes. They struggle to differentiate."

"OK. But why'd the Company do it like that? Why not just train people to use the slip, like they say they do?"

"There's something in our genes. Tyrone says they tried different things, back at the beginning. Embryos. Clones. None of it worked. We got sick, or the slip crushed us, or we were just... wrong. Now they let it play out in the slip, giving us a variety of lives, selecting what they need, adding their little bits of data as they go."

"The Company said my Pop died. They took me in when I was a kid."

"Of course they did," Krezzler says, glancing up from her magazine. "They wouldn't want you to know the truth."

"What? I wasn't ever a kid, is that it? That they ran me through God knows how many aberrant pasts and then mixed it all together in a tank?"

Krezzler says nothing, but her expression has a definite *I-said-you-wouldn't-like-it* vibe. She's right. I wish I'd stuck with her explanation.

"Yes and no," Lois answers. "You aged in an aberrant timeline and in the tank, all at the same time. They pull you out for a second or two, overwrite anything they don't like, put you back again. Rinse and repeat until you're ready to join the team."

"So each time they tank us, that's what's happening?"

Krezzler finally closes her magazine. "No, dumbass. Using the Stasis Bank takes a massive amount of energy, which is costly. Plus, even with the Stasis Bank, it's more an art than a science. Tossenberger says they've got a nifty program that runs it, but even so, things go wrong."

Ice down my spine. My grip tightens on Joe's foot. "Joe. What if-"

"He'll be fine. If his brain had turned to jelly we'd know by now. It's why skulling is such a big deal – can't repair a splattered brain, have to start from the beginning."

"Is that why you've been skulling operatives?"

The magazine crumples in her hand. Krezzler stands, every muscle in her body a threat. "I've told you already, I kill people to wake them up. Skulling them doesn't serve the mission."

"Well, somebody's been doing it," I say, ignoring the lump forming in my throat at the sight of a woman covered head-to-toe in blood squaring off at me. "So what about the regular tanks, then? You said we wake up in the regular tanks, right, during recovery-"

"Reset."

"Sure, fine. My point is, why haven't more operatives woken up? It seems to me it's just us four – unless you got a army of folk I ain't been introduced to yet?"

"The recent versions have a few more failsafes in them. We've tried, but they never wake up," Krezzler answers, disgust in her voice. "Makes them worse in the slip, but if the Company can get pre-Fracture then all bets are off, anyway."

"Well. Shit." I look down at Joe. The person I've lost and found more times than I can remember. The person the Company have stolen from me, time and time again. And the girl, trying to save her brother. Her brother trying to save the world. The domes, and the teasers, and the endless, pointless choices. Catherina snorting her drugs, terrified of the outside world. All because the Company want to keep things just as they are. Keep them and their friends at the top. "We've got to stop them, then. Right?"

"Wow, thank God you're here to explain that to us," Krezzler says. "We need a plan. The Company will be all over our shit."

"Tyrone'll keep them busy for a while," Lois replies, picking at the sleeve of her paper jumpsuit, her brows tight and lips thin.

Krezzler shakes her head. "We can't wait any longer. We've got to find Longsworth."

Lois looks up, alarmed. "No. We're not ready."

"We never were," Krezzler replies. "It's now or never – literally. Tossenberger can get us what we need."

Lois' eyes dart in their sockets as she thinks. Krezzler waits for her to speak, so I do the same.

"OK," Lois finally says. "We'll go for it. I need a shower and a change of clothes. You fill Kong in on whatever's left he doesn't already know."

She exits the bedroom; a moment later, the sound of water hitting tile drifts through the thin door from the bathroom.

Krezzler perches herself against the dresser. "What do you know about Barry Longsworth?"

Briefly I consider keeping what I know to myself, and the irony of that makes me smile. Besides, it'll be nice to show I actually know *something*.

"I came across some Company records a while back, saw a photo of some folk with his name in the mix. He was part of the original Antarctic mining expeditions, I reckon. Back before Clear2o were Clear2o. Must have been either a scientist or a board member, on account of his proximity to the actual dig."

Krezzler tilts her head. "Well done. But we don't think it was Clear2o he was working for, we think it was the TTCP. Or at least, what will become the TTCP. All the major Industries in the One True were originally subsidies of one concern, back in the day."

"Makes sense. But what makes you think this Barry Longsworth was TTCP?"

"He turns up all over the records – he's there for the mining, like you say, but he's also recorded in meetings for companies with interests in, lemmesee..." She pulls up a screen and starts reading. "Pomegranate juice, pistachio nuts, breast milk replacements, anti-depressants, bottled water – that'd be the proto Clear2o, we're assuming – hamburger restaurants, cane sugar and palm oil, vitamin supplements, chocolate bars. You get the picture. Barry's been a busy boy. We know what he's been doing but not who he is."

I burst out laughing, and it takes me a minute to calm down. Krezzler stares at me, annoyance and curiosity fighting it out on her face. It'd be fun to keep her in the dark a bit longer, but her gun is next to her and I ain't keen on getting shot again. Still, I press my luck a little bit.

"You mean you ain't worked it out? You've been awake how long, chasing this sceever, and you still don't know?"

"Just spit it out, Kong."

I smile my sweetest smile. "We gotta catch ourselves a tempo."

Krezzler makes a low whistle, shakes her head. "Can't be. We've got records of him pre-Fracture."

"So?"

"So no one can travel that far back."

"We did. Sure, it hurt some, but we made it."

"Ten years. And Joe and Lois were a mess. I couldn't shoot straight. That's hardly a resounding success."

"I made it. Besides, if the TTCP have super chloros in our future, that means it'll be no problem for them to send someone back, doesn't it? *We're time travellers, Karen.* Anyway, ain't that what you need me for? I'm your operative, sure as silver."

Krezzler opens her mouth, closes it, then pinches her lips up tight as any asshole I ever seen. I wait for her to come up with some smart remark, but instead she says, "Let's see what Lois says."

And that's it. Krezzler switches me off, starts flipping through her magazine again, face unreadable. I watch Joe breathing. Five minutes pass, in which I don't think I think about anything except the feel of Joe's foot under my hand. I let my touch drift to the top of his ankle, my fingers working away the gloop matted in his hair. I got thoughts, sure as silver. A million of them, I reckon. But they're buzzing at the back of my head, wasps drunk on sugar, too distracted by their own madness to bother me.

Lois returns. She's dressed in some clothes I'm guessing Krezzler had ready for her, her wet hair dark, slick against her skull. The shower's ironed out some of her creases, leaving her less jittery and more certain than she was ten minutes ago. It occurs to me that she must remember what the TTCP did to her in interrogation, and I reckon I understand the look on her face, the familiarness of it: anger, deep-banked and burning cold. Krezzler fills her in on our conversation.

Lois pales, her eyes wide. "I think we need another plan, we need to, ahh, reconsider." She looks at me, anxious. "Kong, you do know how far back you have to go? One hundred years before the Fracture. You haven't had enough training, enough exposure."

"How much training does a person need to get turned into paste? If I ain't up to it, I ain't up to it," I say, ignoring the way my stomach flips and my balls feel like they're crawling up inside me. One hundred years is a damn sight further than I'd been imagining. "Leastways, if anyone's gonna-"

Just as I'm about to say something smart and heroic-like, Joe sits up.

Loop 19.1

My hand is still on his ankle... he looks down at the shape of it under the blanket, then up at me, face knit in confusion. Fuck. A second too long to realise I shouldn't be touching him, and when I pull my hand away all I can feel is the sticky lumps of gloop I pulled from his leg hair.

Lois kneels next to the bed; Joe turns his attention to her.

"Do you know who I am?"

"I... yes. Lois."

"How old are you?"

"Thirty-four." He pinches the bridge of his nose. "No. Older. Right, yes. Much older." A pause. Then he grins at Lois. "Not as old as you."

She grins back, the tension leaving her face for the first time since we de-tanked her. "Smart ass. Do you remember how you first died?"

"You shot me, punctured a lung. I woke up in the tank. Took me about, uhhh, three more resets after that? So I guess I've died five times, now?"

Lois nods. "The last one was pretty bad. What do you remember about it?"

Joe closes his eyes, a line appearing between his brows. "We were in the desert, me and Bai... no, running... no. No. We were in Paris, pre-Fracture, testing the chloros. We were jumped by an operative, I got shot."

His eyes snap open, fixing me dead centre. "You. You attacked us."

I can feel Krezzler and Lois looking at me, but I keep my gaze on Joe. All the intrigue and scheming about the slip and the Company dissolves like sugar in water. I ain't got a clue what to say to him, but I ache to say something. I got that feeling again, the sense we know each other, that we always have. That he's constant, in my bones, and always has been.

I hope he feels it, too.

"I didn't know," I say.

Alltimewise, things ain't never changed. People are people, slack-jawed sceevers ready to be herded through their lives by the likes of Clear2o and FRESHAIR and NesPep and politicians and kings and queens and Gods. It comes to being the same, when you seen it cycle round enough times. That's why the operatives get so mean. Leastways, that's what I've always thought.

"I thought you were the bad guys," I say.

We're all commodities. Bought and sold to those folks high up, living in the clouds. I'm getting the joke now, about my name. Not this 'Bai' nonsense; Kong, King. The best there is in the slip; the one and only, a freak of nature and science. A great big, stupid creature that the Company throw onto the stage to make them money. A dancing monkey.

"I remember you better, now," I say.

In the films, King Kong always dies. Then they just pick him right up again from where they left him, repackage him, and send him back out to the multiplexes. Does King Kong remember being black n' white, 3D, fighting other monsters, 4D, being in the chips, in the heads of people, selling them a story about subjugation and all the while feeding in the teasers for popcorn and toffee bars and soda?

If King Kong ever did remember all the times they captured and sold him, had him dancing on the stage only to be shot down... Every time he met his woman, only to have her snatched from him... If he could remember it all and do something about it...

Well, what tune would that monkey dance to, then?

I turn to Lois and Krezzler; like to think I fix them with a steely gaze.

"Speak to Tossenberger. Get me the chloros."

The two women share a look and then, as if by psychic consent, both stand at once.

"We'll be back," Krezzler says. "Don't fuck anything while we're gone, yeah?"

I decide I'm going to interpret that to mean 'don't mess anything up'. Krezzler takes five minutes to wash the blood off her and get changed, and then she and Lois leave the hotel room to arrange whatever it is they need to arrange to get me my chloros.

Joe stares at me a moment, then wraps the duvet around him and heads into the bathroom.

I mean, I guess that makes sense. He's naked as the day he was... day he was... well, whatever the hell he *was*, and he's covered in gloop. Course he'd want to get washed and dressed. Even Krezzler decided to get herself presentable, eventually. I pick at the bedsheets, pulling free clumps of gloop and rubbing it between my fingers until it forms little worms like dead skin, soft and grey and disgusting. I can't say I blame him for wanting to get the stuff washed off. Obviously, that would be most people's first priority.

The air is too hot. Try to open the windows, but they're sealed tight. There's a thermostat on the wall but it's broken, says the temperature's an even 22° which it obviously ain't as my hands are sticky, my neck feels like fire and there's a queasy sickness in my gut. Wish there was a tap in the main room, I could run some water over my wrists or something.

He's been in the bathroom a long while – oh, wait, no. Just under five minutes. How long does it take to wash? I guess ten minutes? Maybe longer, since the gloop can be hard to shift. At the Company, they have these industrial showers to hose us off, but it's unlikely this place has anything more than a pitter-patter. Fifteen minutes, then? Shit, all my life I've been focused on time and now, when I need to know the duration of something, my mind's gone blank.

Maybe I need to think about cleaning myself up a bit? Catch my reflection in the mirror, and there's a dark red thumbprint on my face and a smear on my shirt, both courtesy of Krezzler, along with some general blood splatter that I guess I caused myself. Open the kettle, dab some water on my face and then, fuck knows why, use a little to slick my hair back. Perhaps I can do something about the stain on my shirt...?

The bathroom door opens at the exact moment I'm trying to manoeuvre my shirt into the kettle while still wearing it. I'm cock-about-face and kettle-about-cock and the burning in my neck races up to my cheeks and sits there.

"...OK." Joe leans on the door frame. "Not what I was expecting."

In The Slip

He's washed and dressed in a blue button-up and dark brown pants, his sleeves rolled up, showing off his Holo and, I can't help but notice, his tank-perfect skin. He's thinner now; fitter, too. The tank must have 'corrected' him. Don't know why I didn't notice that before. Don't like it as much as the soft version of him I remember from Paris and... and from before. Before I let him die. Before I left him in the dark.

I need to say something, and it needs to be good.

"I had blood on me."

Kong, you slack-jaw. Make it better.

"Wasn't mine."

Oh, for fuck's sake.

Joe's shrugs his eyebrows. "It rarely is. So... you remember me?"

"Yeah."

Silence follows. Why can't he just do like he did before and lead the conversation – I'm better at replying, I reckon. It'd be better if he just came over and kissed me. He should grab me and pull me close and tight and tell me it's OK. Tell me I'm OK. We're OK.

He walks over to the other bed, sits on the edge.

"What do you remember?"

I tell him, giving as much detail as I have. Explain about the blackness, about holding onto him. About Tossenberger and fighting my way through to the Stasis Bank and Krezzler explaining to me that we're all the same person. But I don't tell him I'm sorry, and I don't know why.

After a moment, he lets loose a sigh heavier than anything I ever heard. "Do you remember *you*?"

Something pinches, deep inside me. "Bits. I guess. I remember skulling myself. I remember sitting on the sand at night, with you. And a... yeah... a forest, when I was small."

"Yeah. I remember that one, too. Camping, right? The stars and the smell of the trees, the earth. It's not your memory, not really. You know that, don't you? We all have it, Lois, Krezzler. Me, you."

I shrug. I got words flying around my head, but none of them seem to want to line up into sentences. Keep my own counsel.

"The way I see it is, somewhere, way back, is this person," Joes says. "This kid who went camping with their mama and papa in the forest. I think that's the original, the one the Company uses to make us."

"Oh. I always thought, maybe... I like forests, you see. And wood, and plants. The smell. So.. uh, how did you 'wake up'?"

A smile darts across his features. "Wow. Straight to it, huh? Well, I always kind of felt... lost, you know? Before I woke up. Looking at the slip and seeing the same thing happening again and again, knowing I had no power to change anything, that nothing I did would ever affect anything or anyone.

"Then I got injured on a job, and I started having these strange dreams. Feeling like everything I did was contradicting something cosmic. Something huge and dynamic and important. That the world was just so *wrong*, and it didn't need to be. It wasn't long after that I woke up. And you and Lois and Karen were there. And you all felt it too, that need to make things possible again."

He pauses, fiddles with his fingers. Am I supposed to say something? I don't think so... he's not looking at me. If I had to speak, he'd look at me, wouldn't he? Maybe I should-

"You felt it the most," Joe says suddenly, quick like the words are hot and he wants them off his tongue... like they might hurt him if he keeps them. "You were so angry, but you weren't hateful, not then. I kept waiting for you to come back. I thought you had, that time before last, when we had you in the other safe house. That you weren't the same man Lois reported spending time with, the liar and the pessimist. The thug. You were almost mine again, almost, and I thought... But then, in Paris, you killed Lois. Smashed her head into a wall, and you didn't even look twice at her. Just another body in the slip, dead already so what difference does it make?"

"I didn't know-"

"And then you let them kill me, and the last thing I saw was you checking yourself for bullet holes."

And there it is. The thing I need to apologise for and the thing I can't find the words to speak to. There's a pounding in my ears suddenly, my skin crawling, hands twitching. A deep, solid anger builds in my gut, making my mouth taste like metal and my heart beat too fast.

"Yeah, well, that ain't right at all." My voice is low and hard, spiteful, but I can't seem to change it. "The last thing I remember is reaching out to you as you bled out on the floor. And before that is you three kidnapping me. You playing nurse and me falling for it, until you saw what I really am, anyways. And before that? You trying to seduce me in a bar, flirting with me and pretending like I mean something to you. That's what I remember."

Regret hits me instantly, a throat punch that makes me feel like I need to gasp for air or else suffocate. I didn't mean to say those things, I know I didn't, but I did and now I've said them. They exist in the space between us, sure as the dust and air. And yet I can't bring myself to retract them – it's true what I said. I ain't the only person who's done wrong, and I don't see why all the blame should be pinned on me. Just... I should have said it better, maybe.

"It was Lois' idea for me to meet you in that bar, not mine," Joe snaps. "I told her it wouldn't help. I said you needed to come to it on your own, but she kept insisting and I was desperate so I agreed, just as I agreed to be the one to help you when you were freaking out after Krezzler brought you in. And I didn't plan to kiss you, either times. I didn't mean for things to get that far, not that quickly. It was a mistake, and I'm sorry. But you *killed* us."

"And how many times have you killed me? You and Krezzler and Lois?"

He stands, eyes narrow, muscles jumping in his jaw. "Because we wanted you to wake up. Because you kept almost remembering us, then pushing us – me – away. When Krezzler killed you, she wanted you back." He draws a long breath, like he's drowning. "When you let us die, you wanted us dead."

"But I don't anymore! How was I supposed to know about any of this? And then when I did it was too late and you were dead and there were operatives everywhere and I couldn't think straight! It all went wrong and I don't know why or when or how, but alltimewise it's been wrong and I hate it all, and I hate myself most of all on account on letting it be so!"

The words leave in a torrent, and by the end of it I'm empty in a way I can't account for, the weight in my gut disappearing like smoke, the metallic taste in my mouth a dream fading in daylight.

There's nothing left inside me except a deep well of regret and loneliness. I wipe my face and my hand comes away wet.

I wait, every single atom of my body vibrating like crickets on a kettledrum.

Joe takes another long, shuddering breath.

"The thing is, Kong, when we reset, when we wake up, we're not new and we're not old. We're both, neither. I don't know. I'm not the same as I was before I saw you kill us. And you're not the same person you were before you put a bullet in your head or before all those times Krezzler killed you. Shit – you know, she kept trying to warn me and I wouldn't listen? I don't know who you are, or who I am." A smile ghosts across his lips, sad and sweet. "How much of a person is what they remember and how much of it is what happens to them that they can't remember? That they choose not to remember?"

"I remember that I love you."

That's it. The words are out there, dry and raw and vulnerable.

Joe shakes his head. "I don't think that's enough. You need to learn to love... everything. Everyone. Including yourself. Like you used to."

I want to tell him he's wrong. I want to reach out and take him in my arms, kiss him and show him he's wrong. I want to rewind the slip and start the conversation again, answer him better, make him say something different. Erase that look on his face. I want to be wrapped up in him and safe, to breathe in his skin and hair. I want to show him all the absences on my body, all the things that ain't there that should be. I want to feed him up, make him soft. I want to change him back, change myself back, even though I can only just about remember what 'back' even means.

But I can't do any of those things, so I do nothing.

Joe presses his mouth into a thin line, his hands hanging at his sides like dead weights.

The door bangs, making us both jump. Krezzler stomps in, sits down on one of the chairs and starts talking like she ain't never been away. Like the whole world ain't ended in this room while she was gone.

"So, Lois is sorting out the chloros with Tossenberger. I've got a slip point for you to meet him in the One True."

In The Slip

I drag myself out of the hole Joe pushed me into. "What about this Longsworth sceever?"

Krezzler reaches into her pocket, pulls out some paper with a location and a year.

"That's vague," I say.

"It's an address. What more do you need?"

I shrug, look across at Joe.

"Alltimewise, I'll take as much as I can get."

*

I arrive bang on when and where I'm meant to be, which is a small private office in the lower levels of Mall 22, one with privacy paid for up front. Tossenberger is due to meet me here, hand over the mega chloros, and then I'll jump into the slip.

A hundred years pre-Fracture. Joe might think there's nothing to me worth having, and it might be he's right, but he can't say I ain't the sort of person who'll take a risk. That's gotta be worth something. Gotta be. And once I've done the big hero schtick, shown myself to be more than another sceever, he'll come around.

It's all going to work out, I know it – the slip is what I've got, what I'm good at, who I am. In the slip, nothing can stop me.

Only there's one more problem I gotta deal with first.

Tossenberger is dead.

F. D. Lee

Loop 19.2

Well, shit on a stick and spin it sideways.

There ain't no way I'm mistaken, people needing their heads and all. The room is full of the smell of blood, which, now I think on it, ain't all that different from the tang of the slip. What with him being skulled and the privacy shrouding the room, there ain't no way to check his feed or recover what might have happened before he entered the room. Whoever did this sure did take a belt and braces approach to their killing. Kinda impressive, in its way.

I crouch next to the body, turn his head towards me. Bits of brain *shlurp* onto the floor, the exit hole big and ugly. The killer got up close and personal: a bullet don't do that much damage at a distance, but the muzzle of even a small gun pressed direct to the skull can make the kind of mess that would stop a fella eating jello pudding for a long while. Especially raspberry flavour.

So, what happened? Obviously Tossenberger got shafted, but whoever done it was someone he knew. An inside job. My thoughts hover a moment on Krezzler, but I push them aside. I'm still unconvinced by her denials of skulling those other operatives, but I don't believe she'd have done Tossenberger. There ain't no want Krezzler has that skulling him would service.

I could try jumping back prior to his death, but with the privacy and the fact that, outside of this room, I'm top of the Company's hit list... well, that's a lot of variables to contend with. Given that, seems to me Tossenberger is dead-dead, leastways for as long as the One True remains. Maybe even afterwards. Who the hell knows what'll change once we've got Barry Longsworth and can start making sense of it all? Hell, maybe nothing will change. Maybe what Lois said is true, and it's the best of a pile of bad options. Maybe the One True is where humanity is just meant to be. Maybe we deserve it.

I sit on the floor next to the body, pick up his hand and check his chip anyway. The connection between the brain and the chip is an intricate one, and the electric storm that went off in the microseconds before his grey matter hit the wall has rendered most of the information that weren't already private useless. Nothing there to be salvaged. I didn't expect there to be, but the disappointment still packs a punch.

OK. What else have I got? Not a whole heap. The TTCP will be after my blood – hell, they might even've done Tossenberger, though I reckon if so, they'd have hung around. Either way, it makes it hard for me. Right now, I'm safely nestled in Tossenberger's privacy. The minute I step outside the door, the feeds will pick me up.

Oh... *damn, damn, damn.* How much privacy is left? Clearly, there's some – the fact I ain't surrounded by operatives speaks to that. But with Tossenberger's chip wasted, I can't tell what I got remaining.

Limited privacy, limited time, no hot-shot mega-chloros.

God damn it. OK. First rule of any job, report what you got, let them know where you are. I send a brief wave back to Lois, Krezzler and Joe, explaining that Tossenberger ain't with us no more. It's not the kind of news I wanted to send back to them, no sir. I wanted to do something right, not bring even more trouble to their door. To Joe's door.

...but...

I've still got Krezzler's pre-Fracture jump coordinates. A city way back in the slip, just waiting for me to visit it... An end to things never ending... A chance to change what can't be changed...

I need the mega chloros. Need to finish the mission.

Check Tossenberger's suit carefully, running my hands gentle across all the folds and lining, looking for the places where a crafty tailor might hide a pocket, but there's nothing. I strip the body, checking the other place a desperate person might hide a small tub of pills, just to be sure. Nothing. Either whoever murdered him took them, or he never had them with him to begin with.

So, who would want the mega chloros? The TTCP got their own supply, though I guess it stands to reason they'd kill him for smuggling and take their wares back with them afterwards.

The only other folk I can think of who would want the pills are the tempos, but those sceevers ain't organised enough for anything like this. I always thought their habit of working the slip solo was born out of greed and selfishness, but I'm guessing now it's because the Company keep burning them up. Dangerous game to be in, then. Better to work alone, can't rat out your buddies and get them incinerated, too.

Flash of the girl I brought in. Push it away, no good wasting privacy on the memory of her face as she begged me to let her go.

"Tempos, tempos, tempos..."

Still, they gotta have a way to get hold of some chloros, right? I've brought in tempos with the real deal, after all. Usually the rich ones, the tempos who got enough but just want more. So, where do they get their branded chloros from...?

Something tickles at me. Not the girl, something else. Some*one* else: I reckon I know of at least one tempo who likely avoided the burners, one who'll know where to get the good stuff on the black market. Hell yes, I reckon I do.

I can feel it now, the beginning of an answer. The start of something. My skin tingles, my breathing slows. It's not a solution, not yet, but it's not the failure I was sitting in two minutes ago, neither.

Now I just gotta get out of this room and across town, take a ride up to the clouds and go visit a patent family without the TTCP finding out I'm back in the One True.

I check my account, somewhat pointless as I know already they'll have drained me of my money and right enough, the display reads 00.00$¥. Not that it makes much difference; even if they hadn't taken my citizenship, I wouldn't have had enough for the privacy I need. But I'm thinking now, working the factors, and just as there's some rich sceever who might help with the chloros, I reckon there's another patent owner who can deal with my privacy issue.

I pull up a screen, dial Catherina.

The little disc spins, waiting, waiting, waiting...

She don't ever answer her screen. People trying to get her, she says. People trying to get all of us, she says. Happens she might be right.

Waiting, waiting, waiting...

She should see it's me connecting. My details will come up, sent from this bubble of privacy to her permanent shell of the stuff. C'mon, Catherina, take a chance on me.

Waiting, waiting, waiting...

A little red light flashes in the corner of my screen. Emergency news beam on the broadwave, overriding everything else. An all eyes alert for me, Krezzler, Lois and Joe. I don't know how much privacy is left; if it runs out, it won't be long until there's a boot to the door and I'm forced to jump. C'mon Catherina.

Waiting, waiting, waiting...

Catherina's face appears.

"Kong, they've got you all over the waves. What-?"

"I need you to cover me, Catherina, right now."

She looks blank for a moment, then her eyes widen. She waves her hands in front of the screen, access menus I can't see, and then my Holo pips up. Five hours of privacy, all for me. Guess five hours is the most she feels she can explain away, should anyone come knocking – and for once, I can't fault her anxiety. To be honest, I was expecting less, and I'm giddy grateful for what I get.

"Kong, what the hell is going on?"

"Thanks, Catherina. I owe you whatever is good value for saving my life."

Her eyes dart up and to the right, looking at a smaller window on her screen. "They're saying you're a tempo."

I shrug, causing her image to wobble up and down. "I guess I always have been. Just didn't it know it 'til now. You, uh... you OK with that?"

A smile splits her face, drawing delicate lines across her skin. I reckon there was a time in her life when she smiled a lot.

"Are you going to break it all?"

"Yes, ma'am, that's my aim."

"Good."

She cuts the connection.

F. D. Lee

Loop 19.3

Now, Catherina ain't never been the cheeriest of souls, but at least she's real. Ain't nothing about her made to be easy, to be quick and clean and desirable. Being in Catherina's company, for all her anxiety, you feel like you're OK just as you are, on account of the fact she don't make you feel needful of anything else.

Unlike where I am now.

I'm high up in the clouds, well above the city. Hell, I'm so far up it almost feels like I could run my fingers across the inner shell of the dome. All around me are elegant white buildings, more glass than fabrotec, and a hell of a lot more grass than I'm used to seeing in the One True – they even got a few trees up here, tall spindly things with pale yellow leaves. Guess there's one thing the teasers don't lie about: money can get you *anything*.

This is the Quiet Zone, floating in the cleanest air, where the money lives. I'm trying very hard to look like I fit in and failing miserably. For the first time in however long my life has been, I wish I'd bothered with the fashions. I am definitely not 'in', which means I'm out.

It's not the being here that's got me nervous. It's who I'm visiting and what their lawyers might do if it ever came provable I was here that's got my palms itchy. But I'm here now, standing outside the right mansion. All I need is a second, right? A second less than a second.

I take a breath and press the comms set in the wall. A voice crackles from the speaker, neither friendly nor hostile.

"Hello? Can I help you?"

"Hi there, sir. Yes. I'm here to see Mr, uh, Forster. Wyatt Forster."

"Mr Forster isn't taking visitors-"

"I'm here about his case. I work for the TTCP." This is a gamble, but I'm betting on the fact that these folks won't want someone discussing their baby boy's tempo terrorism out on the street. "I've got some information that might help."

A pause.

"Let me scan your chip."

Here goes nothing.

"Sure." I step up to the comms and put my wrist to the reader.

"You're private?"

"I figured your employer would prefer it like that. TTCP set me up with it. I can go public if you'd like...?"

Silence.

Come on, come on, come on. Judge the factors. What'll happen to you if you cause a public stir for your big important family?

"Wait there."

Ten minutes pass, and then another. Everything relies on the chips; shopping, finances, medical, and identification – when you can change your appearance with the fashion, ain't much point in photo ID. Guess that's useful when the TTCP have a warrant out for you, but not so useful when you're private and trying to convince some rich sceever to let you into their gated mansion.

Thinking on it, I suppose that means if you got the money for privacy and aesthetics, you ain't got much to worry about. A fine just means it's free for the rich, that's what they used to say, ain't it?

I'm itching to ask what's taking so long, but I figure I gotta appear casual, bored even. Let them think they're wasting their time, not mine. I'm an operative, after all: time ain't exactly an issue for me, or so they need to think.

The voice returns. "Follow the path. Mr Forster will be waiting for you."

The gates swing open, and a line of yellow arrows appears on the ground beneath me, leading up the drive and into the estate.

The kid's looking better than the last time I saw him, when he was trying to change the diox patent. He's sitting out by a large swimming pool, wearing some kind of house suit with a logo on it of a black cat, animated so it prowls across his torso. Expensive. Obviously, he's trying to put on the front of a good citizen.

"What do you want?" he says, still whiney like when I booked him. God, that feels like a lifetime ago.

"I need to know how you got into the slip. Who your jumper is." Not much point in being coy about it. I ain't got a lot of time left.

He laughs at that, and I guess I can't blame him.

"Why the hell should I help you?"

I pull up a seat at his table. He flinches, but recovers himself.

"I can put in a word for you, say you came in easy," I lie. "Maybe get some time knocked off your sentence."

"Brother, I'm not going to serve time. How do you think all this works? How dumb are you?"

My hands dig into my knees, and I see him notice. He shuffles his seat, increasing the distance between us. Twitchy boy. "I caught you red-handed in the slip," I say. "That's fifty years minimum. Officially."

I wondered if the kid knew what really happens to tempos, that's he's likely to fry, and if the knowing might add weight to my empty threat. But judging from his reaction, it seems even his money can't buy that kind of intel.

"God almighty. I'd heard the TTCP employs stupid, but this is insane. My family owns... you know what, it doesn't matter. Firstly, I've seen you on the wave. Even if that were true, the TTCP seem more interested in you than me right now. Secondly, people like me don't go to prison. We don't get punished. We keep on doing whatever the hell we like – isn't that the problem? You're lucky I didn't charge you for beating me up back then."

"Listen here, kid, I didn't hardly touch you-"

"You broke three of my ribs, knocked out my teeth, blackened my eye, fractured my wrist."

The kid stares me out, only the tiniest flicker of fear in his eyes. The black cat on his jacket stretches, little clawed toes splayed. This ain't going right. He was supposed to jump at the offer of a favourable testimony.

He's right. I missed the most important factor: people like him don't need no testimony, favourable or otherwise.

"So why did you let me in, then?"

"Curiosity, I suppose. Why did you *want* to come in?"

Here we go. "Back when I brought you in, you called me a cog, you remember that? Said I was a sceever and a liar and the reason it's all gone to shit. Well... might be I've come around to your way of thinking."

"And why should I believe that?"

"Apart from my face being all over the waves? How about the fact you also said you forgive me. Seems to me, if that's true, you believe folks can change. Can get better. Well, I'm aiming to get better, and to drag this whole stinking mess along with me on the ride."

His eyes dart to my wrist, noticing the privacy ticking away on my Holo. Something like guile washes over his face. "You did something wrong? Is that it? What did you do?"

"I'm... suspended, that's all."

"So why do you need a jumper? Suspended isn't fired. Suspended isn't 'I'ma gohnaah save the whole gaw-dam world', is it?"

"Heh. Funny. I just need to get into the slip, check something. You wanna make a deal or not?"

Kid purses his lips. "Sure. I'll help you out. But it'll cost you. All the world's a trade, isn't it?"

"Sure. But I ain't exactly liquid right now."

"Not money. I want you to go on broadwave, tell the world why the TTCP are after you. Tell them what the TTCP is."

I laugh. Who wouldn't? "You have got to be joking. It's hard enough getting around as it is."

"That's the deal. Take it or leave it."

"Fine. Give me the info on the jumper and-"

"No." The cat on his suit curls its tail around its body and starts cleaning its ears. "You'll go on the wave first, then I'll give you the details."

God damn it. Right. Factors.

Factor one: he ain't giving me nothing without me agreeing to his terms. Factor two: I'm a damn sight stronger than he is...

I'm up and got the kid over the table before the thought clears my head, his stupid cat caught in my fists, his perfect invit face inches from mine. "You'll help me, or I swear to God, you'll-"

My whole body shakes, burning fire in my blood, my teeth pressing into each other like they're trying to snap my jaw. Pain everywhere, blue spots where the world should be. Slow, everything resolves itself, the blue lingering at the edge of my vision longer than the shock sits in my muscles.

The kid tries to help me up from where I've fallen, the little shit. I shrug him off.

"You can't hurt me here, brother. Didn't I explain that already? I'm untouchable." He shakes his head, almost like he's regretful.

My head feels like a broken neon, fritzing and buzzing. "You electrocuted me?"

"You attacked me. Again. So, do you want to make a deal or not? You won't beat the information out of me."

Shit, shit, shit.

Ok, new factors. Factor one: kid's got me over a barrel, and we both know it. But the One True's already burnt, my face over the waves. What difference does it make it I go public, announce my change of loyalties? Factor two: if I succeed in the slip, none of this will exist, leastways not as it does now, right? So what will it matter if I burn the One True? Factor three: if I fail, I'm as good as dead anyway. Either the time pressure will have done for me, or the TTCP will get me. Factor four: what the hell else am I gonna do, anyway?

"Fine," I say. He inclines his head in a kind of thank-you that shows he knew my agreement was coming and he's just being polite. I'm getting sick of people planning out my moves for me.

Forster holds out his hand to shake. I spit on it. He pulls it back and wipes it on his pants, face scrunching up with disgust, and gets to work on setting up the vid, using his own screen to do it. When all's ready, he asks me if I know what I'm gonna say.

"Ain't you got it all writ out for me?"

"No. We dealt for the truth. It's not true if I say it for you." His eyes are fixed on his screen, which he's left clear. I can see a slightly fuzzy image of my own face in the light hovering above his forearm, like looking in a dirty mirror. I turn my gaze away.

"What if I don't say what you want me to say?"

"If what you said before was true, you'll say what I'm hoping you'll say, brother."

Well, he's got me there, ain't he?

I take a moment to think, but the words are there already. Been waiting there a while, maybe, they come so fresh and eager. A little red dot blinks on the opaque screen floating above the kid's forearm. We're recording.

"Uh. Hi." I cough "My name's Kong... only that ain't always been my name. I worked for the TTCP, working the slip – that is, going back in time, I mean, to make sure that nothing they don't want to happen does. But I guess you all know what the TTCP does? Or you think you do, maybe.

"See, the TTCP... they keep us prisoner. The domes, the five cities, the One True. They don't want none of that to change because then they'd lose their power. Their control. They keep us blinded by empty choices so we can't see, don't bother to see, what they're doing. That they're making sure nothing can ever get better. Yeah, or worse, I guess. That's what they say to us, ain't it? It could always be worse, look at what happened with the Fracture. Now you've got medicine and shops and burgers and gadgets and all sorts of things, all thanks to us. What more could you ask for?"

I look up at the kid, uncertain. He nods at me, smiles. OK.

"And that's the point really, I reckon. What more could we ask for? Maybe a future that doesn't include the endless, mind-numbing, soul-shrinking chase for the next product or fashion, but maybe something else... maybe like free air and free water... maybe a chance to build something that doesn't need money to enjoy it, like the, uh, the Eiffel Tower.

"I've been unhappy, I reckon, for most of my life. Leastways, most of what I remember. I didn't even realise I was unhappy, you know? It wasn't like I was crying all the time or anything. It just sat inside me, this... heavy emptiness. This feeling that nothing I do will ever matter, will ever be worth anything. Made me angry sometimes. Made me distant other times. The TTCP did that to me – to us. The TTCP and all the companies they keep safe, they keep in power. They promised us safety and stability, but they took away hope, possibility. It's a bum deal, leastways that's what I think. So that's why I turned on them. Why my face came up on the broadwave earlier and why I'm saying this now.

"The chance to have some control, some impact, some measure and meaning to your life, that's important. That's just as important as anything else. I ain't saying it's all bad here in the One True, because it ain't. But neither is it so perfect we shouldn't be given a

F. D. Lee

chance to change it. No one, not even Clear2o or NesPep or FRESHAIR or any of them, should have the kind of control they have. That's what I think, anyways. Er. Thanks."

Filming finishes and the kid turns off his screen. He stares for a moment at the still image of my face, and then he looks up at me.

"That was good. Very good."

"Yeah. Well. You gonna keep your end of the deal?"

He reaches into his hand and pulls out a pen and paper. I nearly laugh, it's so cliché. Pen and paper... kid's been reading too many spy novels. But then it occurs to me that I'm the one with an apartment full of old paperbacks and retro tech and mended clothes, while this kid's sitting by his pool in his cat suit, his pretty little invit face concentrating on making his marks on the paper, and yet he's been awake longer than I ever have. His pen and paper don't seem so funny anymore.

He manages to get something down with only a minimal amount of ink smudges and hands the paper over to me.

"I'll get you a private car for the journey," he says. I'm about to say I don't want nothing of his, but then I check the address he's given me and change my mind.

Kid's sending me to the Flea Markets.

Loop 19.4

Sitting in the car, I keep an eye on my Holo. Speaking true, I'm willing Joe to send me a message, but nothing comes through. Sensible, really. The last message I sent was about Tossenberger dying, and there's no way for Joe to know if it's safe to message me. Still, I wish he would.

Something does come up on the broadwave though. A bounty on my head for more cash than I reckon most people see in a year. The TTCP clearly didn't like my video message as much as Forster did. The bounty would be a damn pain in the ass whatever the situation, but heading to the Flea Markets... well, in terms of ass pain, this is on the same scale as an endoscopy performed without drugs by a drunk surgeon with the shakes.

See, while the reward might be a year's salary to them who live and work in the centre of the dome, for those pushed to the edge, where the Flea Markets are, it's a lifetime's supply. For all my waxing on about people needing hope and possibilities, the truth is for the people who live out here, money *is* hope and possibility.

All in all, the Flea Markets ain't a good place to be visiting.

See, the five remaining cities of the One True are all clean and beautiful. Metropoles Made For And By The Best Of Humanity. They're what the One True is all about: wealth and prosperity and freedom of choice, all wrapped up neat and easily consumable.

Everyone left lives in one of the cities, under the domes. At the top end of it are the invit set, like the Forster kid, whose families got patents and companies and such, who live high up in the sky. Next is those, like me, who live right in the middle of it all, everything they could ever want there for the buying. Most folks live here.

But then there's the working poor who live on the fringes of the city, their lives short and envious and full of hope that it'll get better if they can *just catch up*. That are sold the lie and buy it in droves because, see, the lie is for them most of all.

And I feel for them, I do. But I also ain't stupid enough to think that walking around with a bounty on my head ain't gonna cause some issues. Privacy won't do much if they can see my face, after all.

Every shop the car speeds past is open, windows glowing a stuttering blue-white from cheap halogens. Teasers are all around, hovering on either side of the windows, bright and sickly, like beggars pressing up against the glass.

I see a teaser for a version of the cat suit Forster was wearing, but this one ain't the same class as his. Shiny material, the animal, a bear, poorly rendered. But it's in style, and that's all that matters. The teaser makes promises on the suit's behalf, showing off two women locked in an embrace while $¥ signs fly around them, like they're caught in a hurricane of money and sex. Just Thirty Easy Payments And All This Can Be Yours.

The bear suit is replaced by a teaser for an aesthetics clinic, Look Like The 'You' You Know You Are, this time on discount if You Hurry And Buy Now. Next comes one for Clear2o because Water Is Life, then a red car with high, diamond wheels, Get To Where You Deserve To Be... a holiday on Pleasure Beach, Join The Beautiful People... Cram schools offering degrees in business law so that In Just Four Years Your Future Could Be Assured! Sign Up Now, Pay Later... Credit Available... Low Rates...

The car pulls to a stop outside one of the Malls. I take a breath and make a dash for the steps, swatting away as many teasers as I can without losing my footing. Make it inside and the teasers disappear, thank God. I'll get an hour without them on the understanding I buy something within that time. They'll come back if I don't, but hopefully, I'll have jumped slip before that happens.

I turn my collar up and try to make myself look inconspicuous. Not sure how much it'll help – a lot of the folks around me have dye jobs or augmentations, so my general blankness stands out. Pretty ironic really. Better try to get this done quick.

Inside the mall, I realise how tall an order that is. Head ducked, I take off at a measured pace down the first avenue, trying to keep my bearings. The whole design is such that you can get lost easy once you're inside. There's no daylight, no clocks, no straight lines. Everything is planned out to keep you in as long as possible. I pass a shop, use the slip to steal a baseball cap and a new grey overcoat. Pull the cap down and my collar up. Would have

In The Slip

preferred to get my face re-sculpted, but there ain't time on my privacy.

I'm fifteen minutes into the Mall, my privacy down to fifty-eight minutes, when I notice the three sceevers following me. Guess my disguise ain't exactly foolproof. They're keeping back, playing it safe, but there's no denying they got my scent. I'm being hunted.

I reckon I could take them easy enough. Two guys and a girl, all three of them looking scrawny and underfed. The tallest guy is covered in jewellery, chains running from a dozen piercings on his face, more around his neck and wrists. The second guy is small, but there's a set to his shoulders that makes me think he'll be nifty in a fight. He ain't wearing anything easy to grab – so either too poor to afford the loans or too experienced in a tussle to disadvantage himself that way. The woman is the fittest-looking among them, spry muscles visible on her bare arms, hair shaved short and spiky, heavy rings on her fingers.

Still, all three of them are no match for a trained operative. Hell, all I need to do is get them in a reasonably predictable space, and I could jump the slip, smash them to a pulp before they've even worked out what they're facing.

Except they must know, right? My little video message is all over the One True, along with the Company's bounty. Hell, now I come to look, there're a fair few people eyeing me up, just they ain't got the balls to do anything about it. These three do. These three scrawny-ass, dirt-eating sceevers are in such a way that they're gonna risk taking on an operative in the chance – slim as they must know it is – that they'll get some reward for it.

Want... there's always a want. Mmm.

I slow my pace, follow the signs to the nearest restroom. Fifty minutes left. They follow me in. The fella who was pissing in the urinal takes one look at the four of us and hightails it out of the john.

"Hey," I say, friendly. "I reckon I know what you want, right enough. What would you do with the money, if you got it?"

"None of your business," says the tall one with the jewellery. "Besides, when we're done with you-"

"Medicine," the girl cuts in. The other two glare at her. "What? It doesn't make any difference if he knows."

Good for her. Not bothering to pretend this is anything more than a shakedown. Hell, it's not far off being basic commerce. Do a job, get paid. Shame they chose the wrong job.

"You know you ain't no match for me? I'm guessing if you've seen the wave, you know what I am. Medicine won't help you if you're dead."

They share another look. Then the short one folds his arms. "It doesn't need to help us."

Ah, right. Reckon I know what the want is now, right enough. It's a good want, far as such things go. "So you got someone you care about? That what you want it for?"

A pause. Then the short one answers, "Our kid."

There we go. Reckon that's the kind of want I can get behind. "So, this is how it's gonna go. You're gonna beat me up, right enough – especially my face. Get in some good punches, let off some steam. Then you can take a photo or a vid file or something, send it to a woman called Nafre Murdache at the TTCP. Tell her you'll let her know where you left me, but you want the money first. Likely you'll only get half, but that's better than the alternative, right?"

"And what's the alternative?" the tall one asks, puffing his skinny chest out.

"Well, now. The alternative is that you try to bring me down for real and I kill you." I offer them a cheery smile. "Your kid might still get the reward, who knows? But I bet they like having their parents around, right? Bet you want to see them grow up?"

Silence. Confusion on their faces.

"You got about one minute to decide," I add, hoping to get this moving. "Then I'm gonna have to carry on my way regardless."

They glance at each other, weighing it up.

"Tick tock, kids."

The short one nods, and that's the decision made. The girl clenches her jaw, turns to me. Those rings on her fingers look a lot heavier up close.

"Remember, a beating – I ain't looking to wind up in a Medi. You go further than I'm happy with and I'll start to fight back. Oh, yeah, and aim for the face."

The three kids move in. I brace myself, focusing on keeping my hands held onto the cold porcelain of the sink. They keep their end of the deal, and I'll keep mine.

The girl's rings slam into my jaw, sending my head rattling and my vision spinning. She steps back, uncertain.

"...carry on..."

With that, all three of them go at me, and they go at me good. Each punch and kick bleeds into the next, swirling heat expanding across my body like a sandstorm, each individual grain indistinguishable from the next. My face starts to numb, shock more than likely, and I lift my hand up to end it.

There's a moment when I ain't sure they're gonna stop – don't think they're sure either. I really would hate to have to fight back. But I will.

Might be they read my thoughts in my body. Might be they're just good folk who keep to a bargain. Either way, they step back, breathing hard.

I check myself out in the mirror. My face is swollen something horrific, my left eye lost in a mass of purple and red bruising, my lip split and bleeding, my cheek cut open. I open and close my jaw, and it clicks. They done a good job.

"OK, give me a moment." My voice sounds thick and woolly. I ease myself onto the tiled floor, ignoring the rancid smell of old piss, and lay in what I think is a good position for a body. "Take your vid, then get the hell out."

I close my eyes and keep them closed 'til I hear the door go. Clamber to my feet. Take a moment to splash some water – brown, sulphuric smell – onto my face, and then leave the toilet.

Thirty-five minutes of privacy left. At least now, no one will recognise me.

Finally I arrive at my destination and, honestly, try not to scream or burst out laughing. Either seems a reasoned, measured response. Forster's sent me to a health clinic. Guess at least my new look will fit in nice with the other customers. Fashion conscious to a fault, me.

Inside, it's what I'm expecting it to be. There are folks all over the place in various states of ill health, coughing and spluttering, bleeding, sweating. Most of them will be aesthetics gone wrong, accidents, ODs. Diseases are rare in the One True but not impossible, not out here. Feel a pang of gratitude to the Company for getting me all my shots as I walk up to the reception screen and type in the name on the paper. The screen prompts me to scan my chip, which I'm hesitant to do, but I figure I ain't got much choice.

A number flashes, telling me I'm next but two. I'm pretty happy about this for understandable reasons, but it appears others ain't. A man marches up, his face leaking orange dye, and starts yelling at me. He's been waiting for hours, he screams, and who am I to get in before him. I offer him my new baseball cap, not having much need for it now I look like a fish that's been slammed into a wall, and he seems happy enough to fuck off back to his seat.

I take a seat at the other end of the waiting area, let my thoughts spin out. Barry Longsworth is way back in the slip. Krezzler's got a date and a location, but that's all. It's gonna take some work to find him, I reckon. What are the factors I got right now?

Factor one: Longsworth is tied up with the Company, must be. They keep a tight ship, so he's probably someone big. Factor two: big means difficult to get to. He'll be protected, no doubt. Security will be simpler back then, but money always offers an extra layer of protection, so I'll need to be careful. Factor three: I won't have much time. For all that I'm good in the slip, I ain't Superman. The chloros I'm hoping to acquire ain't gonna be the good stuff, and the pressure will get me if I dally. Factor four: someone skulled Tossenberger. Someone's trying to stop us.

Factor five: this is very likely a lost cause.

My number gets called before I can think any more about it. It's time to save the world.

Christ, that sounds dumb.

Loop 19.5

Well, she ain't what I expected.

The woman's about sixty, I'm reckoning, though it's a hard guess on account of the work she's had done. Underneath her oversized cat ears and weird branch-like eyebrows, she's got green eyes, sun-blush skin, and orange lips. No idea what her heritage is. People don't come from places in the One True, they come from catalogues.

"What do you want doing?" she asks as the door slides shut behind me.

"Wyatt Forster sent me."

"I don't know any Wyatt Forster."

"You ain't Zehra Lupe?"

She lifts an eyebrow, which impresses me, given how much those branches must weigh. "I might be. What have you got to offer to confirm it?"

Oh, for God's sake. I empty my pockets – the paper instructions Forster gave me, two tubs of regular chloros, Company branded, some currency for the slip, and a pack of gum I don't remember buying. She picks up Forster's note and my chloros. I guess that's to be expected, but I ain't gonna lie and say it doesn't hurt seeing the pills disappear into her hand. The pain in my head amps up, probably on account of the beating I took. I rub my forehead, surprised to find I'm sweating a touch.

She unfolds the note, eyes darting across the page, then turns on her screen and taps at it. Finally, she looks up at me.

"Dr Zehra Lupe at your service. And you are?"

"The fella whose chloros you just stole."

"Hardly. Trade is the oldest form of commerce. And commerce is-"

"Constancy. Yeah, fine. So, you know Forster now or what?"

"Calm down, mister man," she says casually, checking the label on the tubs. "You won't get very far if you beat me up."

"I weren't planning on beating you up," I counter.

She looks up at me then, catches my eye, and lets her own fall to my hands. I look down, and I gotta say I'm surprised to find that I've got fists on the end of my arms, knuckles white, and my hands are shaking. Shaking like they want nothing more than to be moving, if you get my meaning.

"I saw what you did to Wyatt," she says.

"He resisted. I subdued him. That's all."

"You tell yourself that. I think we both know the truth."

"Look, doc, he'd have got a lot worse if one of the others had caught him, and that's a fact."

"So because you're not as bad as the rest, that makes you good? You sound like the teasers outside."

Cheap. She means I sound cheap. I guess I might have gone a bit hard on Forster, but he *is* lucky it was me and not one of the other operatives that caught him. Them others, they've been known to do some stuff that ain't worth thinking on...

"I need a pill."

She looks up. Sighs. Opens my tub and chucks me a pill, which I catch and swallow.

"They get you like that," she says, returning to her work.

"I ain't addicted."

"I never said you were, though you wouldn't be the first."

"I need them for my job. Can't survive in the slip without chloros. Which is why I'm here."

She nods. "You need the new ones, correct? They're for you?"

"Yeah."

"Right, well. First things first." She pulls out a Kwiq-Dissolve masque and plugs it into her computer. "Can you come a little closer, please? I need to scan your face."

I hesitate. She rolls her eyes. "You're planning on going into the slip looking like that? No? OK then, so stick your face into this machine and let me scan you. Blimey."

I do as she asks and then, after a few moments of her tapping information into her console, she puts the masque over my slashed-up face. Instantly, I start feeling better. I think I even sigh.

"There we go," she says, more than an air of smugness about her. I let it slide, too busy enjoying the way my face doesn't feel like it's made of ground meat anymore. While I'm busy being healed,

In The Slip

Doc Lupe pours out all the chloros she took from me, scattering them across her desk. Picks one up, places it in a machine and pulls up her screen from her chip.

"What are you doing?"

She doesn't look at me. "Re-engineering. A mutual friend sent me the code a few weeks back, said it was for use in emergencies. I suppose since I've got a strung-out operative in my bay and the OK from Wyatt, this is the emergency. It'll take about ten minutes," she continues, "Then you can have them back. See? No thieves here. How long have you been taking them?"

"I ain't here for a check-up."

She makes a point of running her eyes over the MediMasque. "Could have fooled me. Look, I need to know some things about you to get the mix right. Unless you want to jump the slip raw...?"

She lets the question hang in the air, knowing what the answer'll be.

"Fine. I've taken chloros as long as I've been working in the slip. Which I think is about... Shit... I don't know."

"Let me see your Holo."

I offer her my wrist and she accesses my chip, pulling data from it onto her screen. She frowns a bit at whatever it is she's reading, which ain't never what you wanna see a doctor do, even a tempo jumper one like this.

"I probably got some wear n' tear recently," I offer. "In addition to the face, I mean. Did some fast jumps, shaving time."

"How old are you?"

"Thirty-eight. But I think I've been thirty-eight for a while."

She stares a moment, then makes a kind of shrugging motion with her mouth. "You're in good shape, however old you want to admit being. DNA is strong, a few odd kinks – no, don't worry. Most of us have some mutation or another, depending on how our ancestors got us into the dome. Though I will admit, you've got a few things I've not seen before. Interesting to come across someone with something new. Some mutations actually help with the jumps, bet you didn't know that? We try to screen for people with the best markers. Yours are *very* good."

"Is that so?" Course it is – the Company has all the time in the slip to test and trial it.

"Oh, yes," the doc says. "Now sit back, please, while I run the program."

She taps away a bit more, seeming intent on her work. About twenty minutes pass, her tinkering with her screen, occasionally asking for access to my chip again, occasionally doing stuff with the chloros, while the MediMasque repairs my face. I don't know what I was expecting, but the truth is the whole thing passes quietly. Peaceful, almost. If I weren't so anxious about my chloros and my privacy and Joe and the slip and all the rest of it, I reckon this might even be pleasant.

Shame really that I am anxious about all that stuff. All that stuff and more. While I ain't so sure about all that's happened in the last few hours, I sure as silver know this: if I get my head smooshed in the slip, I won't know if I've been born, if I'm alive, or if I'm dead. Chances are, I'll be all those things at the same time, which don't strike me as being at all peachy.

And yet, there's a thrill to the thought of it, in a way I can't really explain. Feels like... feels like it's something I should have done a while back. Not the getting splattered across time bit, but the just doing *something* bit. I can't speak to where that feeling comes from, but it's been there a while, I reckon. Hiding even deeper in me than the chip.

Lupe says something, interrupting my thoughts. I guess she must sense my confusion as she speaks again in the tone of one repeating themselves:

"They're ready. These will hold you together for an hour, tops. Maybe. I've done the best I can, anyway, and I've done it square."

Lupe drops about ten chloros back into one of the tubs. Ten. Seriously. *Ten*.

"What about the rest?"

Her lips thin. "Deactivated. They might as well be chalk tablets now. But the ones I've given you are legit. I want you to remember that. I could have palmed you the duds. Sent you off to die and had one less operative attacking my friends."

"So why didn't you?"

"Well, your, hah, anti-PR video helped – yes, I saw it. But also because we're not your enemy and we never have been." She leans forward, her eyes wide and sincere under her branching eyebrows.

"You were right: there are things that should never be for sale. Trust and hope are among them. And..."

"And?"

"And I forgive you, brother."

F. D. Lee

Loop 19.6

My heart is gonna escape my chest; I can feel it crawling up my throat and into my mouth, my lungs are pressed so hard against it. I cough, spit; a lump of thick, yellowy mucus lands on the pavement. There're red spots in it, which can't be good.

My elbow screams murder at me as I reach into my pocket for some more pills, and even after the fourth one in ten minutes I barely got the warmth in my joints to melt away the pain. Need to make the most of my time here, but with the pressure weighing so heavy, it's hard to move, let alone think. Every action seems like it costs me a day's worth of energy, my joints popping and cracking, all the squishy bits inside me squeezed tight.

I struggle down the wide street, crashing into people as I go. No one seems to notice, which is a bonus for me and a shame for the state of their social weave. The place is busy, the sidewalk overflowing, causing folks to walk in the road, cars honking and tooting fruitlessly. More than a few people are drunk, despite it being early afternoon, local time. Still, it covers up my own shambling distress, so I ain't complaining.

I heave my way across a long bridge, trains coming and going below me, cars and buses streaming past, the sun – 37° – beating down on my skull. A teenager with yellow hair and an accent that makes her sound like she's eating her consonants shoves a flyer in my face, telling me to come see the show, it's free, in the attic of a pub around the corner. I tell her to fuck off, and she shrugs and flyers the couple behind me. Thirty seconds later, an old man in a red and black skirt bellowing obscenities manages to get his flyer into my hands. I push past him, blinking as I try to read the text: *USNEA Wants You (To Die!): A physical theatre/dance hybrid explosion – watch it before the bombs drop for real! FREE entry. Bucket collection. Venue 76.*

I think I might have ended up in hell. I was aiming for Edinburgh.

I fight my way down the street, surrounded by a nightmare of noise, smog, heat and people. So many people. Takes me thirty minutes and another two pills to make it off the main street and down one of the many narrow, blessedly shaded alleyways, stumbling some against the steep incline.

I'm gonna run out of chloros if I don't get this done quick. Gonna get pasted. Need to work above the pain – just need to survive this and then someone else, Krezzler maybe, can take the lead on the next near fatal mission. I'd laugh if my mouth didn't feel like it was full of pins.

The alleyway is only slightly less busy than the street. My elbows feel like there's burning lead inside them. About six bars dotted around me, people loudly drinking pints of beer and discussing all and everything, seems to me, except the one thing they ought to be talking about, which is why somewhere so far north is baking in the heat. I try to roll my shoulders, get the blood moving. Hear the bones creak and feel my muscles pull against me. The air smells slightly of melting plastic and the sky has a reddy-brown haze. No one's talking about the fact that one of their little islands, even further north, just got swallowed up by the ocean.

Take half a pill. Krezzler's directions lead me to a narrow wooden door set in a recess between a bar and a digital investment kiosk. There's no bell nor buzzer, just an old brass ring. I go to knock; my hand won't lift. It's swollen and purple, like some kind of fruit. I flex my fingers and just manage not to shriek at the agony of it, the fluid building up around the joints refusing to dissipate easy. Fucking hell. Eyes water, flex flex flex, hand slowly revives and I use it to take the other half of the pill. Then I knock at the door.

It takes longer than I'd like, but eventually a panel slides back in the wood and a pair of eyes appear, looking me up and down.

"We're not a performance space."

"I'm here to see Barry-"

"Right. You're late."

Well. Been a while since I was accused of that. Cough, swallow the phlegm that rises. "Yeah, sorry. I was, uh, held up on the bridge."

"Bloody festival. You got the fish?"

"Er..."

The eyes roll. "You're not coming in without the fish, right? I've been here all night and I've had enough. Call Darren if you have to, I don't care, just get the fish."

The panel slides back with a click.

It's getting harder to breathe. Not impossible, but harder. Heavier. Swallow another half pill while I wait and try to think. One and a half left.

Watch the people go by. Get handed another flyer, this one for a play about the last giraffe, which apparently decides to escape to the moon.

My head hurts too much to make sense of the factors. Need to get this done. I was expecting guards, security, God knows what. Not a pair of eyes and a request for fish. I look at the door. Kick it down? Maybe if my body weren't trying to turn itself into paste. OK. Fish, then. Where? For a second I consider jumping the slip, taking my chances on a future in which, somehow, I've managed to find a fish mongers or something.

No. Stupid. I don't know where I am, and I'm turning to paste already. Jumping into the future could land me in a brick wall where I'll die and never be found, under a bus I didn't know was coming. Anything.

Half a pill. One left. Flex, blink, flex. Keep myself alive a little bit longer.

There are bars and restaurants all around me. Should be easy enough to find somewhere selling fish.

I stumble into the nearest bar. Veer to the counter, get the attention of the server, ask for some fish. To her credit, she don't seem overly bemused by me and my order, but then I guess she might just be relieved I ain't pressing a flyer into her hands.

Lean against the counter, try to get my breathing regulated. My hands are starting to swell up again, weird spots blocking my vision. Blink. Flex. Breathe. Wait. Breathe. Flex. Blink.

My fingers are turning black, bruises spotting my arms.

Fish arrives.

Leastways, I think it's fish. It's covered in some orangey-brown flaky stuff that looks like hard pancake mix. The 'fish' is flung across a pile of thick cut fries, a slice of lemon and some green gunk that looks like toxic sludge. The server drops a paper bill on the bar and goes off to get flyered by a group of men in black turtlenecks.

I pick up the orangey-brown thing and shove it in my pocket, ignoring the bloody cracks appearing around my blackening knuckles. Make for the door as subtle as I can, given my wavering gait. Lucky for me, the bar is busy and more than a few of the patrons are drunk, so if my weird wobble-walk is noticed, it's at least explainable.

Back to the door, knock, panel slides, eyes appear.

"That was quick. You got the fish?"

"Ye... yeah."

There's some noise from the other side and the door swings open. Last pill. Swallow it whole. Push my way in, get the sceever against the wall, my forearm resting across his windpipe. A promise, not a threat. If he's got guts, decides to make a dance of it, I won't last one round.

"Where... is... Barry Longsworth?"

Eyes grunts a bit, nods down the hallway. I pull him off the wall, holding him by the scruff. "Show me."

It's a bit of a scuffle, me unsteady and Eyes too scared to walk right, but we make into a room at the far end of the hallway. It's got tall, wide windows on the opposite wall letting in the muddy light while a aircon machine keeps the space cool enough that my breath is misty. There are two cheap cots along the right-hand wall, a computer bank along the left.

In the middle of the room, taking up all the space, is a tank. Not a *tank* tank, like the Company use. This is a glass box filled with water, and, near the top, some kind of ledge covered in SoftiGrass or whatever the presenttimewise equivalent is. I blink, trying to focus on what's inside.

I blink again.

A penguin dives and dances in the water.

"There," Eyes pants. "Barry Longsworth."

Well, I guess now I know why I needed the fish.

F. D. Lee

Loop 19.7

"What the fuck?"

Eyes wriggles out of my grip. "Don't hurt me, please, I've got a family, I've got money, please-"

"Listen, I ain't..." Take a breath. Pull myself together. Concentrate on the thing in front of me, ignore the crushing weight on my body. "I ain't gonna hurt you, long as you tell me exactly what is going on. And get me something to sit on."

Eyes doesn't even think about keeping his cool. He grabs a chair, helps me on to it, and then the explanation begins:

"So I took this internship at the zoo, right, 'cause I want to retrain, you know, get a better job, and the fees are still cheaper here than over the border, you know, since the Alliance came in, and I don't mind working for free because they give me an allowance for my boy to go to school, and so I took this internship and one day this guy, Asian guy, like you, but real Asian not, uh..." He struggles, probably trying to place my accent, then rallies. "I mean, er, like from China or Japan or somewhere... shit, shit... Oh god, I'm sorry, I didn't mean you're not real, just, you know, with the registrations coming in after the war, and-"

Good God. I'll be a pancake before he's through. It's like he ain't never been interrogated before. "Listen, kid, just get to the point."

"Sorry, sorry, sorry," he says, barely taking a breath. "So I took the internship and this Asian guy comes in one day and he was obviously someone important, some big man, because they shut down half the zoo and this is the summer, right, tourists, and then we have to show him around all our different zones and he comes to mine and I show him the penguins and, well, I show him the Brigadier and-"

"The Brigadier?"

Surprise and fear mix on his face. "You don't know who the Brigadier is?"

"Tell me."

"Well, see, it started in the last century as a bit of a joke, I guess, or diplomacy or something. Anyway, the first Brigadier was

In The Slip

adopted into this foreign army – sort of like a mascot? – and then he got promoted up the ranks, you know, like a joke. And so by the end of it he was a Brigadier and then when he died the title sort of got passed on, and it became a kind of tradition, brought in the tourists, and so... yeah. You see?"

I spit red gunge on the floor, look at the penguin in the tank. He turns a somersault, showing off. "That's the Brigadier?"

Eyes snorts out a laugh, catches himself and tries to turn it into a cough. "No, no. That's Barry Longsworth, CEO and COO of AquaMesh. I mean, just as a joke, right? A publicity stunt? They're hosting a conference or an AGM or something up in Aberdeen, the Asian guy said."

Get to the fucking point kid. "So why is... is Barry Longsworth here, then?"

"He's just waiting to travel up. There was another incident in the North Sea and-"

"OK. Yeah, I get it. Right. You – what's your name, kid?"

"Er. Michael."

"Right. Michael, you go sit over there and shut the fuck up. No, wait, you got a screen on you?"

He frowns. "I've got a phone and a watch. Is that what you mean? I haven't had the I-Do implant – I'd like one, but there was this story about this woman who got one done and died. They say the tech won't really be ready for years and-"

"Hand them over."

My left arm won't move. It's... I can't even feel it anymore. Maybe that's a blessing. Offer the kid my right hand, take his screen. He scoots over to one of the desks, his hands conspicuously lain out on his thighs, his face a mask of innocence and don't-beat-the-shit-out-of-me cooperation.

What the fuck are the factors now? It's getting harder to breathe – my chest moves like I've been running hard, lungs expanding and contracting, but it feels like I'm getting my air in teaspoons.

Ain't got time to unravel this mystery. Shit, couldn't sort it out here even if I weren't slowly getting squashed. Too far back in the slip, my Holo's useless, no information, no factors.

Think quick, Kong.

This penguin here is Barry Longsworth, CEO and COO of AquaMesh. Never heard of them, so either they didn't make it past the Fracture or they evolved. So, business is good at surviving, then. Probably one of the Big Five or if not, then a subsidiary high up the food chain. Ties in with what Krezzler surmised. So, some business man came visiting the zoo, looking at all the animals. Liked the penguins – no, liked the story about the Brigadier penguin. Romantic sceever, or just got himself a sense of humour? Crappy one if so – the kind of sense of humour that'd come up with names like Bai Yu, Joe King, Carrie Bagges, Lois Pryce, and King Kong, the monster in the slip...

Laughter... mine? The pain ain't even there anymore... it's a cloud...

No. Euphoria. That ain't good.

Focus.

This skeever took Eyes out of his internship and had him look after this penguin while they wait for the after-effects of the tsunami to settle and travel to be possible again. Means we've got ourselves some kind of businessman with a shitty sense of humour, a company about to go large on something or another, and a penguin as a folksy publicity stunt.

I can't figure our what the want is, nor how any of this ties up with the TTCP and the One True. Running out of time. Need more time. Need space to think. Gotta work it out. I'm gonna die very, very soon.

An idea occurs.

A really fucking bad idea.

"Hey Michael, you said the penguin was due for transport?"

"Er. Yeah?"

"Get him ready to go. Me and Barry are taking a trip."

Krezzler's hand rests on her gun, her fingers twitching all eager. That ain't never a good sign, but there are worse ways for the woman to handle her weapon, God knows. Still, she's jumpy as a tap-dancing frog, which ain't like her. Joe seems to have picked up on it, too. He's sitting by the window, picking at the plastic screen, but his gaze is fixed on her. Lois ain't here.

I rub at my arms, helping the blood flow. My fingers are red now, sore, and I'm covered in dark blue bruises, the blood caught in pools under my skin. But I'm alive, and feeling better after a shower and a chloros, regular kind. Joe came to check on me twice while I was putting myself back together, a look of horror on his face when he saw the state of me which, I'll own, cheered me up no end. He made me the cup of hot, sweet tea that now sits nestled in my hands.

Still, despite all that, the relief I feel at the blessed lack of pressure is soured by the atmosphere in the room, I don't mind saying.

"Best you tell me what's gone wrong," I say, knowing something has.

"Lois hasn't come back," Joe says, quiet.

An image of Tossenberger, skulled, on the floor. I'm guessing the other two are picturing the same thing.

"Shit."

"She'll be back," Joe says. "She goes off sometimes. You know she does, and she always comes back."

This last bit must be for Krezzler's benefit. She grunts.

"You tried waving her?" I ask.

"No, gosh, what an amazing idea," Krezzler snaps. "Thank God you came back with such wonderful advice. Obviously, you must be the clever version."

"Must be, yeah. Did she say where she was going?"

We both wait a moment to see if Krezzler will answer. When she doesn't, Joe does. "No. She went to sort out the pick-up with Tyrone, and... and obviously we know what happened there. I don't know if she even knows he's, uh, he's passed away. I guess she would have got your wave?"

"Yeah. I probably should have thought more about that... worded it better, I mean. Hell."

Joe offers me a smile, or an approximation of one, anyway. "It's not your fault. Lois and Tyrone-"

"Lois and Tyrone were close," Krezzler interrupts. Her voice is flat, no anger or scorn or even amusement in it, and the emptiness carries more meaning than anything I've heard her say this far. "It will have hit her harder. That's why she's not come back yet."

Joe catches my eye, nods at the door. I follow him into the hallway, a pang of anxiety about leaving Barry as I do. But the kid, Michael, set him up in this fancy carry case thing with a screen on it for his vitals, and so far, he seems to be OK. At least pressure ain't an issue coming forward – we'd never be able to come back to the One True if it was. The future carries its own problems, but at least it won't turn you to paste.

Joe leans against the wall, hands in his pockets. Too casual to be casual. "So, uh, what happened? You looked... you looked pretty bad when you landed."

"Which part? The One True or the jump? Both were a mess, that's a fact." I explain about Tyrone in more detail, then about the tempo and the jumper doc. I'm just expounding on the off-brand chloros when Joe grabs my shoulders hard enough to hurt.

"Wait – don't tell me you were stupid enough to go back one hundred years before the Fracture with some cobbled-together tempo chloros?"

I'd shrug, manly-like, but he's got my shoulders too tight. I make do with a wry smile.

"Sure, that's what needed to be done."

Joe stares at me, his expression a jigsaw puzzle of different emotions. His hands drop from my shoulders.

"No, Kong. You should have come back here. We should have worked out what to do together, as a team."

Ain't the hero's welcome I was expecting, that's for damn sure. Ain't I supposed to be the one who goes off, gets the job done, deals with the factors? I'm the best in the slip, me. I did the job, succeeded where all else have failed, right enough, and if I've got a few things wrong with me as a result that's only right and proper for a noble endeavour and, leastways, can't be that much more wrong with me than already is. Don't understand why Joe's getting all pinchy, frankly.

"There wasn't time," I snap, not sure how true that is. "I did what needed to be done – I got this Barry Longsworth you've spent God knows how long looking for, didn't I?"

"That's not the point."

"Way I figure it, you should be thanking me."

In The Slip

"Don't you get it, Kong?" Joe snaps, his eyes narrowing and his voice hardening. "This isn't about you trying to win me over or prove yourself. Who the hell do you think you are to make a decision like that? What gives you the right?"

"Being the best gives me the right, that's what. Besides, you seemed happy enough to do whatever it took to get me on the team, far as I recall it."

"Fuck you. No, actually, you know what? Since you bring it up – we did that to help you. We were trying to get you back. To help you remember. And how come when you did, you always remembered Lois and not... not Krezzler? Or, I don't know, that time we were in Salzburg, or when I changed my name and you made us have that stupid party?"

"You changed your name?"

"Of course I changed my name – you think I want to spend my life being called Joe King? Jesus, *Kong*. Changing our names is the first thing we do."

A flash of a memory. "José?"

Joe blinks, his anger rerouted into surprise. "Uh, yeah. José."

"So why'd you tell me to call you Joe?"

There's a moment of silence, and I think maybe he ain't gonna answer. He don't seem like he knows what to say, which I guess is understandable as I sure as silver can't keep up with this conversation.

"It was part of her plan," Joe says at last. "Lois thought you might remember us better that way. Like, a connection or something to when we were at the Company together? I don't know. It seemed to make sense at the time."

"José," I say, testing out the sound. "José Cortez... No... Otero. Right?"

"That's me."

"So why don't Krezzler or Lois call you José?"

Another pause. He drops his eyes, his voice barely a mumble. "I told them not to, just in case... just in case Lois was right."

"Ah. OK."

"But she wasn't right, was she? You didn't remember me – us." He shakes his head, pushing aside whatever it was he was feeling. Back to business. "So what happened in the slip?"

OK. I can take the hint. But I won't deny I'm feeling a little bit more cheerful than I was a moment ago. *'Just in case'* – who'd have thought three little words could make everything seem so much better?

"I went back to where Krezzler sent me. Her coordinates weren't for shit, had to walk about half a klick through some screwy locals. No wonder the world went to ruin the way it did, not one of them sceevers was paying any attention to the signs-"

"I don't think you can talk about people missing signs, Kong. That's where you found Barry Longsworth?"

"Yeah."

"And?"

"And I guess I better show you and Krezzler together."

Joe's, no, José's lips thin, but he stands back, opens the door to the room, and ushers me through. Krezzler is still fiddling with her gun, which ain't exactly heartening. Considering these two are supposed to be versions of me, I don't see why they have to make my life so God damn difficult. She looks up.

"You finished welcoming each other home?"

I'm ready to say something cutting, but Joe's – shit – José's in there quicker:

"What can I say?" He grins, his tone light. "I'm a handsome guy and Kong has impulse control issues."

Krezzler rolls her eyes. "So romantic."

"You've got no idea. So, now that's out the way, Kong's going to tell us both about Barry."

I notice he doesn't leave any room for me to talk about Tossenberger or the manner in which I got into the slip, and I ain't stupid enough to think that's done on accident. OK then. Time for the big reveal. Deep breath. Reach down to the large plastic box, making sure my hands are visible, movement obvious. Don't want Krezzler's twitchy little gun fingers getting any ideas. I can almost feel my teeth meeting, I'm biting down on my lip so hard.

Undo the latch on the top of the box, pull open the flaps, lift out the penguin.

"It's all this here fucker's fault," I say. "The whole God damn mess of it."

"Huurrll," squawks Barry, somewhat unhelpfully.

In The Slip

Krezzler's fingers stop dancing on her gun.
Shit.

F. D. Lee

Loop 19.8

Krezzler doesn't shoot Barry or me, which is a better reaction than I was expecting.

Still, she ain't exactly happy when I explain to her what I found. José sits with the penguin, stroking his smooth head and feeding him the fish that Michael packed. Barry chunters and squawks.

Five minutes or so pass, and then José picks Barry up and carries him into the bathroom. The tap runs. Krezzler glares at the wall like it's personally offended her.

"We can't keep him here," José says, coming back into the main room. "Penguins need... ice? Saltwater?"

"We should kill it," Krezzler replies. "You should have killed it in the slip."

"Yeah, maybe. My head wasn't working so good." I look at José. "Besides, I guess we should decide, as a team, what to do with him and what him being a penguin means. Right?"

José's lips twitch, almost a smile. I'll take it. "Alright," he says. "So, this guy here is Barry Longsworth, head of some kind of water company? Do we think-"

"Lois isn't here," Krezzler reminds us. "We're not a team yet."

"But you, me and José can work the factors 'til she gets back. No harm in that."

Krezzler's eyebrows shoot up her forehead. "José, is it? That took long enough. Good for you." She takes a breath. "OK. So, it seems clear that AquaMesh becomes Clear2o, agreed? How does the penguin fit in?"

José pulls up his Holo and searches through their files on Longsworth. "Nothing here matches a penguin, obviously, but the name shows up in companies all through the slip, right up to the One True. Let me see if I can get something on Clear2o – no, no, no, no, shit!"

José closes his screen down, looks to me and Krezzler with fear in his eyes.

"What?"

"The system's thrown me out on a code 78. That means-"

In The Slip

The air fills with the coppery tang of the slip. Krezzler's on her feet before either José or I react, her gun ready. The air starts to spin, the old magazines caught in a draft that's coming from nowhere and everywhen all at once.

"Where can we go?" José shouts above the noise.

"What about Lois?"

"She's not here," Krezzler replies, aiming her gun at the little tornado that's building over the bed. "We have to go. She'll find us."

"Wait!" José runs into the bathroom.

Five figures appear in the middle of the tornado, dark and sinister. Newbies, not so good at the jumps. Nevertheless, through the haze of time, I can make out weapons and armour. Krezzler's wearing a suit in loose cotton, and José and I ain't dressed any better for battle. When they finish their jump, they'll have us out-manned and out-gunned.

Can we fight them anyway? I'm quick in the slip, but after my adventures pre-Fracture, I don't know how close I can shave time nor if my body can cope with it if I do. Maybe I can get behind them, shoot them out the second they arrive, once I know when that is... Or I get it wrong and shoot Krezzler... Or José...

José appears with the penguin in his arms. "Where are we going?"

Where? Where's safe? The whole of time, and we can't outrun them, not if we need to access the data feeds. We need somewhere safe. Somewhere we can regroup and work all this Barry shit out. Somewhere no one would think we'd ever go.

Right. Of course.

I jab the coordinates into my Holo, wave them to the other two.

"You can't be-"

Krezzler's complaint is cut off by the arrival of five operatives in full field armour, black and shiny and fucking terrifying. Their weapons are already lifted, but it takes them a couple of seconds to overcome the lurch from the jump.

All the time I need. I hit the 'activate' button on my Holo and take me, Krezzler, José and Barry out of this soon-to-be mortuary.

Back to the only place they'd never look for us.

Back to the One True.

Catherina ain't even slightly pleased to see us, but after some desperate pleading and promising, she agrees not to throw us out of her apartment and her privacy. It's then that she turns her attention to Barry Longsworth.

"Kong? Is that a penguin?"

"Er. Yes, ma'am, that it is."

"Where's it from? Who sent it?"

José and Karen share a look. I get it. Catherina's jumping anxiety takes a while to get used to, sure enough. "No one sent it. Leastways, I suppose I brought it – but you know you can trust me, Catherina. Sure as silver, good as gold, ain't that so?"

She doesn't look like I've convinced her, but she doesn't give in to hysteria either. Another win for me.

"It better not make a mess on the floor."

"We can put him in the bathroom if you like?" José says.

Catherina turns to José, noticing him properly. I don't know what I'm expecting, but it sure ain't what I get.

"Haven't seen you in a long time," she says to José. "I guess you've forgotten me too? You've lost weight. Makes you look like the rest of them."

"Ahh, well," José rubs his ear like a little kid. "I intend to get back to myself as soon as possible, Cat. And no, I've not forgotten you. How have you been?"

"They've been trying to get at me. They hacked my windows. They're always listening... Have you got any medicine for me?"

I take a moment to realise she's turned back to me. I reckon I must be staring at José and Catherina like a goldfish watching a circus trick. I'll own to being somewhat relieved that Krezzler's looking as shocked as I feel.

"Uh... not on me. In my apartment, next door. I'll go get you some in a moment, yeah?"

"It's not safe, you can't leave." Catherina's voice rises to a wail. "You have to stay here. It's not safe, it's not safe."

Shit. The last thing I need is her going off on one. "I'll get you a peppermint tea, instead. For now. You like mint tea. And, uh, José can catch you up on what he's been doing."

José nods, and I make my way across her apartment and up the steps, into the kitchen. It's a damn good thing I know my way around, I'll say that, because I sure as silver ain't concentrating on the tea. I'm not sure what I'm thinking about – my mind is jumping around, thought to thought, like staying too long on one idea will burn it.

Clear2o from the tap. *How does José know Catherina?* No teaser to wave away, not with the privacy on. *Did I bring him here once?*

Put the kettle on to boil, choose the good voltage. *Why didn't Catherina say anything to me?* Get the cup from the cupboard. *Maybe she did, and I lost it in the tank?*

Teabag in the cup. *Has Krezzler been here before? Shit.* Sugar, two spoons, cover the bag. *José and Catherina sitting together, her telling him about the folks out to get her.*

Kettle boils, clicks off. *José and Catherina talking about everything wrong with me.*

Pour the steaming water into the cup, letting the fog heat my face just a little too much to be pleasant. *All four of them, Lois, José, Krezzler, Catherina, sitting around discussing what to do about me.*

Stir the tea, help the sugar dissolve. Can't rush a good cup of tea. *Do I ask them how they know each other or do I pretend I remember?*

Tea's ready.

Shit.

I carry the cup back through. José and Catherina are sitting on her long couch, chatting. Krezzler is standing by the window, the glass obscured as ever, her arms folded. She's frowning at the two of them. Guess that means she's no more clued-in than I am. The knot in my stomach loosens a touch.

"So, Catherina. We've got some stuff we need to check out on the wave. Will you be OK if we do it here?"

She looks up from her tea. "What stuff?"

"Just some research. Factors. We need to find out who owns the penguin."

"You're going to bring it all down... Are you here for me? Is it finally time?"

I'm ready to dismiss the comment, but José chimes in. "Time for what, Cat?"

"My grandmother warned me, you know," Catherina says, her tea held tight. "She said that sooner or later, you'd come for us. You'd find out. She said it wasn't our fault, but that didn't matter. No one would see it that way. She tried to keep us safe. She put everything into the privacy, all the money we had. They come for you in the night, she warned us. They listen in."

Krezzler catches my eye, a question in her expression. I shrug. *I don't know what she's talking about, either.*

"Who's 'they', Catherina?" I ask her, gentle as I can.

"The people who stole the company from Baba, from my grandmother. She didn't like it... what they were planning. She made a deal, promised them she'd stay away, that we'd all stay away. Bought the apartment, bought the privacy... When the TTCP moved you in next door, I knew, I *knew*, you were here to kill me. But then you didn't, and I thought maybe you weren't here for me... You were so sad, so lonely. So angry with them all. I thought I was safe." Catherina is shaking, her hands gripping her knees. "Kong? Kong, you won't hurt me, will you? Are you here to hurt me?"

"No, ma'am," I say, moving to the couch. "I look after you, ain't that right?"

She sniffs, runs her hand across her nose. "You forget me."

"I forget a lot of important people," I reply, not daring to look at José. "Don't mean they don't matter to me. Tell me about your grandmother. You know I like hearing about her."

"Liar," Catherina cuts back, her mood shifting on a dime. Drugs or fear, I don't know which. Probably both. "They take you away, all the time. I don't want them to take me away. You're going to let them get me."

"I won't. We're gonna pull it all to pieces, me and my friends."

Catherina shakes her head, her brown-spotted hands flexing, knuckles and veins pushing against her skin. For some reason, all I can think of is how beautiful she is. How real. Her whole life is there, in her body. The child she was, the young woman, the lady. Her skin is thin and tight, but I can tell where once it held the fat of youth, and the lines from the jokes she used to share with friends, jokes she's shared with me, maybe, over the years. All of it painted on her like the colours on a butterfly's wing, fragile as the same.

I take a deep breath and try to pretend José and Krezzler ain't listening. "Catherina, I don't remember when or how I first met you. But I remember knowing you. Every time I come back to my apartment, I want to visit you. I spend as much time as I can with you. I ain't no friend to the TTCP, I swear it, but I'm a friend to you. And I... I reckon I trust you, right? I gave you that voksac disc to look after, and I bet I've given you other things besides. Bet I..." Shit. Here goes. "...bet I gave you José once, right? Brought him to meet you? Only... only he's been going by a different name, and I didn't know that, so there was no way for you to know, either. But I trusted you with the thing I love the most in the whole world, right?"

She nods, hesitant like a child.

"And you trust me, too," I continue. "I bring you food and medicine. I keep you company. Put you to bed when you... when you need to be put to bed. Tell you things about my day, about the slip. Tell you what I really think of it all. Ain't that so? I ain't gonna hurt you, Catherina. Hell, I love you. I love the fact you ain't dolled yourself up. Love the fact you ain't pushed your feelings aside and replaced them with perfume and sneakers and microbial skin treatments and invit and acceptance. Ain't no way I'd ever hurt you nor see you hurt, neither."

I daren't take my eyes off her. Can't look to José or Krezzler. Can't think. I just need her to know I'm telling the truth. I ain't lying, God's own. This is it, and it's not perfect and it sure as hell ain't neat enough for a teaser, but it's all I got and I need her to know it. It ain't for the others. Ain't even for the mission.

"You can trust me, Catherina. Like I trust you."

Silence. The dim light in the room seems to darken, the air growing thick with the promise of something important about to happen.

"The penguin was a joke, my Baba said." Catherina speaks low, her hands still gripping her knees. "She wasn't even born then, but her grandfather told her all about it, and she told us. My father and I. When she set up the privacy, when she got us away from them. She told us to be careful."

"She did you good, Catherina. And the penguin...?"

"The penguin... they thought it was a joke. They'd been working on the sea levels, worrying about the ice melting – this was before the Fracture, before it was too late. Kong, you remember?"

I ain't got a fucking clue. "Yeah, I remember."

"They were working on ways to clean the ice water. There were diseases in it, frozen, but as it melted, they were coming back. No one was paying them any attention. The world, then, hadn't realised what it all meant, how... how big the problem was. The governments were trying to pass the Thunberg amendment and-"

"We don't need a history lesson," Krezzler grunts. "Get to the point."

Catherina blinks. "Oh. Yes. I didn't... We have to speak quickly. You're right. My great-great-grandfather was a board member of one of the big companies," Catherina continues with a wary glance around the room, as if she might suddenly notice a spy hiding behind the coat rack. "The one looking into the water, Aqua something. We needed more water, then as now. The rains were dirty, the sandstorms had started in the Middle East. The ice was melting, oceans rising, tides shifting. It was a race – whoever could get the ice clean, get the viruses out, they'd control the future. Our company – Aqua whatever – won. But it was in the Antarctic, and there were problems. Disagreements. No one knew who had sovereignty, so in the end, no one did. They were free to do what they wanted. There was no oversight, no compliance, no laws that they couldn't work around. They owned the world, and no one noticed they'd done it. Not until after the Fracture, anyway."

I take a moment to unravel what she's talking about, but I think it makes sense. So, someone in her family, way back when, was part of that Antartic project, the one I saw the image from. Private company, taking advantage of the confusion the world was in, pre-Fracture. Not hard to do, I'm reckoning, considering in that part of the slip folks were still arguing whether the world dying was even a real thing. So, what next? They worked out a way to purify the ice, get rid of all those viruses and shit hidden inside it. So when the Fracture did hit, and the world burnt and melted and drowned, they were there, ready and waiting, with clean water. Which, I'm guessing, came at a cost for everyone still left alive.

That explains some of it. AquaMesh becomes Clear2o. Clear2o were the main investors in the dome tech, the fans. Everything really. They had a hand in the locations chosen for the five cities, in the lotteries. Hell, they're still the biggest fish in the little pond that is the One True.

But it don't explain all of it.

"Where does the penguin come in?" I ask.

"It was a joke," Catherina answers softly. "A middle finger. Our company tied everything up in international law. Companies inside companies, a head office that was located everywhere and nowhere, tax havens... It wasn't that hard, Baba said. Most of the politicians were in business then anyway, and the ones that weren't directly had partners, children, lovers who were. That was the joke, really. How *easy* it was. That's why they made a penguin the head of the company. Set it in the company charter. Always a penguin."

I speak before Krezzler can. "That doesn't make sense – I mean, the corporate bullshit does. But why a penguin?"

Catherina chuckles. There ain't no happiness in it. "Because penguins are always in suits. Always ready for the next meeting. It was a joke. They got the idea from some country that had a penguin as a King or something like that."

I let a long sigh, hallow. "It was a Brigadier. They took over the world, and they made a joke out of it." Jesus. So that's it? All this work, all this struggle, and all we've got to show for it is a shitty joke?

Krezzler coughs. She's standing right next to us. I hadn't heard her move. "Catherina, me and Kong and José, we're going to check on the penguin. We won't be long."

Catherina grabs my hands. "You won't let them get me?"

"No, I won't let them get you. I promise."

I squeeze her hands and stand, trying to summon up some feeling. But there ain't none. It's all just a joke.

José leans over and gives Catherina a hug. Very softly, he asks, "Catherina, who are you afraid of? Who do you think's coming for you?"

Catherina lets out a sob, hugs him tighter.

"Everyone out there, everyone left. All the people my family stole the world from."

F. D. Lee

Loop 19.9

"We're screwed."

Krezzler's sitting on the toilet, legs crossed, glaring. Barry Longsworth is swimming lazily in Catherina's frankly ridiculously large tub – damn thing's near enough a swimming pool.

"There must be something we can do," José counters. "I mean... It's just so stupid. We've been chasing a, a, a penguin for years. There has to be something."

Krezzler pinches her mouth up small and then releases it. "Ha. You sound like Bai, how he used to talk. What do you suggest we do? Kill all the fucking penguins that've run Clear20 and the TTCP? You get that's the company she's talking about, right?"

I shake myself out of my silence. "What do you mean?"

"The TTCP, idiot. They've got that stupid penguin logo, and they always prioritise the water. Good God, you two really didn't put that together?" Krezzler slams her elbow into the tissue dispenser on the wall. It buckles with a painful metallic screech. "We spent *years* tracking down that name. Bai, Kong, whatever, skulled himself for it. And now we've lost Lois, we don't have any leads, any clues, and no one sensible to kill. But yeah, let's keep jumping pre-Fracture on knock-off chloros until our lungs explode and we get spread across time like fucking pats of butter on fucking four-dimensional toast, and we still won't have stopped any of this happening because it's too God damn fucking tangled, and it's being run by *fucking penguins*!"

OK. So Krezzler clearly ain't taking it very well. José seems to be in much the same state, just not erupting. Can't even blame Krezzler, though I wish she'd keep her voice down. She's right. All this for some stupid joke some dead sceever in a suit thought was clever.

"Hurrrrl," Barry offers, before splashing around some more in Catherina's tub.

"What do we do now?" José asks. "Give up? Hit the slip?"

"Not much else we can do," Krezzler replies. "We need to find Lois. Either she's safe and lying low, or she's already dust."

"If she is, can we reset her? Like we did for José?"

"Doubt it." Krezzler spits on her fingers, starts rubbing at the graze on her elbow. I guess she could be genuinely disinterested, but I reckon I know a diversion tactic when I see one. Besides, it's what I'd do. "Tossenberger's skulled, so we can't get the codes to rebuild her, even if we could get into the TTCP without him."

"So we find her then. She's alive, I reckon. She never came back to the hotel room. Maybe… Maybe Tossenberger was able to warn her before he got done."

Krezzler glowers a bit but nods. "Yeah, maybe. She's got training. She'll be OK in the slip on her own."

Silence falls, except for the sound of Barry splashing around happily in the tub.

"There has to be something we can do," José lets out all at once. "We can't let them keep erasing the past. We can't let the TTCP, Clear2o, all of them, get away with it."

"Listen, José, I think Krezzler's-"

"No, you listen to me. I get it – it's awful. It's… it's *insulting*. But Barry there, he just highlights why we've got to stop them. They saw the planet dying, and they could have helped, they could have done something, but instead, they took what was left and packaged it up and sold it back to us on terms we couldn't refuse or negotiate. And they had the nerve to make a joke out of it." He takes a breath. Flexes his fingers. "And now the TTCP have their mega chloros. Imagine what they'll do when they can go right back to the beginning, to AquaMesh and the start of their Empire. You think the tempos can take the TTCP down? Come on. Kong. Karen. Please. We can't… we can't give up."

"José – we already have. You know it." Krezzler walks over to him, lays her hand on his shoulder. "You know it because you know we've lost. It's OK. We need to find Lois and we need to run, and hope we get something of life before they catch up to us."

His realisation she's right plays out on his face. I see it happening just as if I'd been able to hear his thoughts churning. His eyes, dark brown now like mine, start to shine as the sorrow hits him. The way his jaws drops slightly, taking the corners of his mouth along with. The tilt of his head. The avalanche of his features as hope crumbles.

"It was naive to think we could stop it, José," Krezzler says. "Tossenberger and Lois... Bai... they all thought we could do something about it. But how could we? We were never going to succeed." She looks over at me. "Kong knows it, that's why he didn't come back to us in all those resets. Isn't it? *Alltimewise, nothing ever changes. Ain't that so?*"

She says this last straight – no funny accent, nothing. She ain't mocking me; she's agreeing. Offering up my own words, laying them bare, raw and naked and absolutely, horrifyingly true. It is what it is, alltimewise.

And what can I say to that? She's got the truth of it, no one can deny. *Save the world.* As if people ain't tried to save it a thousand times over, and each and every one them has failed, taking the long view.

José looks at me, fear and hope mixed in his expression. Barry offers a friendly squawk. Through the door, I hear Catherina's big screen playing. I almost imagine I can hear the teasers running on the streets below.

Nothing ever gets better. Nothing ever changes.

Except when it does. Except when it *can*. Might be nothing happens. Might be everything does. But the point is being able to try. The point is having the chance. Having the choice.

"Bullshit," I announce, folding my arms in a manly, heroic pose that ain't in any way lessened by the fact I'm standing in front of a double-wide bathtub with a penguin nosing at my pocket for more fish.

A smile flutters across José's face. Krezzler freezes.

"What?" she says.

"Bullshit," I say again. "I told Catherina I was gonna smash it all, and that's still what I aim to do."

Krezzler cocks her head. No threat, not yet. "And how do you suggest we do that? We're a member down, we've lost our man on the inside, we've got no leads, and the TTCP has your face splashed over every feed in the city."

Damned if I know, but I've started now. Might as well see what comes out. Barry squawks his support. Or his anger at the lack of fish. I'm taking it as a vote of confidence, anyways.

"Look, 'alltimewise', right? That's the problem, right there. We can't fight the past. It's done. The Company's got it sewn up tight. And we're just following their rules when we try. They set it all up – the whole board's owned by them. Hell, even the tempos are part of the same bunch, leastways the ones that survive getting caught. Everyone playing the game the TTCP and Clear2o and all the rest set up, way back when they were naming penguins their CEOs. Even when we're winning, we're losing. I'm right when I say it: ain't nothing ever changes. Because we keep playing the same game."

José's grinning now. Even Krezzler seems somewhat less icy.

"The way I see it, all these sceevers and slack-jaws got this whole thing packed tight. No way in or out except that which they allow. Hell, even Tossenberger was one of them, and what did he do? Kept killing us and waking us up, kept us on the same cycle. Now, don't misunderstand me, I ain't saying his heart wasn't in the right place or nothing. I know he was a friend of yours – mine too, probably, only I don't recall that – but what I'm saying is, even he was a damn fool about the whole thing because he was thinking in their terms. Thinking relative to their construction of reality. But... but maybe we can change the rules out from under them. Play a different game."

"How?" José asks.

Ah, well. OK. "I'm not sure," I say. It's the truth. "But there has to be a way to change things up. Something we can do that no one's ever done before. Something new. We just need to think on it, is all. And look, we got time here. We're private."

Krezzler snorts. "Great plan."

She's right, of course. For all my pretty speeching, it isn't a plan. It isn't anything. I should have lied. Should have said I know what to do, but it needs to be kept secret right now. Would they have bought that? Maybe? Why didn't I lie? Why didn't-

"No," José says. "It isn't a great plan. Not yet. But it could be."

Both me and Krezzler gawp at him. José stands a little straighter, his shoulders squaring. It's like someone ran a jolt of electricity through him. "Kong's right. We need to change the game. So what if we don't know how to just yet? We'll work it out. The point is, we've got to keep trying."

I'll own that I take more joy from the fact it's him vouching for me than the endorsement itself, but I reckon that doesn't matter much. Then Krezzler goes and ruins it all.

"You realise this is madness, right? For Christ's sake, there's some video all over the feeds of Kong telling everyone how terrible the TTCP is. We're done. Hope won't stop bullets, and there's no way the TTCP will risk rebuilding one of us again. When they catch up to us, and they will without Tossenberger's help, they'll shoot us and we'll *die*."

"Yeah, I reckon so," I reply, shrugging. "But who wants to live forever, anyway?"

I didn't know I was gonna say that, but a weight lifts off me as soon as the words are out my mouth. I catch José's eyes, hold out my hand. He steps forward, takes it.

"I love you," I tell him, hoping I'm on a roll and won't throw no snake eyes at the final toss. "And I ain't that other guy, that Bai guy, not any more. He sounds like he was a better man than me, right enough. But I love you, and I'm trying with the rest. Maybe that can count for something? The truth is, I'd rather live once and remember you than have it taken away again. Even when I forgot you, I missed you. I missed you in a way no person can survive, like missing their brain or their heart. And yeah, sure, that's schmaltzy, and I don't know whether that's something Bai would have said or whether José would have liked it, but I reckon Kong and Joe are kind of schmaltzy, underneath it all. I reckon... I reckon Kong and Joe would rather die together than live apart...?"

Krezzler is practically retching. I ignore her, keep my focus on José.

He puts his hands on my face, gentle.

"Yeah, I reckon that's about right."

He kisses me just like I remember and nothing like it, all at the same time. He runs his tongue along my lower lip, pausing for a moment at the point above where our scars used to be. But he waits, denying me the thing I want so bad.

Except this time, I think I understand why he's pausing. What he's asking. What this means, this thing between us, this weird, messy, complicated, no doubt downright incomprehensible need I have for him and that I think, I hope, he has for me. I want him to grab me, want him heavy and bristled like he was before the Stasis Bank, when he was owned by himself, through and through. But it doesn't matter. We got each other, whatever shape we come in; whenever, forever.

Alltimewise.

I fold into him, taking charge and kissing him. He stills for a moment, and then his hands move from my face to my hair, his fingers knotting in it, tugging just the way I want him to. I'm vaguely aware of Krezzler muttering blue murder and the bathroom door opening and closing, and then all I'm thinking on is the man in my arms, the man I desperately want to bed, but, more than that, the man I want to see me. To know me, broken and fake as I am.

The man I love, and who loves me back.

José and I exit the bathroom some fifteen minutes later. Yeah, I know. But we got a world to save and all that. Besides, Barry started getting curious about what we were doing after the first go.

"Howdy, cowboy," Krezzler says, waving a lazy salute. I don't know if that's a dig at my accent or other things. Don't care.

"Ma'am," I say, returning the salute.

Catherina pulls her gaze from her big screen. "You're still all over the feeds. All three of you. It's been three cycles."

She sounds worried, her voice picking up that thin quiver that warns she's gonna spike soon. I suppose that was to be expected, but what comes next isn't.

"You have to go," Catherina says. "They'll try to find you, they'll come here."

Krezzler and José share a worried look.

"We're private, Catherina," I say, taking a seat next to her. "They won't know we're here. And we'll jump the slip as soon as things quiet down, I swear it. But we need to hide out here a spell longer."

"I don't... They'll know it was me. They'll come for me." Catherina's fingers rub against each other, faster and faster. I'm about to say something to calm her down, or at least try to, when she takes a deep breath and her fingers slow. "I'm... I don't mean to be like this. I don't want to be. I want to help you, I do. I'm so scared all the time... I hate it. You have to go."

I look at the other two. Krezzler's face is a mask, but her knuckles are white, her hands gripping her hips. José's gaze is fixed on Catherina, a sadness in his eyes that ain't meant for nobody but her. No point asking them what they think – besides, I reckon I'm caught between them, anyways. There's probably something philosophical in that.

Right then. On to plan.... D? E?

"It's OK, we can go," I tell her. "I just need to get some more chloros from my apartment, OK? We can't jump without them."

Catherina wrings her hands. "I'm sorry, Kong."

"I know."

"You have to leave."

I place my hand on top of hers, stilling them. "We will. But I have to go next door to get my medicine so we can leave. You're gonna have to give me some privacy to do it."

"That's not a good idea," José cuts in. "We won't know where you are, either."

Panic washes across Catherina's face, her eyes darting to mine, her voice rising. "What if they get you? I don't know what to do! Kong, I can't-"

"I'll be next door," I say, keeping my tone mild. "Just next door. I won't be gone five minutes, and Krezzler and José will be here the whole time to keep you safe. But you need to give me a bit of privacy, Catherina, to get to my apartment."

Catherina takes a long, shuddering breath, and then nods. She taps her fingers on her screen and a second later my Holo pings. Ten minutes of privacy. It's enough.

"Thank you." I pick up her hands – such lovely hands – and press them to my cheek. "You've been a good friend to me." I stand, shoot a reassuring smile at Krezzler and José that I know they'll see is fake. "I'll be back in ten. Less than."

I'm at the door when José grabs my arm. "If we're going to do this, going to go back into the slip, if something happens. If they come for us again and it looks bad-" He stops himself, perhaps aware of Catherina listening. Perhaps unable to say the words that sentence finishes with. "You don't leave me, OK? Not again."

I pull him close. "Deal."

"Don't take too long."

"I won't."

"If you can't find the pills, just come back."

"Promise."

"We won't be able to find you if-"

"Ten minutes, yeah? Then we'll hit the slip, live on the jump 'til we work out our next move. Hell, we'll be our very own folk heroes – we can write songs about ourselves. Krezzler can play the tambourine."

José smiles, but it doesn't quite wash the worry from his eyes. We kiss goodbye, and I hightail it down the corridor. The couple across the way are probably in, but I doubt they're watching their keyhole. They ain't never shown any interest in the outside world before. Wonder if that'll change if we do manage, somehow, to fix it all. I realise I'm hoping it does.

My door slides open before I get a chance to wave my Holo over the lock.

"Kong," Lois says, her arm extended, inviting me in. "You took your time getting here."

"What? How'd you-"

"Quick, get inside before anyone sees us."

"Right, yeah." I step past her. "So how'd you-"

Something pinches my neck. Coldness floods my veins. I turn, stumble.

Lois recedes, likes she's lifting up into the sky.

No, wait. I'm falling...

F. D. Lee

Loop 20.0

Lois steps out from behind the Stasis Bank. She looks... tired, I guess, but there's an energy to her, too. Reminds me of the vids of tigers turning circles in their cages. I don't know why she's here. I don't know why I'm here, nor why I feel like I've been drunk sleeping for about twenty hours.

"Hey, Kong. How's your head?"

"Fuzzy..." The room dips and spins. I blink hard. "Real fuzzy. What happened?"

"I drugged you. Quite heavily. Sorry about that, but you know yourself you've got a high tolerance."

I go to move my arms, expecting to be tied down – cuffed even – but to my misty-minded surprise, my hands come forward easy. I nearly unseat myself, in fact, misjudging the strength I needed.

"You're not a prisoner," Lois says. "Besides, the sedative works just a well as rope, and after you ripped your Holo off last time, I didn't trust the cuffs. Do you want some water?"

Water... Water's important... Penguins?

"What's happening?"

Lois pulls up a chair and sets it near me. Not next to me. She ain't stupid enough to put all her faith in her drugs. "I got caught once, and they brought me here. Maybe a few years after you skulled yourself? It's hard to keep track. Everything bleeds into one, doesn't it? Same old same old. We talked about that, do you remember? When we'd meet in the bar?"

"Sure. We talked about how shit it all was." My tongue feels like a wet sock.

She nods. "Yes, we did. I'm hoping we can talk now, too."

"Where's... where are the others..?"

A shadow passes across her face. "Wherever you left them, I assume. I don't know, yet, how you were able to take Tossenberger's privacy, but it'll run out eventually. They're not important, anyway. Karen's a lost cause; she's too far gone. Joe, maybe-"

"José."

In The Slip

"Ahh. Yes. José. You remembered? I'm pleased – no, really. I don't pretend to understand it, but I don't begrudge you both your happiness. I hope you're going to make the right choice, Kong, I really do. For you and for José."

My head dips, woozy and sleepy, and I pull up with a start that sends the room turning all over again.

"Here, let me get you that water."

Lois' figure turns hazy as she steps away from me. It seems for a second like she's talking to someone, but all I can make out is an orange-ish blob next to her. She returns to focus, puts the glass on a tray and slides it over. I go to pick it up; the whole room swerves then goes momentarily black, but I got the glass. The water is cold and clean and sharp, and when it's done, I feel a pang of sadness. Put the glass down slowly.

"For what it's worth, it's not that I *wanted* you to forget José," Lois says like I understand what she's driving at. "But memories are such slippery things, aren't they? Get the wrong ones, and it changes everything. It was felt... no, *I* felt you'd find it easier if you could forget your old ties. That it would be less painful for you to understand what has to be done. But Karen and José were so determined to get you back."

I must show some surprise, because her tone changes to something more real, more like herself. Like she's sharing an interesting fact she knows I'll enjoy. "Oh no, honestly. Karen wanted you back just as much as José did. She's broken, but she's not stupid. You're the best in the slip, best of the best, really. José, Karen and I being the best."

She laughs a little at that, and I get the joke. She's not being falsely modest. She's laughing at the situation, at the four of us being the same and still one being better. It was that cynicism that drew me to her in the first place, back when I was asleep and we'd meet at the bar.

A new thought slides into place... Lois shouldn't be here. Shouldn't be drugging me. What's going on?

"So, look," she says as if she's read my mind. Maybe she has – is it her mind, too? "I'm not keen on this whole explanation thing – I'd rather you'd come to this yourself. But things are moving too quickly to wait. So here we are. Time to put the plan into action."

"Huh?" Nothing she's saying makes any sense. "How do you know about the plan? We only just came up with it, back in the bathroom. You weren't there."

"No, Kong. My plan. Everything's rotten. You said so yourself, a thousand times. We used to talk about it for hours – I know you remember that."

Something in the way she speaks cuts through my confusion, bleeding across my brain with all the slow and sickening dread of seeing a dark shadow on an x-ray. People are all the same, alltimewise, sure enough.

"You... the tanks. You made sure I remembered you?"

"We worked the variables as much as we could, yes." She sounds colder for a moment, flatter. More like Krezzler. "Every time we met in that bar, you were closer to the person I needed. Closer to seeing it all the way it really is. How pointless it all is. The tempos, the fight. But José and Karen, they wouldn't let you go. I guess in hindsight I shouldn't have changed strategy – ironic, right? Hindsight for us? But it is what it is."

"...what it is..."

"Exactly. I thought if I put José in front of you, he'd realise he had to let you go, stop going on about resetting you, waking you up. Hell, I thought they might both realise the old you, Bai, was gone. That he died the day he skulled himself."

Silence between us for a moment. The drugs are fogging me up, thickening the layers of meaning and intent, of spoken and hinted at, until they lose all definition. Until it doesn't matter anymore because what difference does it make how you justify something when the moment comes to take the shot? The truth is, you either do it or you don't. You either make the good choice or the bad.

Seems like Lois has been making all kinds of choices and there ain't one of them seems good to me.

"You... you doctored my memories when they reset me. Helped me forget things, remember things. That it?"

"I advised, yes."

"Why?"

"Because you're the best. Because you came back even after you skulled yourself. You shouldn't have been able to, and yet you did."

"Always been persistent."

She smiles. "True. But it showed the Company that something new was possible. I was caught trying to find out what happened to you. They brought me here and then showed me a... a place. A secret place. You'll see it too, soon. Things were explained to me. Just as I'm trying to explain to you."

"Why?"

"Because I want to make the world better, like Bai wanted. Like José and Karen want. Only our way wasn't working, so I found a new path. A new team to work with."

"You switched on us."

"Yes."

"You skulled those operatives."

"Yes."

"And Tossenberger."

"Yes."

"Didn't think you were that good."

"We're all that good."

"Yeah, but I'm better." I try to smile. Might dribble a bit. "I got you in Paris."

She tuts. "You're not going to annoy me into making a mistake, Kong. Come on, even doped you must realise that?"

"Worth a shot. So, you got a plan you need me for? A jump? That what all this is about?"

Lois nods and waves her arm, beckoning someone, not taking her eyes off me. The orange blob separates from the dripping, breathing walls and slowly settles into the shape of a man. Lois gives him her chair; it takes a moment and then I've got him placed.

"You... You're that sceever from the party... Clear2o."

He nods, beaming wide. So many teeth. Like a shark trying to sell me a deep-sea diving experience. "You made quite an impression, I must say. I'm Simon Tyrrel-Bourdieu."

"Never heard of you."

"Of course not," he says, brushing his fingers over his beard. It's black, now. His suit's orange. "I'm too important for fame, Kong. Just as you're going to be. We're here to save the world, after all. Can't get more important than that."

He takes a step toward me, but Lois halts him, and his face hardens. Feel like I should be noticing something in that. Think straight, Kong.

Factor one: he's annoyed by Lois stopping him. Factor two: he's more reckless than she is. Factor three: he reckons I'm too doped or too stupid to be any danger. Factor four: he's a big boss man, likes to talk.

Want: he wants to be in charge. Wants power. Respect.

I can work with that.

"I have a plan for the future," Tyrrel-Bourdieu continues. "For Humanity. These domes, you see, there are some among us, your friends included, who see them as some kind of prison. But the domes saved us. My company's water tech saved us – with, of course, a few crucial developments from the other interests in our consortium."

"You're gonna build more domes?"

Lois sighs. "Just listen, Kong. Simon will explain."

"Thank you, my dear. Now then, Kong, I understand you're not the type to suffer fools gladly. Made that clear enough at your party! So, let's talk brass tacks, man to man." He fixes me with a matey smile that makes me wanna punch his face through the back of his skull. "Population's on the rise, the domes won't last forever. It's not a problem at the moment, but it will be eventually. Clear2o have some short-term solutions, and I won't deny the bump in revenue's a good thing, but we're not the sort to ignore the lessons of the past. Things are getting out of hand. This time around, we intend to get ahead of it. Control it."

Can this guy hear himself? I might be a doped-up, chloros-addicted, slack-jawed sceever that ain't no good for nobody, but I know a God damn monster when I meet one. "Oh yeah?"

"Yes, indeed. We will build more domes, absolutely. In the interim. But we've set our sights higher than that. Higher and farther."

I lean forward, spit on his shoe. The world tilts, but I get it under control. "That's what I think of your type of control, you orange fuck."

Lois steps forward, arm raised to elbow me, but she stops just short of getting in range. Interesting factor though: both of them want to hit me, but only Lois has any level of self-control.

Tyrrel-Bourdieu coughs. "Yes. Well. I suppose to the uninitiated this might all sound a little sinister. But we need someone of your talents, Kong, if we're going to pull this off. Lois assures me we can work together without having to re-process you every time you step out of line."

"Why me?"

"It's like we explained to you, Kong," Lois says. "The newer operatives are less likely to wake up, but-"

"But they ain't worth shit in the slip."

"Exactly." She smiles, proud of her student. Used to be I lived for those smiles. "We're the original four. Good in the slip but unreliable in, ah, other ways. Everything was at a stalemate until you skulled yourself. The TTCP's never been able to reset someone with that kind of injury before you or since. We have tried."

"The other operatives."

Lois nods. "Yes. But you're different. Special."

"Huh. Being special don't seem so great right now."

"Everyone's special Kong. Everyone's unique." Tyrrel-Bourdieu leans forward. He's gonna come too close, he's gonna come too close, he's gonna – and he leans back. "That's why we need you, you see. You're the only one we think can survive it."

And here it is. The choice they're pretending to give me. The option that'll see me dead and reset if I choose anything except what they got lined up for me anyway.

"Alright, go on then. Survive what?"

"The future," Tyrrel-Bourdieu says. "Jumping into the complete unknown. No coordinates, no knowledge of what you'll find out there. Someone who can survive; or if not, can be brought back again. We don't know what the world will be like 100, 300, 1000 years ahead – perhaps the planet will finally have died. Perhaps Humanity will have splintered even further. Or, perhaps, we will have blossomed. We want you to find out what's coming so that we can ensure we're heading towards the future we want. A future we control, just like we control the past."

"So what was all that with the mega-chloros then? Why send me pre-Fracture? Seems like you're scrabbling around trying to find your ass to scratch it."

Annoyance paints his face. He takes a breath, his fingers digging into his orange-clad thighs. "To see what you can do, how far you can push your body. And because we had the biologicals. No reason to walk away from something that's working just because a new opportunity has arisen, is there? Imagine what we could achieve, Kong, if we had that kind of insight."

I think I'm supposed to react to that. Be all like 'ooooh' and 'ahhh' or some such. Ain't never been lectured to by a madman before – leastways as long as all the times I've talked to myself don't count. I cock my head a bit, shrug. "Seems to me you're doing OK as you are."

"I'll admit I was hoping for a bit more enthusiasm," Tyrrel-Bourdieu says. "Still, big ideas take time to gestate. You'll come around."

I try leaning forward a bit. Gut flips. Swallow back the sickness, head clears. "Go on then, sell me this future you got planned."

"'Planned' isn't quite the right terminology. More... reverse engineered. As I say, you're going to go forward for us, Kong. Hopefully Lois, too, once we know a bit more about what to expect. But for now, you're our man. You're going to learn what we do, what happens, and report back. Depending on what you see, we'll adjust accordingly. The overall plan is to improve the dome tech, get off world. The Moon first, naturally, but then Mars. There were some promising scientific developments on Mars, before the Fracture made such things unfeasible."

"Unprofitable, you mean."

Tyrrel-Bourdieu's eyes widen like he's just been bit unexpectedly, and then narrow. His fingers press into his legs again. "Two sides of the same coin, Kong. Without profit, how can there be innovation? Things cost money. Progress has always been at the expense of charity."

"And, just out of interest, but who'll get to live in this bright new world you're gonna create? See, 'cause I've recently been learning that your company was in place a hell of a lot earlier than your records say. That you could have done more for those folks back then and you didn't. You let it get as bad as it could, then you brought in the domes and the lotteries. Seems to me, you already picked a future you could control."

He smiles, but there's an edge to it. "Before my time, Kong. But give me, give us, enough resources, and we can resolve a lot of the issues that seem to so pain you. What did you say at the party – you were going to give your apartment over to some stuckers? But you wouldn't have that nice big apartment if it wasn't for the TTCP, would you? How would you save the scroungers and the malcontents if you yourself weren't a hard worker, if you didn't have value?"

OK. Head's working a bit better, movement's easier. Lean back, smile, meet his eyes.

Here goes.

"Depends how you rate it, seems to me. Currency exchange, ain't it? See, your value is based on promises, ain't it? Tomorrow, we'll pass a little more down to you. Tomorrow, they'll be a space for you at the table. Tomorrow, tomorrow, tomorrow. But it don't ever come, does it? That's your currency, sure as silver. And if you think I'm going to do anything to help you package up the future same way you've done the past, you can go fuck yourself with your own credit score, you cheap, greasy, shit-for-brains, low-down, no-good, slack-jawed, *revolting* scee-"

Tyrrel-Bourdieu's up and pulling me forward by my shirt, his face filling the whole of my world, the whites of his eyes perfectly pale and his skin smooth as china.

My forehead crashes into his nose, *crunch*, and comes away hot and sticky. Hands up, grab his neck, ram his face against my knee, roll down, pick up the glass of water, smash, shove, push – *gush*.

Tyrrel-Bourdieu topples over, the glass sticking out of his neck, blood spewing around it.

And then Lois is on me.

F. D. Lee

Loop 20.1

She kicks my chair out from under me, slams my head into the floor and jumps back.

I blink away the stars. Blood on the floor; could be Tyrrel-Bourdieu's, but the numbness in my face and the iron tang on my lips makes me think it's mine. Pull myself up on my elbows. Exhaustion washes over me, and I have to bite the inside of my cheek to stop myself from yawning, my body screaming out for oxygen. Stand with the help of the chair.

"You got a thing for sucker punching me, huh?"

"If the shoe fits."

She's steady, watching me, her weight centred in her legs, ready to fight or dodge. TTCP trained, just like me. I prod at the lump forming on my cheekbone and around my eye. Blood – definitely not mine – pools around my feet. I push Tyrrel-Bourdieu's body away with my boot. Try not to think about how much effort it takes.

"Jesus, Kong. Show some respect."

"Ain't seeing anyone here deserving of it. What the hell were you thinking, Lois?"

She shifts her weight onto her right leg. Too obvious a move to be genuine, but then this is the woman who turned traitor on the traitors, so who knows anymore? She cracked my head good, that's for damn sure. Between the drug – wearing off, but nowhere near absent – and the bump, I ain't so trusting of my judgement. Nor how well I'll do in a fight with someone who actually knows what they're about.

Damn, I wish Krezzler were here.

"Look, we're evenly matched," I lie. "We can keep puffing up to each other, or you can explain to me why you did all this."

"Or I can kill you, reset you, begin again."

"Yeah, sure." I spit on Tyrrel-Bourdieu's body. "Harder without Pop here to help, though."

I'd hope I might anger her, get her off guard, but nothing doing. Lois shrugs. "He's not our father. You think Simon was around when we were created? Clear2o will have a new boss soon enough. People like him come in packs."

"Like rats."

"Yup. Just like rats."

She lunges forward, leg swinging in a roundhouse kick that lands against my ribs so hard I swear I hear them crack as the air rushes from my lungs. Flashes of light fill the world, and for a moment all is quiet, just the blood rushing in my ears and the hot, white pain in my side.

I cough up some blood, try to get my lungs working again. Takes a moment to uncurl my body. When I do, Lois is backed away, bouncing slightly on her joints. Ready to dodge what she thinks is coming.

"Jesus, Lois. Give a guy a break, yeah? I'm having a really long, really shitty day." I breathe in, my ribs grinding like cock-eyed gears. "So you're just gonna wait it out for the next one to take his seat at the table?"

"Better than going around in circles with you, José and Karen. At least on this side of the fence, things might actually change."

"You think sceevers like him want to make it better for the rest of us? Seriously?"

She darts forward then back. Anxious, or looking for an opening? Reckon she thinks I'm playing possum, trying to lull her in close like I did Tyrrel-Bourdieu. That's fine with me – longer she thinks I can put up a fight, longer I got 'til she beats me to death.

"That's why I'm here, to make sure they do it right." Lois' eyes soften. When she speaks next, she sounds young suddenly. "What if it isn't nonsense? What if we could have a world again?"

I could cry. I really could. "You chose wrong, Lois. People like that, they won't ever give us a world."

"I used to think so, too – but look around you. Look at the One True. There's no disease, no pollution, no prejudice. You've seen the slip – the dirt and the grime and the sickness. Remember the wars that followed the first drought in Syria, or the people who were left to die after the storms in the Pacific, the children dying in Africa because the water had been poisoned by a God damn chocolate bar company? The oil spills and the oligarchs. The popularism, the weapons manufacturing. The deforestation and the mad, ravenous farming. What about all the gay, bi, trans, whatever, people stoned to death? The kids murdered by cops as the rest of the world watched on their screens and tutted – surely that doesn't sit well with you? And all of that was before the Fracture, before the so-called point of no return. It's crap, Kong. We were a dead planet long before the Fracture. Compared to that, is the One True really so bad?"

"I... yeah. I know it, true enough, but things also got better. Slowly. Once, people would have cheered someone like me getting murdered, or wouldn't even have seen it as murder. If Clear2o and the other companies get control, nothing will ever get better."

"Or will never get worse."

"Lois, this ain't right. You know it ain't." I try to speak soft, to keep the desperation and fury out of my voice. "The slip *is* shit, Lois, true enough, but it's more real than any of this."

"You've changed your tune."

"Yeah, I suppose I have. Because I can, see? I can change and, hell, if I can change, anyone – anything – can. Look at this, right now; here's me trying to get someone else to feel hopeful. Who'd have seen that coming?"

She looks me in the eyes, sorrowful and loving. "That's the thing, Kong. Very soon, we'll be able to see anything that's coming. We won't be caught out a second time."

The punch comes quick, landing against my shoulder. Stagger back, the blood underfoot and the drug making it touch-n-go whether I'll land on my ass, but I manage to keep my feet just long enough for her to come around again with a left hook that sends me teetering in the opposite direction, a high, painful note ringing in my ears.

My forearms come up and her next punch lands against the bone – a shock of pain, but less so than if she'd hit my face dead on. She pulls back, her knuckles split, drops to swipe me with a kick. Grab her by the hair, bring her face into my knee, once, twice. Third time's barely a tap, my arms like overcooked noodles. It's a cheap trick, but it's effective. Also probably the only move I've got, and I've used it now. She won't go low again.

We stumble away from each other, momentum pushing us in opposite directions. Her nose is a smear of blood and bone spread wide across her face. Fuck knows what I look like, but the pain and the sticky wetness on my face and head, at my ribs, tell me it's gonna be worse.

Take a breath, the scratching sharpness reminding me I've got at least one broken rib. Lois touches her fingers to her nose, pulls them back sharply.

"Lois... please... it don't have to play out like this."

She fists her hands. "No, it doesn't. We could go back to Karen and José and keep on throwing ourselves at inevitability." Her voice is nasal, her words thick. "Great options there, Kong."

I need to do something. Can't keep fighting, hoping for lucky shots. If she's got sense, which I know she has, she'll keep darting in now, aiming high, wear me down. I need to get out of here, but I can't jump, not with the Stasis Bank in the room. Maybe I can get around her, get to the door, get outside and jump away... Need to get past her, distract her, or...

Or have her beat me in the right direction, towards the door.

Now that's a plan only an idiot like me might come up with. Me, Lois, Stasis Bank, door, slip. OK. OK. Easy. Keep her talking, keep her fighting.

"Yeah, I guess I ain't got much to offer," I say. "Why'd you skull Tossenberger, anyway?"

"You were waking up, joining the team. I thought if José and Krezzler saw you fail, they'd toss you out. Or you'd die in the slip and we'd rebuild you. Win, win."

"Yeah, OK. Suppose that was obvious." I wave at my face, take another sidestep left, getting the exit lined up. She mirrors it. "Head's a bit fuzzy."

When she smiles, her teeth are pale red. "Sorry about that. You've never been one to choose the easy path."

"Sure." Step forward. "Guess we got that in common, huh? So, what makes you think this future will be any better, anyway?"

Lois widens her stance, watching me, trying to work out what my plan is. Christ, it hurts to breathe. I cough up some blood, wipe it away with the back of my hand. Lois sees it, and I recognise the calculations going through her mind, working out the factors. *How damaged am I? What can I do? How good am I, really?* This ain't gonna last long once she realises she can win. Take another step forward. Just gotta last long enough to get to the door. The Stasis Bank is on my left now, the door just beyond it. Lois in the middle. Need to get past her so when she starts killing me, she'll be working me towards the door.

This idea is madness, ain't it? I'm probably gonna die a bad death here – but I guess I won't remember it, so there's that at least. But I won't remember José, neither, will I...? OK. Scratch dying in this Godforsaken place. I gotta make this plan work.

"I don't know if it can be better than it is now, Kong," Lois answers, her shoulders squaring, fists ready. "But we both know it could be a damn sight worse. People can't be trusted – you want everyone to have real choice? Real freedom? But look at what they did when they had it. You know what they chose? They chose to ignore it all. Chose to fight and bicker about sex and race and who wore what dress better, and what kind of victims deserved rescue and what kind could be left on the boats to drown. You want *these* people to have choice again? They'd squander it. Alltimewise, people never change. Nothing ever changes."

She's the second person today to repeat my words back at me. And I can see it. What she's saying makes sense, true enough. That's the thing, ain't it? She's not wrong. But she ain't right either.

I take a step forward, legs unsteady as a fawn. Lois brings her fists up, ready. I guess we both know where this is going. Now it's just a question of when she decides to throw the punch.

"This is it, huh? You're gonna beat me to death, right?"

"That's not my preferred option, no. Not why I brought you here. But I will if I have to."

I nod. "And then what? Reset me?"

"Something like that."

I eye the door, so close. So very close. "I keep thinking on when we were in the bar, talking about how shit it all is. About me, and how I thought I saw it all proper. But I was wrong – I was alone and angry, and... shit... and helpless. Scared. I shut myself off and told myself I was nothing but a cog. But it ain't like that, see? Took me a long time to work it out, but now I have. What you're focusing on is the worst of it. There could be better, too."

For a moment something of the woman I know and love settles on her. Her voice is softer, and it's all I can do not to stumble towards her and wrap my arms around her.

"And that's what you really think?" she asks, something like regret in her eyes. "Despite everything you've seen? Everything you've done?"

"Yeah. Yeah, I reckon it is."

"Good for you, Kong. I mean it."

She lunges at me, landing a punch bang on my breastbone, knocking the air out of me so hard I feel my broken rib scraping against my insides as my lungs struggle to fill. My jaw explodes, blood filling my mouth as two teeth come loose. Spit them out as my broken cheek cracks, bones crunching under the weight on her fist. A foot lands in my gut, vomit filling my throat and leaving behind the sting of bile.

This was a bad plan.

Something – a fist, a foot – slams into my head, blackness and noise and nothing else, and then a lightning storm of pain on the small of my back, sending me hurtling forwards. I crash into the Stasis Bank, struggling to see straight through the pain. My right eye's swollen closed, and the only reason I know I'm still alive is because every fucking part of me is screaming to just let me die. The lights on the screen blur, the keyboard flecked with my blood, one of my teeth sitting in the crack between the 't' and the 'h'.

The door, my escape, my hope, stands too far away, blood red as I blink, trying to clear my vision. I drag my gaze from it, hating it for being so close and distant.

"Lois… please…"

My left arm makes a wet, popping noise as she grabs my wrist and twists.

"It's going to be OK, Kong," she says into my ear. "You'll understand, I promise. He'll explain it to you, like he did to me."

I want to struggle. Need to. But there's nothing left in me. My breath gargles in my throat.

"…please… don't… don't take it away from me…"

She pushes her knee into the small of my back, pinning me. Grabs my wrist and does something to my Holo.

"It's all going to be OK," she says. "It doesn't have to hurt like this. I was where you are now, and it gets better, once you understand."

I groan and creak as she rolls me over, yanking my arm so she can better access my feed. I watch the blurry shape of her, the hazy light of my screen.

"What are... are you..."

"Hush, brother," she says. "Almost done."

"No... Lois... please..."

"Shh."

"...I forgive... forgive you..."

She turns her face to me. "Thank you."

And then she slams my wrist down on the data-port, connecting my chip to the Stasis Bank. Everything I am and was and might ever be flows from my brain, down the wormy little wires to my chip and into the Stasis Bank. Into whatever it is the Company keeps separate from the slip, from us, from time.

A second less than a-

Loop ----

The metal is cold for a second, and then burning hot. I don't think I hear the sound of the gun, but I imagine that I do.

Something – the bullet? – digs into my shoulder blades. No. It's José, screaming, shaking me.

I open mouth to speak but-

We're all dead in the slip.

Chest shot. Nice. If that doesn't wake the bloody bastard up, nothing will. Wonder what José and Lois are doing? Probably arguing. Wish they'd get their shit together. They're wasting time. Pull up my Holo, ready to fly. I don't know why, but I take a moment to look down at Bai, Kong, whoever he is now, the blood pouring out of his chest, the light in his eyes fading.

"Come on, you arsehole. Wake up."

I'm trying.

Bai's chest rises and falls beneath me. We can't stay out here long. The Fracture's done and now the world's dying. The domes are coming. We both know this, but he won't say it and neither will I. Time presses us, an old friend offering one more drink before we go. Time never knows when to stop. When to call it a day. I let my fingers drift down to his shirt buttons, playing with the little plastic discs. Feel him startle, then relax.

When will he realise he's perfect to me? Not because of his body – he has to look like that so the Company don't suspect him. I *know* that. He knows I know that. Because of who he is.

I tickle his skin, my fingers dipping between the gap in his shirt. Bai squeezes me tight.

I try to tell him how much I love him.

Time listens and laughs.

Alltimewise, nothing ever lasts.

F. D. Lee

We can't keep doing this anymore, why can't they see that? We have to think about things differently. *Can't you see I'm doing this for us?*

That's how I explain it, every time. In my imagination. Sooner or later, I'll do it for real. But it's been so long now – how do I explain why I kept it a secret for so long? They'll understand the murders... yes. Yes. Even the skulling.

If I can just explain it all, if I can think of the right words. It's simple: things are bad now, but they could be so much worse. What if we change everything and the Fracture still happens, but we don't have the domes or the invit or the water? We've been doing this all wrong. How many times have we given our lives for the cause? How long can we keep doing this?

Yes. I can explain it to them. Make them understand.

I love them. I'm doing this for them.

Time to meet the new operative, Lois Pryce. They told me she's younger than me, but I don't think that counts in our job. What does age matter in the slip? The doctors seem excited, anyway. And at least they won't need to keep tanking me – '*oh, Bai, just one more test*'. Yeah, right.

Worth it though, to have a partner. Someone to keep me company. I guess I'm excited? Hope we get on. Hope she likes me. They really screwed up the last one, that's for sure. Knew there was something wrong with her from the start. Wonder if Tossenberger feels stupid for not listening to my warnings, now that Carrie Bagges has gone AWOL? Hope so. Anyway, this new one can't be any worse.

And... Yeah. It'd be good to have a friend. Someone who understands what it's like, this job. The slip... it's not what they think it is-

My head, my head, my head, please make it stop, please.

In The Slip

It's cold, my feet feel like ice and my side hurts. Wish we had one of those air beds. Rocks digging in through the thin, rubber ground mat. Roll over, unzip the tent, stretch my legs. The knot in my side goes away as I wander over to the trees, the sounds of the forest lulling and dreamy. Guess the bullet wound wasn't so bad, after all.

Wait... Bullet wound?

Lift up my shirt. A scar sits just above my hip, pale and smooth. Old. The moonlight glitters on my skin. There's a mess of scars across my ribs, and one running down from my belly button, under the elastic of my PJs. More on my arms, now I'm looking for them.

I feel my lip, the raised line running down my chin.

Brush my fingers across the underside of my jaw, and, sure enough, feel a spot of smooth, tight skin.

I'm covered in scars. All my scars, all the marks they took away from me.

What's going on? Where am I?

Take a couple of breaths. Think, slack-jaw. A second less than a second. Best operative in the slip, alltimewise. Those other sceevers fuck up because they don't pay attention, they assume everything in the past is dead. I'm better that that.

OK, Kong. Take the factors.

So... well. The first factor, the *numero uno*, can't be missed, elephant in the china store factor is that I am now a child in my pyjamas in a forest. I'd say maybe twelve or thirteen years old. No Holo, no chip. How did I get here without a Holo? My head's foggy like after a tank, but I got a feeling I was someone else just before this, and someone else again... The shape of a memory I don't have anymore, the space for a missing jigsaw piece...

I was in the Stasis Bank.

Lois... Oh shit, Lois. Lois turned on us. She damn near killed me, and then she... uploaded me?

I'm *inside* the Stasis Bank.

I'm inside the God damn Stasis Bank, in the wrong body, lost and alone. But the thing is, I don't feel scared, no matter the factors say I should. I know I should be going around the mountain, steam coming out my ears type of thing, but I'm not. It's like I can picture being frightened or alarmed or even angry – I can see how those feelings should be happening – but they just ain't.

Being a kid is... well, 'weird' don't really cover it, but also it ain't weird, either, and that makes it more weird, right? I ain't even sure I've ever even been a kid – I've always been me, mid-thirties, sour and handsome and plastic.

I've always been me for so long. I can feel it, the weight of my past, even if I don't understand it all yet. Even if the factors ain't all in place.

I've been here before, I think.

Deep breath, pine and earth and the sweet smell of old wood. Look up at the stars, sprinkled between the trees, and realise I don't care what shape I'm in. It don't matter right now. So what does matter? Getting back to the One True. Fixing it all. Saving the world. Finding José again, and Krezzler. Helping Lois find herself.

Factors.

Factor one: there's a large family tent over the way, a big old gas-powered car, and the remains of a fire. Factor two: the forest is old, but the clearing with the tent seems well-kept. Factor three: I know this place, which means I've found my way out before. Factor four: If I've done it once, I can do it again.

Flex my toes in the earth while I think.

OK. Got a plan. Figure I can maybe get the car working; we got trained on gas transmissions for the slip, even though it's mostly electric post-Fracture. If I can get the car moving, I can get the hell out of this place, find a city or, I don't know, the CPU for the Stasis Bank, or the weird old man with a big white beard that somehow runs time, whatever. I've gotta try, right?

Last factor: there's a man sitting by the dead fire. Was he there before? Tall guy, maybe late forties, nice eyes – looks a bit like Catherina but less anxious. He smiles when he sees me.

"Hey there," I yell across to him.

"Couldn't sleep again, huh?" His tone is soft, concerned. "Bad dreams?"

Walk over, keep my tone civil. "Mister, ain't no nightmare can account for what's happening right now. I need to take that car, and I'm guessing you ain't gonna want me to on account of you thinking – quite fairly, I'll grant – that I'm just a kid. Here's the

In The Slip

thing: I'd rather get this done quick and without any issue, and I reckon you would, too. So let's skip past any scrapping and get to the bit where you do what I want, yeah?"

I'm not expecting any of that to work, but it can help to have people too busy trying to work out what you're talking about than to focus on what you're doing. Figure if I can keep him off-balance long enough to get close, I can get the keys off him and make good my getaway. Even with this little body, I know a few tricks. Plus, he won't be expecting a tussle.

Turns out I'm about as wrong as a person can be.

"It's been a long time. You've got bigger – growing like a weed," the man says, standing up and rubbing his sooty hands on his pant legs. The fire burns hot, flames dancing. Wasn't it dead a moment ago? "How old are you now?"

"Thirty... thirteen."

"Such a big boy! Don't you want to sit and talk a spell before you go rushing back? I've missed you."

I stand, frozen, staring. "Who are you?"

But I know who he is.

The man gestures to the fire – another cushion next to his. Didn't notice it. "Sit for a while. You've got time."

My feet carry me closer, like the earth itself is some kind of conveyer belt beneath my bare soles.

"So, champ, what brings you here?"

"I... my friend. She sent me here." My voice is high and alien in my throat. "I gotta get home. Gotta save the world."

"Well, that certainly sounds exciting, doesn't it? But there's no hurry. Not here, you know that. How's life treating you – you sound like you've been watching too many films. You know you need to get outside at least sometimes, don't you? Go visit the animals at the zoo."

"The animals in the zoo ain't nothing special."

"No, I suppose not," the man says with a little twist to his mouth, "But we used to enjoy them, didn't we, champ?"

"I... Yeah. Maybe."

"Only maybe?"

Memories of walking the Sky Rail near the dome. Sitting in the backyard. Visiting the animals in the zoo. I take the offered seat. "Yeah. It was… it was fun."

"That's my good boy. My clever boy. So, tell me about saving the world."

I press my hands into the soft, damp earth. The smell of burning wood, and behind it, the sweet scent of pine. "It's all gone wrong, and they want to make it worse. I'm gonna stop them. Yeah. I gotta get back – this isn't real. I know who you are and what-"

"Hey, I've got some marshmallows." A pink and white bag sits next to the extra cushion. My cushion. "Let's roast some, huh? Make some smores before you go?"

He settles back down, tugs the bag open. Sugar and the smell of the fire. I pull my cushion just a little away from him. I see him notice, and the sadness in his eyes as he does. But he don't say nothing, just starts stabbing long, silver spears through the pink and white fluff balls.

"I have to go," I say, my hands raking the earth, freeing the smell. "I can't stay here."

He doesn't look up at me. "Let's make a deal. I've missed you, and you're really in no hurry. So, if you stay and chat, I won't let you die."

"What?"

"Do you remember when you broke into my office? That was very naughty. We've talked about that before. You shouldn't be trying to get into my office."

His office? Where… Memories flicker like the flames. A room filled with glass and chrome coffins. No, that doesn't make sense… An office with all his history books along the wall, and his computer, his private computer, on a desk in the middle.

"I… I'm sorry…"

"I know. But you made a mistake, and for a second, a second less than a second, there were two of you in the same place at the same time."

"Two of me?"

"Yes," he chuckles. "Strange, isn't it? Well, really, I should go back and do something about that. But if I did, you wouldn't have had all those exciting adventures, would you? Wouldn't have spent

In The Slip

the day with your friends, playing cops and robbers." A pause. "Perhaps you wouldn't have got José, Karen and Lois out…"

He shoves a marshmallow skewer into the fire. The stink of melting sugar rises, cloying, suffocating.

"So, here's the deal," he says. "I'll leave that as it is, and your friends can keep playing their games. How's that? But you have to stay and chat with me for a spell. Besides, don't you want to spend a bit of time with me?"

Burning sugar. The fire jumps, sparks flying into the air. The others can play for a bit without me. He's going to let them keep playing. That's… that's good. I want them to keep playing.

I nod.

The man murmurs his approval and hands me a skewer. "So, what have you been up to, champ? Breaking hearts and winning fights, I'll bet!"

"Er… yeah. I, uh, I met a boy." Either the fire is too hot, or I'm blushing a storm.

"And school?"

School? What… oh, yeah. "There was a test. A history test about France."

"I heard all about that – you did very well, according to your teachers. Everyone says you're on your way to big things. I'm proud of you."

"Really?"

"Of course!" He grins at me, orange light flickering on features which look familiar, somehow. But then, I've always known his face. "You're turning into a real stand-up young man. Now, why don't you make a start on those marshmallows, huh champ?"

I feel myself return the smile and, a moment later, the emotions that go with it. Happiness. Pride. Embarrassment.

"Oh, don't forget to clean your hands first," he says, producing a packet of wipes from somewhere.

I look at my palms, covered in earth. I don't want to wash them. I like the earth, the trees. But the sugar smells so sweet, so delicious. His marshmallows are bubbling in the flames, almost ready to eat.

"Come on, there's a good boy."

I take a wipe, clean away the dirt. Wiggle a bit so I can sit comfortably, put my skewer in the fire. Watch the sugar boil and brown, dripping down the metal like… like… like-

"Tell me about this boy," the man says suddenly, his tone light, encouraging.

"He's just some kid from school." I spin the skewer around a bit. "He's nice."

"Not that boy from the special class?"

Stare into the fire. "Uh… yeah, maybe. I don't know."

The man spins around to look at me. "Look, you're getting older now. You've got to start making better choices. This boy, he's been in trouble, hasn't he? Him and that girl he hangs around with. There've been complaints about them."

Hang my head, the fire stinging my eyes.

"I'm not trying to be unfair," the man continues. "But I care about you – about your future. All it takes is one bad influence and *poof*, everything you've worked so hard for is gone, just like that. You don't want that, do you?"

"No."

"The trouble is, champ, there are some people in the world who just don't care about what's right. They think they know best and they'll do whatever they can to get what they want. I'm sure this boy isn't *bad*, but from what I gather, he doesn't listen to his teachers. Doesn't even try to understand the way the world works. Isn't that so?"

"I… yeah. Maybe."

"Maybe?"

"Maybe yes?"

The man leans over and squeezes my shoulder. "That's my clever boy. You don't want to get caught up with a boy like that, do you? A bad boy? Not when you're doing so well. Not when the next big test is coming up."

"…no."

"Your smores are ready. They're best when they're hot, aren't they? Go on, dig in."

He watches me closely, his own skewer still sitting in the fire, the marshmallows burning, black like death. The smell is overwhelming, sweet and sickly, hitting the back of my brain where my spinal cord does the thinking, driving my stomach wild with centuries-old desires.

"Go on, champ, don't let it get cold."

I lift my skewer from the flames. The closer I bring the bubbling, melting, gooey mess to my lips, the more certain my need becomes. My stomach gurgles and crunches, getting ready for the treat.

I hesitate. "You'll let them – let him – keep playing, though? You won't… you won't punish them?"

"We made a deal. I'll cover up your mistake, I'll forgive you for breaking into my office. I'll even let them go. But you have to promise me you'll start flying straight. You've got so much potential; I don't want to see it wasted."

The marshmallow smell is driving me crazy. "I hate you."

"But you love them."

"Yes." I look up at the stars, at the trees. "One day, I'll come here, and I'll be grown up."

"Perhaps. But not today."

"When I do, I'll kill you."

He laughs. "Maybe. But for now, do we have a deal?"

"Yes."

My free hand, hidden by my side, digs into the earth.

The marshmallow hits my tongue and my brain spirals, the heat and the sugar seeping into the walls of my mouth, cooling inside me into something chewy and filling and delicious. I take another bite, and then another.

"That's my good boy," Pop says proudly.

F. D. Lee

Loop 1.0

Light spikes my brain.
 I roll over, scrunching my eyes closed. I want to stay in the darkness. There's something soft under my head... A pillow. Slowly I crack my eyes open again, ready this time for the light. Sit up, yawn. Scratch my stomach, roll out of bed.
 I shake my head, dizzy for a moment, like I stood up too fast or... or was falling down something deep, like a canyon or a well. I stand, naked, and look at the world stretched out below me. And I don't know why exactly, but I'm overcome with a wave of sadness so unexpected, I have to lean against the sill or I think I'll fall over. Tears prick my eyes and my throat tightens, dry and scratchy.
 Unsettled, I shower and dress. I walk around the apartment, watering my plants. Checking the soil. Breathing in the smell of them. It centres me, as it always does. My big screen buzzes. Murdache appears, her leopard print face looking me over, excitement in her eyes.
 "The briefing's been moved forward." She sends me a wave with the new time. "Pryce is here already. Don't be late." And then she's gone.
 This is the day. The jump into the future. No wonder Murdache looked so eager. Check the new time – briefing's in thirty minutes. But what's thirty minutes to me? Besides, I've got an appointment.
 I go to Catherina's, bring her some medicine and some fish for her penguin. She calls him Barry – who'd ever think of calling a penguin Barry? I make us tea, and we sit in the cushion of her privacy.
 "You're leaving today," she says after a while. "Leaving me again."
 "I'll be back."
 "Do you... do you remember you love me?"
 I smile, opening my arms. She snuggles up close, her white hair brushing against my chin. "You know I do."
 "You forgot me again."
 "I'm sorry."

In The Slip

She shakes her head, pulls away. "It's OK. You're different this time."

"Am I? Well, I guess... I don't know... I just feel like things need to be done differently." I frown. I feel like I've been running around in circles, wasting time, but now... I don't know. I've got this sense that I can do something. That there's an answer somewhere, and I'm on the right track to finding it.

But I have to be careful. Have to be clever. Grown-up...

The slip opens, and José and Karen appear. I don't know how these two tempos met up with someone like Catherina, but I'm learning, and they're patient with me. Hidden in Catherina's privacy, away from spying eyes. Away from the feeds and the TTCP. I should bring them both in, I know it. But for some reason we got to talking and, I don't know why, exactly, but I found myself believing them. Trusting them.

I like them.

I like him, too. José. Like him a lot.

"Hey," José says, smiling his handsome smile. "So, are you ready for another history lesson?"

"Yup," I reply, returning his smile. "As long as you're the one leading it."

Karen rolls her eyes, but doesn't object.

Thirty minutes. But thirty minutes is good enough, and we're safe here. Besides, I want to be here.

I choose to be here.

The End.

F. D. Lee

Thank you for reading. If you have a minute to leave an honest review on your preferred online store or Goodreads, that would be very much appreciated. Your review will help others decide if they want to read this book – it need only be a line or two, and makes a big difference!

Join my mailing list (www.fdlee.co.uk) to learn about the research for the Fracture and receive a free e-copy of The Fairy's Tale.

Thanks

I'd like to thank my critical partner, Kit Mallory, for all her help in getting Kong out of my head and onto the page. I had a number of anxiety attacks with this novel, but Kit's advice and enthusiasm for the project kept it alive. Thank you.

I'd also like to thank my amazing BETA readers, Pam, Theo, Jo, and Simon, for all your support, advice and comments. I hope you like the finished product!

Thanks to Ian Whates for his early advice and encouragement. Thanks also to my husband, James, for always having crazy conversations with me, one of which (about *Back To The Future*) led to creation of this book.

Thanks must also go to my readers and fellow Plot-Watchers. You guys are a wonderful bunch, and I really appreciate your support in letting me try something new and to stretch different creative muscles. Thank you for taking this journey with me.

I'd also like to thank everyone who has gotten this far! I really hope you enjoyed the book, but even if not, I appreciate you giving me your time.

Printed in Poland
by Amazon Fulfillment
Poland Sp. z o.o., Wrocław